STOP THE TSUNAMI

by
Padraig Standun

Gotham Books

30 N Gould St.
Ste. 20820, Sheridan, WY 82801
https://gothambooksinc.com/

Phone: 1 (307) 464-7800

© 2024 *Pádraig Standún*. All rights reserved.

No part of this book may be reproduced, stored in a retrieval system, or transmitted by any means without the written permission of the author.

Published by Gotham Books (February 2, 2024)

ISBN: 979-8-88775-733-9 (P)
ISBN: 979-8-88775-734-6 (E)

Because of the dynamic nature of the Internet, any web addresses or links contained in this book may have changed since publication and may no longer be valid.

The views expressed in this work are solely those of the author and do not necessarily reflect the views of the publisher, and the publisher hereby disclaims any responsibility for them.

CONTENTS

Chapter One 1
Chapter Two 19
Chapter Three 23
Chapter Four 36
Chapter Five 51
Chapter Six 58
Chapter Seven 63
Chapter Eight 68
Chapter Nine 72
Chapter Ten 81
Chapter Eleven 86
Chapter Twelve 93
Chapter Thirteen 110
Chapter Fourteen 116
Chapter Fifteen 123
Chapter Sixteen 131
Chapter Seventeen 139
Chapter Eighteen 146
Chapter Nineteen 151
Chapter Twenty 160
Chapter Twenty-One 184
Chapter Twenty-Two 191

Chapter Twenty-Three 198
Chapter Twenty-Four 205
Chapter Twenty-Five 224
Chapter Twenty-Six 234
Chapter Twenty-Seven 253
Chapter Twenty-Eight 257
Chapter Twenty-Nine 265

Chapter One

The great wall on the island clifftop was first noticed from outer space. Many islands off the west coast of Ireland such as Aran or the Blaskets are famous because of the writers they produced, while Sceilig Mhicil is famous because of early monastic settlements, followed fifteen hundred years later by Star War's extravaganzas. The Western Isle was one of the quieter and less famous ones in which Gaelic flourished and life was lived at a slower pace into the early years of the twenty-first century.

It came as a surprise to many in the communications industry to find that this gentle giant was stirring. Soon "Tsunami Tom" was to become a household name as the wall he had organised seemed to rival on a smaller scale that of Hadrian on the English/Scottish border or even the Great Wall of China itself. As in many Irish offshore islands, Tom was better known by a patronymic of parent and grandparent names, in his case Tom Tadhg Rúa, than by a name and surname. Real peer recognition came in the form of the nickname, "Tsunami Tom" that summed up a person's character.

Residents of The Western Isle were unsure of where the money came from to build the great wall on top of the towering cliffs. Tom had left the island as a young man and little enough was heard about him until he returned about a quarter of a century later with a wife and two young children. He came ashore followed by a dog called Topsy, a number of lorries and large machines, the likes of which many islanders had never seen. Work began almost immediately on the wall, helped by returning emigrants who had worked with Tom on major building projects in many parts of the world. Building began on land belonging to his family and quickly extended to small farms owned by fellow workers. Strips of land along the clifftop were bought to put money into the hands of the builders and ensure that there would be no questions about ownership later on.

Tom explained at a public meeting that climate changes were the main reason for the building of the wall: "I don't need to tell anyone who has lived through recent storms, many of which were sub-tropical hurricanes, that our island is under constant threat. We have all seen waves rise higher than the cliffs. Another few metres and they could be spilling across the island and washing us out of house and home. Our lives as well as our livelihoods could soon be in danger. I just want to do something to lessen that threat."

A questioner from the floor asked: "Are you trying to tell us that the big cliffs on the south coast are not tall enough to hold back the waves? People have lived safely on this and other islands since the time of the old saints fifteen hundred years ago, and maybe even before that and nothing like what you are talking about ever happened."

"Was there ever talk of global warming until now?" Tom asked.

"I remember when we had hot summers," was the answer. "We spent most of the day at the beach if we didn't have turnips to thin."

"I remember that too but were the ice-caps melting and the sea rising. How many hurricanes do you remember?!"

"What about Debbie back in the early sixties?" an older man asked.

"And the night of the big wind in 1839?"

The mood was lightened when a smart Alec said: "You would remember that alright."

Tsunami Tom took a piece of paper from his pocket as if he needed to check some facts: "There are similar sized cliffs in Inis Mór in the Aran Islands, or maybe they are even a little higher. Fifteen men were washed of the clifftop on the fifteenth of August in 1852 as they fished with long lines. All of them were drowned not far from Poll na bPéist where the Red Bull divers jump in nowadays. Check it. Google it when you go home. It happened, and tides are higher now than they were then."

A hand was raised in the middle of the hall, and when Tom suggested he would be next to speak, the man said: "Everyone knows that it was because they went fishing from the cliffs instead of attending Mass on one of the holiest days of the year, the feast of the Assumption of Our Lady that those men were drowned."

"Is God that cruel?" Tom asked. "Does he take that kind of revenge? I don't know. I gave up all that old stuff years ago. But if they had a wall like the one that I am talking about, that tragedy would not have happened."

"I agree with you," another speaker said: "If they were daft enough to go fishing in a storm, they deserved what they got."

"It was apparently one of the finest days that ever came," Tsunami Tom said quietly: "There wasn't a stir in the sea until the great wave came out of nowhere."

"You would need a wall to the sky," the first woman to speak at the meeting said, "to stop a wave like that. What difference would your wall make is ten feet or so extra going to stop a tsunami."

"I am talking more than thirty feet," Tom answered. "Ten metres. The top of the wall will be high enough to add another five feet or more if it is needed!"

"Is it your intention to build it right around the island as well as across the top of the cliff?" another questioner asked.

Tom answered: "The biggest threat is from the south and the southwest, but it would be possible to build right around the island to stop coastal erosion. We have the technology and the equipment to build walls of any kind, and to do so quickly."

Then came the question that it seemed that everybody was reluctant to ask: "Where is the money coming from?"

"From my pocket," came the quick answer.

The answer: "Isn't it you that has the big pocket?" drew a laugh from the audience. "What does your wife feel about all of this?"

"She thinks that I am completely off my rocker, but I have her full support. We came into a bit of money. Both of us were interested in the environment, but we could not agree on what to do about global warming, rising tides and all that."

A questioner asked: "Where is your wife tonight?"

"She is at meetings in Dublin all of this week with senior Government ministers and officials. She has her own plan, to provide employment on this island in a very sustainable way."

"And what way is that?" was the next question.

"I am not in a position to go into details about matters that are sensitive just now," Tom answered, "but I can assure you that it is a plan that will provide employment on this island for everybody prepared to work."

"Minimum pay, I suppose," came a shout from the floor.

"A living wage," Tom answered.

"You didn't say where the money will come from?"

"The lotto," Tom's answer drew a howl of laughter mixed with derision, followed by the comment: "Pull the other leg."

"There are questions I cannot answer without my wife's agreement."

"Is it dirty money?" came the next question, "Has it been to the laundry?"

"Where does your own money come from?" Tom asked the

questioner.

"I sign on the dole every week. Honest money."

"Are you suggesting that my money was not earned by the sweat of my brow?" Tom asked. "Ask those who worked for me in trenches and tunnels all over the world."

"There are rumours that you were in trouble with the taxman in England."

"Rumours never dug a drain or bored a tunnel. Her Majesty's Service as they use to call the Income Tax in England did examine my books, but did they find anything wrong? Would I be here tonight if they did? Her Majesty The Queen, before she died, got every pound of my flesh that she deserved. No more, no less."

There was silence in the Island Community Hall until the next question came: "What about planning permission for the wall? Have you got that?"

"I did not ask for, nor did I get such permission," Tom answered. "The work we have done on the wall can be seen as emergency work, to save this island from being swamped by a tsunami. Planning permission will be sought when the work is done, and the island secured. There is no point in seeking separate planning permission for each plot of land or it will take forever. When ownership is secured, we will seek permission then."

A shout of approval came from among the crowd: "Build first and ask questions afterwards."

Not everyone agreed as the next question proved: "Are you telling me," a young man asked, "that all of this unnecessary work as some people would see it, is being undertaken because some men were drowned on a different island about one hundred and seventy years ago. No one on earth can predict if the likes of that is ever to happen again."

Tsunami Tom replied: "No one can predict when or if Mounts Etna or Vesuvius will erupt again, not to speak of the

Icelandic volcanoes that halted air-travel over most of Europe about ten years ago."

"People can keep away from volcanoes if they are not stupid," the young man said, "Do we need to spend millions to fight a once in a couple of centuries wave from washing across us. If the men drowned in Aran had kept away from the clifftop in bad weather, no one would have drowned at the time. Are we taking a sledgehammer to crack a hazelnut?"

Tom tried to explain further: "Tsunamis can travel miles and arrive in the best of weather. They say that is what happened in Aran. They can be caused by an earthquake or volcano thousands of miles away. They say thar the Lisbon earthquake of 1750 sent a wave sweeping into Galway Bay and damaged the Spanish Arch in Galway."

"So, you say," the young man answered.

Tom's reply came quickly: "So history says. So, science says."

"Surely there is enough science in the meteorological service and in the satellites in outer space to see a tsunami coming in this day and age," the young man countered.

"No doubt such eyes in the skies are a help," Tom replied. "But is anyone really watching during the night? Tsunami watch is important in the far east as well as Hawaii and California and other places that have been swamped in the past. But is anyone in Ireland, France, Spain, Portugal or the Canary Islands really on the lookout? Of course, I would prefer if there was never such a wave. But if it comes, I would prefer to be prepared for it rather than drowned."

Discussion and argument continued for some time, the most vexed question still where was the money coming from. Was it a foreign government? "People said you were a bit of a communist before you emigrated?" was the final question asked by the youngest questioner.

"My wife and myself are providing the finance," Tom replied. "It may seem hard to understand but it is from the goodness of our hearts, and for the sake of the environment. I cannot answer further questions about finance without discussing it with my wife. Much depends on the talks she is having in Dublin this week with political leader's civil servants. Are they willing to provide euro for euro for instance for the building of the glasshouses? If they are, then our contribution will go twice as far. When all of this has been ironed out, I will call another meeting to explain everything."

"So, the wife is the boss then?" came a humorous comment from the floor. "She is the one who wears the trousers in the relationship?"

"Are not the way things are in every house on the island?" Tom asked.

This was followed by a more serious question: "How long is the work going to take?"

"That depends on how many landowners get involved."

"What you are really saying is that the wall could end up with breaks here and there? Like an old man or woman with a bad mouthful of teeth?"

"And no dentures," came a wise crack.

"That could happen, but it would still be more protection than no wall at all. It would break the flow of the wave and send a stream rather than a torrent here and there across the island."

"What do you intend to do when your big project is finished?" asked the young questioner. "To build doons or forts like our pagan ancestors?"

Tom answered: "From an employment point of view I would see it as an advertisement of what the workers of this island are capable of doing to prevent coastal erosion anywhere in the world. There have already been online enquiries from the Maldives which could be under water inside a matter of years. But all of that is some way off. We must protect our own island first and foremost."

There was an excitement in the air when the meeting finished. Quite a few people continued the discussions in the local public house. Tom did not accept the invitation to join them, as he had to take over at home from the babysitter taking care of his and Róisín's children, Cliona and Jacob.

A sister of the babysitter had come to walk home with her. The children were asleep, so Tom took the opportunity to call Róisín in her hotel in Dublin to let her know what had happened at the meeting. It was as if everything discussed in the hall was still fresh in his mind as he gave a running commentary on what had been said and who had said it.

Róisín's focus was elsewhere: "How are the kids? Did they go to sleep for you?"

"Fast asleep," Tom answered. "They are as happy as Larry when we are away. They know how to get away with this or that, as if they are on holidays. They can manage fine without us most of the time."

"I miss them so much, even after a couple of days."

"How is the work going?"

Róisín answered: "Everything here is very slow. I suppose civil servants have a lot to do and that they look on the likes of us as a small fry. I find it hard to find anyone who really understands the project. They look at me as if I am off my rocker. They seem to understand very little about the environment."

"I know how they feel," Tom joked. "I have the same problem with your big, sophisticated words."

"There are a couple of four-letter words I would like to use about this crowd. They have no understanding and no interest in anything that has to do with the west of Ireland, and the islands and Irish speaking areas in particular."

"I wouldn't mind," Tom replied, "if you were just looking

for money for nothing from them. You actually have a large amount of money to invest in your project."

"I actually have millions to invest. I am willing to go into partnership which will help to spread the costs and get much more done than I can do on my own, but they are finding it difficult to find a legal way of doing that. They seem to be hung up on the idea of providing grants or nothing."

"You probably need to go higher," Tom suggested "to a Minister or to the Taoiseach herself before they will pay you any heed. Or do as I did with the wall on the cliff: Ignore them and go about the work yourself."

"Your case is different," Róisín said: "You can build first and ask questions later. I would be losing out on the prospect of getting a euro from Government for every euro I spend. There is a big difference between two hundred million and a measly one hundred million on the kind of project that I have in mind."

Tom laughed: "We didn't have twenty euro between us to rub together when we got married, and here we are talking in astronomical sums."

"Those were happy times all the same, with nothing really to worry about but ourselves. I never thought that it would be so difficult to spend money on a worthwhile project."

"Civil servants are not used to people coming to them who have money to spend."

"At least we are trying to use it to do good," Róisín said, "for the island and for the country."

"And the world," Tom added. "It is not just the amount that we can succeed in doing that counts in the long run, but the good example we give in the process."

"You are beginning to sound like some crazy guru now," Róisín mused. "We could have done even more, I suppose, if we had not split the money down through the middle."

"We did the sensible thing when we could not agree on how

to spend it. We did what fellow in the Bible did long ago – what was his name? The guy who threatened to split the baby in two halves."

"Solomon," Róisín replied. "I thought it was the cruellest thing I ever heard when I listened to that story at school all those years ago. I can't understand why anyone would think of him as a wise man."

"I suppose he brought the discussion to a head as far as I am concerned, splitting it was the most sensible thing for us to do. Otherwise, we would spend our lives arguing about who is going to spend this, and who is going to spend that."

"It didn't make some of our relations very happy."

"Didn't each family get a million."

"But did that satisfy them?" Róisín asked.

"I don't know, and I don't care."

"This is my first time staying in a hotel in this city," said Róisín, "because neither of my sisters offered me a room, in spite of all that we did for them."

"They probably think that a room in a house in the suburbs is not good enough for you anymore."

"They have doubts about where the money came from."

"Say nothing to them except for: 'lotto, lotto, lotto'" Tom said.

"They seem to think that it is money that has been laundered?"

"That did not stop them from taking their million each. I didn't hear any of them saying to leave their million in the washing machine."

"You would tell me if it is dirty money?" Róisín said.

"Would the State be dealing with us if it was not?"

"That may be why they are so reluctant to commit to anything."

"We would hardly be as upfront as we are if it is not legal,"

Tom assured her. "We have no need to share it with anyone, but we are using it for community projects."

"Nobody believes that we actually won the lotto."

"We don't either. Let them think what they like. We are doing good with it. What would the British establishment have done with it if we had handed it all over to them? Spent it on weapons to blow people up in North Africa? But if you want to give your share back, feel free."

"I don't like to be shunned by my family and friends because I have money," Róisín said. "I never felt so hurt as when my sisters didn't offer me a room while I'm staying in Dublin."

"You mean to say you would prefer to be in a boxroom in the suburbs than in a five-star hotel?"

"I would prefer if people were not jealous of us. There will be nobody talking to us soon."

"You will always have me to talk to," Tom said.

"I'm talking about having sisters and friends to talk to. Men can talk all day about football or hurling or other sports, but we like to be able to talk about more important things in our lives."

"You mean gossip and backbiting?" Tom joked.

"I'm talking about feelings, and health, and children."

Tom cut in on the conversation: "Not to speak of men, husbands, and partners. Men you would like to have on your 'To-do' list,' if that was allowed."

"Who needs permission for anything in this day and age?" Róisín asked playfully: "As far as men are concerned anyway."

Tom answered: "Right now, the only permission I am seeking is planning permission to get the clifftop wall built and to back up your own plans for the environment."

"I would prefer friends to money any day," Róisín said wistfully.

"Are you telling me you would prefer to be back in the lifestyle we had before coming into a bit of money, with constant bills and a mortgage around our necks? I would much prefer to have millions in the Bank with which we can do anything we like."

"Of course, I wouldn't like to be broke, but there is not much in a life in which your friends have deserted you."

"It is lonely you are," Tom insisted, "without me and the children."

"I do miss Jacob and Clíona big-time."

"And what about me?" Tom asked.

"You are not the worst." Róisín laughed: "In fact at this very moment I would be tempted to give you the time of your life if you were here beside me."

"Are you watching porn or something?"

"What a thing to say."

"Something is obviously making you horny."

"I would just love a nice cuddle."

"Unfortunately, you will have to use your imagination. Or maybe you could order something in: Do they do takeaway cuddles?"

"They do, but they come with a man attached, and it might not be easy to get rid of him when a girl wants to go to sleep."

"So, you are a girl when you are away from home. I thought all of the feminists wanted to be 'women?' I notice that what used to be the ladies football teams down the country are now women's team. Political correctness gone mad."

"We cannot turn back the clock."

Tom changed the subject to ask had Róisín found out anything more about the great glass conservatories in England and Wales.

"Not much so far. I did raise it with some Government representatives. They recommended that we start with good quality plastic tunnels until we would see how things were going."

"A typical civil service answer from somebody who has never stood in this or any other island. I can see the tunnels floating across the sky after the first hint of storm from the southwest. Anyway, is it not trying to get away from plastic most of the environmentalists are, instead of setting up mushroom tents?"

"That was exactly the point I made, but cost is the biggest item on their agenda. I can understand how much cheaper plastic is than glass, but what good is it if it is gone with the wind the following day?"

"That crowd obviously knows nothing about gales," Tom said. "It might be a different story if you were just looking for a grant rather than making a major investment. Get glass or get nothing, I would say."

"Glass is easily broken too," Róisín commented.

"Not if it in good strong frames. See the glass in the Botanic Gardens, for instance that has stood the test of time and weather."

"I'm talking of stones," his wife answered. "A couple of young delinquents could do a lot of damage, and they might even be paid for doing so. Not everyone is on our side, as you well know."

"I would kill the bollixes," Tom said. "Anyway, isn't there law in the land, not to speak of insurance?"

"Says the man who has often boasted of the damage he did in his own time, back when they were bringing the electricity into the place, and you thought they were going to ruin island life."

"Ok. I was young and foolish once."

"What about that ass-cart a group of you put up on the chimney of the school?" Róisín asked.

"It was a Halloween prank."

"So, you might understand if today's young people did something the same?"

"I can tell you now that nobody is going to get away with breaking windows on the glasshouses," Tom answered.

"Who is going to stop them? There is not a policeman or policewoman on the island."

"CCTV cameras will stop them, as it will be perfectly easy to see who is involved. Anyway, they will be shamed by the community."

"Not everyone in the community is in favour of what we are doing," Róisín said. "I am actually having second thoughts about the whole project."

"Don't let a few good for nothings destroy your dreams."

"We could do it somewhere it was appreciated."

"We have plenty of workers to protect it," Tom said. "Their jobs depend on it."

"Wait until you take off to the Maldives or somewhere else to save another island. To save the world."

"It will be well sorted out by then. Islands have been blackmailed by a handful of thugs for far too long. We will win them over or buy them off. This will not be a problem inside a year or two."

"We will see," Róisín said without much enthusiasm. "I certainly don't want to see people taking the law into their own hands."

Tom laughed: "One man watching is better than ten men working."

Róisín asked him what he meant by that.

"It is a line that stayed with me since the first job I ever had. I was working in Westport as a back-up to a man who was a great carpenter, Mike O'Mara. He had a great dislike of bosses, engineers, gangers or anyone else in a position to give orders. It was not that he was not a good and skilful worker himself. He knew more than any of them about timber. He had an obsession or a kind of superstition that if you stopped for a moment to light a cigarette or drink a cup of tea or deal with a call of nature, the arrival of some kind of a boss at the same time was inevitable. Real life seemed to prove this in practice. I will never forget his daily advice that one man watching was better than ten men working."

"You have the memory of an elephant," Róisín said.

"I remember silly little things like that because I was young and impressionable and eager to learn at the time. It was all part of what led me to be able to do what I am doing at the present time."

"I learned a lot too," Róisín said, "from jobs I had on the mainland during summer holidays from secondary school. When the Irish language students were coming one way, we would be going out on the boat to see what we considered to be the real world."

"I sometimes worry that our own kids will not have that kind of opportunity, because we are a lot better off now than our parents were."

"Don't you worry, his wife insisted. We will send them out to work. Anyway, we will probably have blown everything we have in the next ten years. All they will have for a legacy will be broken glass and a tumbledown seawall."

"Isn't it you that is positive?" Tom said.

"Keep doing the lotto," Róisín advised jokingly: "It might be the only hope we have."

"Let's blame the lotto for everything. If we say it often enough, we will come to believe it. It was earned the hard way in tunnels and trenches. Why should we give most of it to the Queen or King of England? Haven't they enough palaces and treasures as they are?" Tom added: "In fairness to them, it was a good country to work in."

"Whatever else, let us not spoil the children."

"They are in the right place. Surrounded by their own people."

"If anyone is to spoil them, it is your father," said Róisín: "They are very attached to him."

"Well, he didn't spoil me."

"The jury is out on that one," his wife laughed: "It was enough for your mother to spoil you."

"It is sad the way that age catches up on everyone. It made me feel guilty today to have to ask a local girl to look after Jacob and Clíona while I was at the meeting. But it would have been too much to ask my Dad. He had already collected them from school and minded them for the evening."

"It is not the ideal situation," Róisín said, "but at least they are getting to know their grandfather."

"He is getting on and my mother has lost it altogether," Tom said. "We should be looking for a plan B as far as minding the children is concerned."

"Even before your mother became ill, I was feeling that your parents were getting too old for child-minding. It was enough to do that once in their lives, without having to start all over again in their sixties and seventies."

Tom suggested that it was for financial reasons that many parents had their children minded by relatives.

Róisín joked: "Why can't everyone be millionaires like us? I suppose trust in family members has to be weighed up against the age of many relatives. But it is hard to find someone who is free to childmind on an island."

"Especially when there is virtually full employment with all that is going on."

"It is not as if we can't afford it, and we pay for the best. It is a pity Mary Poppins or Mrs Doubtfire are not available at the moment."

Tom said: "We will have to do with what we have, but we will be working on it. The old fella might have slipped a bit, but he hasn't left any of the children in a shop so far."

"I would be worried about older people bringing children too close to the sea," said Róisín: "Accidents can happen so easily."

"They are not stupid, and they have not lost or drowned anyone so far."

Róisín sounded hurt. "I am not suggesting that they would deliberately do anything foolish, but if someone has literally lost their mind?"

"People can be too careful too," Tom suggested. "My old man has not burnt down the house yet."

"We both know that your mother will not be coming home for good from that Nursing Home. Your Dad is essentially on his own."

"All the more reason for him to see Clíona and Jacob for a while now and again. The man is lonely. It does him good to meet the kids and they love his stories from the old days."

"He seems really lost without your Mum."

"He is coping," Tom insisted: "And I wouldn't write my mother off yet. That place she is in is supposed to be good. I heard of many a one who has got better there after a couple of weeks."

"Those were people who were there for respite."

"She could improve." Tom latched on to the vain hope.

"Not from Alzheimers, she won't."

"There are new drugs coming out every day, and we can well afford to pay for the best treatment in the world."

"The best thing you can do," his wife advised him, "is to pay her a visit now and again."

"I hate to say it, but I am not able to look her in the face in the state she is in. I know that it is none of her fault. I know she is my mother and I love her dearly, but it breaks my heart every time I see her."

"If you could just go to see her once," Róisín said, "you could get over that mental block."

"We will see. In the meantime, my father can help with the children. It does him good and it does them good, and what else has he for doing?"

"I know he does his best, but we can't take chances with our children."

"What if I drop a load of sand next to his house?" Tom suggested: "Jacob and Clíona love playing with sand at the beach. If they had their own sand by their grandad's house it would keep them from being too bored."

"That makes a lot of sense in the short-term," Róisín said. "We will sort something out when I get home. I have to look over a few forms and plans to be discussed with our contacts here tomorrow."

Chapter Two

Reports and rumours that had reached the Planning Section of the local County Council with regard to the wall being constructed on the clifftop to the south of the Western Isle had caused confusion and worry. A meeting of engineers and other officers was called. The chairperson announced that he had received almost daily updates from a small number of islanders that the wall was being constructed so quickly that the idea of demolishing it would soon be out of the question. "The solution would be worse than the problem:" he said.

One young engineer raised a laugh when he announced that he had been told that it would soon not just rival the Great Wall of China, but would be even tougher to knock, given the amount of steel and cement that had been used in its construction "The guys building it have worked all over the known world, and what they do is done for a very long time."

Another man claimed that there were actually Chinamen who had helped build The Great Wall working on the Western Isle: "I'm told that there is not a wild duck left on the island because the Chinamen are snaring them and cooking them for their dinners."

Another Councillor swung his head from side to side as he marvelled: "Duck and orange sauce. What are we ever satisfied be nicer?"

The Chairperson brought the meeting back to something approaching reality when he wondered out loud did the Chinese references constitute racism. He suggested that a delegation be sent immediately to the Western Isle to investigate what exactly was happening, to speak to those involved and remind them of the law with regard to planning permission. "We have been dealing with hearsay and rumour until now," he said: "It is past time to find out what the exact story is. Are we dealing with some kind of a threat to our democracy or are we making mountains out of molehills?"

"If this matter is as important as you say it is." A woman Councillor said, "Where are the Google maps? Where are the photographs? What research has been done? Is nobody brave enough to bell the cat? To take a boat or a helicopter out across a few miles at sea and have this matter investigated properly."

The Chairperson ordered a twenty-minute recess so that such material could be supplied, as he tried to explain: "All of this landed on our laps without notice. Questions were being asked in Dáil Éireann before it was formally drawn to our attention nearer to home."

"Are you not embarrassed," the woman Councillor asked, "That a huge wall has been built from one end of an island to another, and it was not noticed until photographed from outer space?"

The young engineer made his own comment as the meeting broke up for the short recess: "It is a bit like your man in Achill that built a kind of concrete Stonehenge. As far as I know it is still there a decade or so later, although the Council called to have it demolished. It has turned into a tourist magnet, and this wall will probably be the same."

Another Councillor commented: "That kind of stupidity gives the country a bad name."

"A nine-day wonder," was the opinion of a colleague: "It will be past history in a couple of weeks' time."

"We will be back here in twenty minutes to deal with the fallout from this matter," the Chair announced.

"A pity the wall would not fall out into the water," was a

comment from the young engineer almost lost in the air as the group went for tea and coffee.

It was overheard by the Chairman who suggested half-jokingly that the same engineer be sent out to the Western Isle to prepare a report for the Council.

"Why me?" the engineer asked.

The Chairman answered: "You are the youngest and the most handsome, and there are a lot of young women student teachers on an Irish course out there at the moment."

"I'm up for it," the young engineer answered: "I hear that there is great music and craic on that island during the teacher training courses."

"I can't decide anything," the Chairperson told him, "Without the approval of the full board."

The young man was less than impressed: "I am sure that a statement will be agreed that will blame everyone except ourselves."

The Chairperson was a bit more bullish when the meeting resumed and they had time to peruse the paperwork: "This wall has to be stopped immediately," he announced, "or we will become a laughing stock for the whole country."

"Some things are worse than shame," the young engineer suggested.

"Such as?" one of the committees asked.

"Taking on a battle that we have no hope of winning. Leave the wall where it is, and it will soon be forgotten about."

"We need a court order," the Chair announced.

"When did anyone take heed of the likes of that?" the young engineer asked.

"We can't give in to thuggery or blackmail," one of the members said.

"The wall just has to go," said a prominent Republican.

"How?" asked the young engineer.

"Dynamite."

The Chairperson said: "If the wall is seen as a kind of pollution, what will we have if it is blown up or blown down? Carnage, chaos. It would create many more problems than it solved."

"The army could be brought in," another Councillor said, "as happened in the case of Nelson's Pillar when it was blown up on O'Connell Street."

"The army made a mess of it," the Republican said. "The IRA took down the top half as neatly as you would take the top off a boiled egg."

"There won't be any illegal organisation blowing up anything on my watch," the Chairman said.

Attention wondered to other matters: "Did they ever find Nelson's head?"

"Is it true that his body was brought back from the battle of Trafalgar in a cask of brandy?"

"What a way to go," said the young engineer.

"Order, order" The Chairman tried to bring them back down to earth: "Who is in favour of a court order?"

"A waste of time and money," was the opinion of the young engineer.

"Maybe so," said the Chairman, "but it will show the Government and the public that we are tackling the problem."

"We would be as well to be trying to tackle it with a knife and fork," the woman Councillor said: "An Irish solution to an Irish problem." "Say much and do nothing."

"Would you like to be part of the delegation that will go to the island on a fact-finding mission?" the Chairman asked her.

"I will not be available for a month due to annual holidays."

The Chairman laughed: "An Irish solution to an Irish problem."

Chapter Three

"You are my best friend in the world," Clíona said to her brother Jacob.

They were playing in the big heap of sand dropped by their father Tom beside his own father's house. There was little more than a year of an age-gap between the children and they were often mistaken as twins. They really enjoyed playing in the sandhill as they tackled it with their little shovels and buckets, building walls and castles all over the place.

Jacob stood and surveyed his handiwork. "Look at the wall I have built," he said to Clíona: "It is just like the one Dad built on top of the cliff. I am going to build a lot of castles beside it. It will be like the lost city. I saw a programme about that on TV a few days ago. All of the city was under the water."

"Dad is afraid that the whole island will be under water next year or sometime," Cliona said. "That is why he is building the big wall."

"I would love to be able to talk under the water," Jacob said. "It would be magic, and all the dolphins would be my friends."

"It would be lovely to be able to eat sweets and chocolates under the water."

"Maybe Mom and Dad will be able to get us magic some place so that we can have holidays under water," Jacob said.

"If they had that kind of magic they would not need to build a wall to keep out the water."

Jacob did not have time to answer because their big black Labrador, Topsy walked through his castles and smashed every one of them. The young boy was incensed: "Fuck you, Topsy," he blurted out.

"His grandfather tried to not make a big deal of it said Jacob," and left it at that, as he returned to reading his newspaper on the bench in the garden.

"Sorry Dado. I won't say it again. Topsy is after scattering all the castles in my lost city."

"And my castles too," Clíona said, but I didn't curse because I love him no matter what he does." She hugged the dog and told him: "You are my very best friend."

"I thought you said a while ago that I was your best friend?" Jacob reminded her, as he began to rebuild some of his castles.

"You are my other very best friend," Cliona said. "Well, you were until you cursed. You will have to put ten cents in the curse jamjar."

"Did I curse? What curse did I day?" Jacob tried to trick his sister into saying the bad word so that she too would have to put money into the jar.

"You know well. It begins with an 'f' and ends with a 'c'."

"Isn't it well that you know it?"

"Why do you say that?"

"Because you are everybody's pet, and you never do anything wrong."

"I'm not the pet around here," she said as she put her arms around the dog's neck. "But Topsy is and he does not like bold words."

"Why does he knock every castle we build so?"

"I will help you to fix them." Clíona began to refill her bucket at great speed, scattering sand all over the place at the same time. When she turned the bucket upside down her castle just collapsed.

"Here," Jacob said: "I will help you. You need to use wet sand and to press it down hard." This resulted in a perfectly formed castle, but as soon as Clíona began to decorate it with seashells, Topsy made a mess of it again with his tail.

Jacob raised his shovel in the air, used the same curse as he had done previously, and said: "Don't do that again, you bastard."

The children's grandfather realised that it was high time he nipped this kind of talk in the bud, and he asked Jacob where had that word come from.

"Dad says it all the time," Jacob answered.

Clíona supported him: "And Mom too, and neither of them ever put money into the curse jamjar."

"It is a very bold word and very hurtful to other people," their grandfather told them. "I don't want to ever hear it again from either of you."

"Is it worse than the one that begins with an 'f?'" Jacob asked.

"Much worse, and anyone that uses it can forget about sweets and ice cream."

Jacob said in a low voice that he was sorry.

"And I am sorry that Jacob was bold," Clíona said.

"We won't talk about it again," the old man said. "I am going to read the rest of my newspaper now, but first I need to know is anybody thirsty? Would anyone like a drink of orange juice?"

"Me, Me," The children ran towards him, followed by Topsy as if he wanted orange himself. "Where are the drinks?" Clíona asked.

"The orange juice is where it always is, but you have to go and pour it into glasses yourselves. You can't have an old man running around all the time."

"Will you still be tired after we have finished our drinks?" Jacob asked: "We need someone to push us on the swings."

"Do you think that I am a young fellow that can run around the place from morning till night?" their grandfather asked playfully. "I will start you off on the swings and it is up to yourselves to keep them going."

"Thanks Dado," Clíona said. "You are the very best."

The old man did as he had promised. He pushed the children for a while before returning to his seat. The swings came slowly to a halt, and the children sat in them as they watched what looked like cottonwool clouds in the blue sky.

Clíona pointed in the air as she remembered a terrier that had died a couple of years earlier: "I would say that Ranger is on that cloud. He is in heaven with Jesus and Mary and all the rest of them."

"Can dogs go to hell, Dado?" Jacob asked: "If they are very bold?"

"Some of them are very bad," Clíona said, "They kill little lambs and sheep. I saw it on the television."

Their grandfather turned a deaf ear as he felt that he had no expertise in that department. The children were having none of It: "Are you asleep, Dadó?"

"Old people get deaf sometimes," Jacob said to his sister.

"I'm not deaf. I am listening but I don't have an answer to that question. Only God could answer that."

"God must have a very big head," Jacob said, "Because he has to think of everything old people have forgotten."

"Maybe our Mamó has an answer, but she is not able to tell it to anyone because she is forgetful at the moment."

Jacob turned towards his grandfather: "Are you getting forgetful as well, Dado?"

"Why are you asking that?"

"Because you are old and you don't know what happens to

dogs when they die," his grandson said.

The old man tried a different answer: "They say that Jesus said there were lots of rooms in heaven."

"Rooms for people or rooms for dogs?" Clíona asked.

"For everyone and for everything, I would say," her grandfather answered.

Clíona was not finished yet: "For bad dogs as well as good ones?"

"Maybe the bad ones get good when they go there."

Jacob had his own idea: "Maybe the dead dogs go to the lost city. That is why Topsy wants to knock it every chance he gets."

The children went back to playing in the sand. Clíona thought of a question she wanted to ask. She stood silently for a while as if forming it in her mind. "Dado," she asked, but did not finish. It was as if she was not sure how to word her question.

"What is it, Clíona?"

"Is Mamó your sister? You know the way that I am Jacob's sister?"

Jacob corrected her, as if to show that he was older and knew a lot more: "Mamó is Dado's wife, just as Mom is Dad's wife."

"Did you ever have a sister?" Clíona asked her grandfather.

"I did and I do, and she is alive and well still."

"I never saw her," Jacob said, surprised. "How come she never visits the island?"

"Because Maggie has been living three thousand miles away in Boston in the United States."

"It is me that is talking to Dado," Clíona said to her brother. "You shouldn't be butting in. Mind your own business."

The old man took away the tension between the children in his own way. He put a hand over each ear and said: "Sir, I have ears like a donkey. They are so big that I can listen to you Clíona with one ear, and to Jacob at the same time. As for the question about Maggie, she comes back to where she was born here on the island about every five years. Both of you were very small the last time she was here, so you would not remember her. She will be coming here next year, and she will be amazed to see how big both of you have grown."

"I have a great memory," Jacob said, "and I don't remember her."

"She might have been a síóg, a fairy and we were not able to see her," was Clíona's opinion.

Jacob took the speculation a bit further: "Or a mermaid and she stayed in a cave near the sea."

"Or an angel," said Clíona "and she went away to heaven."

"You both have great imaginations," commented their grandfather: "Do either of you remember when you were little babies wearing nappies and drinking out of bottles?"

Clíona shook her head from side to side: "That was a long, long time ago and I don't remember a thing about it."

"That was the time Maggie was here. Long, long, long ago."

"Was she as small then as I am now?" Clíona asked.

"She was much older then than your Mom is now," her grandfather said, "but I remember when she was a baby in the cot."

"Was she bold?" Jacob asked as he smiled to himself: "Was she as bold as Clíona is now?"

Their grandfather shocked both children by saying: "She nearly killed me."

"Killed? Phew..." Jacob said: "Was it with a knife?"

"Or a gun?" Clíona interjected.

"It was an accident.!"

"A car accident?" Jacob wondered.

"Are you not listening to Dado? How could she have a car accident in a cot inside in the house?"

Their grandfather stretched out his arm and showed them the thumb of his right hand. It looked like it had been split in two halves many years earlier.

"It looks like two thumbs in one finger," Clíona said. She gave a little giggle and looked at Jacob: "It looks like a little bum."

"Don't be bold," he answered crossly before asking his grandfather: "Was it with a knife she cut it?"

"Is it sore?" Cliona asked before he had time to answer her brother's question.

"It has looked like that for more than seventy years, and the only time that it was sore was the night it happened."

Clíona asked how Maggie had cut the thumb.

Jacob had his own idea: "Was it with her teeth? Is she a werewolf? I saw one of them on the TV, but it was throats he was biting and not thumbs."

"She broke her bottle on the concrete floor," the old man said. "She fired it out of her cot."

"The bold..." Clíona held herself back from using a bad word: "The bold baby."

"That is all she was. A one-year-old baby, and I was not much more than a year older. Much as you and Jacob are now. Baby's bottles were made from glass at that time, and it smashed into smithereens on the floor. I could see the little pieces of glass coming towards me. They looked like diamonds in the light of the oil-lamp, so I grabbed one of them. When I looked my thumb was in two halves with blood spraying all over the kitchen."

"Was Maggie laughing?" Clíona asked.

"I don't think she even noticed what was happening. All I remember was that I was sitting on my mother's knee, as she tried to stop the blood."

Clíona asked: "Did she put your thumb in her mouth and try to stop the blood in that way?"

"No, but she squeezed my thumb between her fingers in

order to hold back the blood until my father went out to the cow-barn to get a spider's web. That is what stopped the blood, and that is what saved my life."

Jacob found his grandfather's story difficult to believe, "You mean that it was a dirty spider's web that saved you? That is disgusting." He hastened to add: "But I am glad that it worked."

"Some people hate spiders or are afraid of them," the old man said, "but I have loved them ever since that night."

"I hated spiders too," Clíona said quietly, "but I love them now."

"I wish I was a spider." Jacob jumped around on the sand, swinging his arms this way and that like a monkey and landing on all fours, laughing.

Clíona laughed as she told him: "You would not be able to put on your clothes if you were a real spider because you would have so many arms and legs."

This gave him an excuse to run around this way and that, full of energy: "I would be able to run back and over and sideways at the same time."

Clíona took her grandfather's hand and examined the old wound again: "Did your Mom bring you to the doctor to get stitches?"

"There was little talk of doctors at the time, because we could not afford them. You would be dead and buried before they got to the island."

Jacob had his own solution: "You could have done the lotto like our Mom and Dad and you would have plenty of money to pay the doctor."

"There was no lotto that time."

Jacob chimed in as if he was reciting some kind of mantra or an old boring statement of fact that he had heard all too often: "And there was no electricity or radio or computer or phone." He broke into laughter: "And there was no breakfast or dinner or supper."

Clíona joined in the litany: "And there was no school and no books and no teachers. And life was wonderful."

"Life changes," their grandfather said: "I never thought I would see the day that there would be no harrow or hoe or hames or horse on the island, or any of the things that would be as strange to you now as computers and mobile phones are to me and your grandaunt Maggie or your Mamó."

The yard was quiet beneath the burning sun for a while, as the old man seemed ready to join Topsy for an afternoon snooze.

It was Clíona who broke the silence: "Mom is going to build a great big glasshouse." She stretched out her hands as if she was able to reach out to both sides of the island: "It is going to be as big as Croagh Patrick."

Her brother corrected her: "You mean that it will be as big as Croke Park?"

"Isn't that what I said?"

"Croagh Patrick is a mountain. Croke Park is a football pitch."

His sister tried to defend herself: "You can play football on a mountain if you like. Isn't that what Saint Patrick did in Croke Park for forty days and forty nights?"

Jacob decided to give up the argument: "There will be every single kind of plant in the world in Mom's glasshouse."

"We will have lovely fruits to eat in our dessert," Clíona said, "And they will not just be sweet but healthy as well."

As if his grandfather didn't know, Jacob reminded him: "Dad is building a great big wall up to the sky to keep out the sea and keep everything in the island safe and well. It will be as good as the spider's web that saved your life, Dado."

The old man looked at his thumb as if he had not noticed it for the previous seventy years as wars and revolutions stoked the daily headlines. He spoke almost as if he was talking to himself:

"My thumb would not be like it is now if I had been able to go to a doctor or a hospital to have it stitched. But I prefer it the way it is."

Jacob asked him why.

"Nobody would have ever noticed my thumb if it had not been cut."

"I'm glad you didn't become a thief," Jacob said, "or the detectives would have noticed your fingerprint straight away."

"Aren't you the smart one," the old man said.

"I'm a smart one too," Clíona said.

"Both of you are a lot smarter than I am, but nobody is as smart as Topsy."

"Topsy is a dog," Jacob said. "He is a bit stupid sometimes."

Clíona patted the dog's head, and he licked her hand: "You are full of seafóid," she said.

The Irish word 'seafóid' that Clíona used reminded her grandfather that it was the word used for at least the previous century to describe dementia, an illness that had now stolen away his wife to the extent that she did not recognise him most of the times he visited her. It was mainly called by the generic name of Alzheimers in more recent times, but it had come be almost a living death in so far as many people were concerned.

He heard his granddaughter calling: "Dado, Dado."

"What is it, Cliona?"

"Are you alright?"

"I'm grand."

"I thought you had fallen asleep standing up," she said.

"You are not far off the mark." He thought of the name of a film he had seen on television some months earlier: "Dead man walking."

Clíona took his hand: "You are sad, Dado? Are you thinking of Mamó?"

He pulled himself together as best he could: "I said a while ago that you are smart, and that Jacob is smart. You are the two smartest cookies I have ever seen."

"Tell us about Mamó," Clíona said.

"I'm sure that I have told you everything already."

"Maybe you forgot something," Jacob said, "because you are getting old."

"I can see the two of us now in my mind's eye. I'm sure you know what the mind's eye is. It's what you remember as if it happened today or yesterday. Something that lives on in the mind for the rest of your life."

"Like cutting your thumb?" Jacob asked.

"Or getting a dirty cobweb from the henhouse to stop the bleeding," his sister said. "I never saw that in my life, but I can nearly see it now."

"That is the way I see your grandmother especially now that she lives in that Nursing Home on the mainland. I often see her now in my mind's eye as the young woman I married more than fifty years ago. She was only seventeen years old. People got married young back then. Teenagers without a care in the world. No talk of school or college. Just get married and get on with life as the generations before you did."

Clíona asked: "Do you still love Mamó?"

Jacob tried to answer for his grandfather: "Of course he does. Isn't she, his wife. He has to love her."

The old man laughed: "That reminds me of something funny I'm supposed to have said when I was about Jacob's age. My Dad was helping his sister with the hay because she was a widow. My mother was not very happy about it because she was afraid our own hay would rot if there was to be rain. I took my father's side when I said about my Dad's sister: 'She was his sister all his life, but you are only his wife for the past few years.' My mother used to joke about that for the rest of her life, but I think she was never too happy about it at the same time."

"What kind of work did you and our Mamó do together?" Clíona asked.

"Setting things. Sowing potatoes and cabbage. Thinning turnips. Saving turf. Catching mackerel out in the currach. Lighting a fire on the shore and cooking it. Great memories."

"Could Mamó row the boat?" Jacob asked.

"She was as good as myself at that and many other things, though I suppose that I never told her. I didn't like to think that I was being bested by a woman, or as a girl, as she was then. We were always competing with one another whether it was footing turf or thinning turnips or rowing the currach. I still remember a silly plan that I tried at one stage. To try and get ahead I used to pull the turnips and the weeds altogether. I used to separate them then, replant the turnips and throw the weeds away. By the end of the day my turnips were lying tired looking in the drills while your grandmothers were as fresh as daisies."

"What did she think of that?" Clíona asked.

"I can still hear her saying it inside in my head 'Look at your little soldiers dead in the ditch.'"

"We are going back to the sand now," Jacob said when the stories ended.

It occurred to his grandfather that neither of the children understood half of what he was talking about. For them a drill was an instrument their father used to bore a hole in a piece of timber rather than a low continuous mound of earth the length of a field. He thought of all the other farm or fishing words that he had mentioned earlier. "Different worlds," he said to himself, but it did not stop young and old from loving and caring for each other.

"That's life," he thought as he stretched back on the easy chair he used while outside keeping an eye on his grandchildren. Soon he was dreaming of himself, and his young wife pulled a lobster pot at the base of the cliffs to the south. Past and present were woven into each other in his dream. He hoped to see the great wall his son was building on the clifftop from the water below. There was a slight swell in the sea. He was using the oars to keep the currach away from the cliff while Nora, his wife, filled a lobster pot. Suddenly she seemed to have disappeared without a trace. Had she fallen over the side. How come he had not heard a splash? He woke up with a start. It was not the past but the present that frightened him now: "Where were the children?"

Topsy was still asleep. There were many new sandcastles on the sandheap but there was no sign of Clíona or Jacob. It was when he called out their names that he heard the skit of laughter from behind the flowers by the footpath. "You scared me," he said. "I didn't know where you had gone to, unknown to me."

"We pretended that we had disappeared, because you were asleep."

"We were just there behind the flowers," Clíona said.

"And I was just pretending to be asleep."

"You were snoring," Jacob told him. "Like an ass roaring."

Tsunami Tom, the children's father had just arrived on the scene: "Who was snoring?" he asked.

"Dado," Clíona and Jacob shouted together as they rushed over to hug their grandfather.

The old man tried to dismiss what had happened: "It was just a bit of hide and seek."

Tom made no comment on what he had heard as he urged the children: "Hurry up. Your Mom will be waiting for you."

Chapter Four

Work continued on the clifftop wall on the Western Isle at a steady pace despite the court order that Tom Thaidhg Rúa had received through the post to down tools and stop the work immediately. Tom neither replied to the letter nor told his fellow workers about it while he considered the situation. What they did not know, they could not be blamed for, was his attitude. After a couple of days, he decided to use it as a spur to incentivise his workmen. He nailed the letter to the inside of the door of the cabin which doubled as an office and a little canteen, and at lunchtime he read out the contents of the letter.

"Anybody who does not want to continue working on this project can leave immediately," he announced. "Anyone who fears being jailed for ignoring a court order and who wants to leave will be given a job on the house building project I have in Galway.!"

"How great is the danger of being sent to prison?" he was asked.

"Big enough, if they can catch you. This and other islands off the Irish coast have a long history of failing to catch up with renegades who broke the law of the land in one way or another."

"I would have no problem with prison," one of the men stated, "but there could be a downside to it if work was scarce and I was trying to get into the United States or on some of the sites in the Middle East. It could even come back to haunt a man's children in future years if they were blackballed too."

"That is the very reason I am giving you the option of

taking a job in Galway," Tom stated.

"The money is better here, and there are fewer expenses because we are living at home," another man said.

"Does anybody in Government or the police really give a damn what we do?" was the next question.

Tom answered: "Questions in the Dáil always make them nervous. Did you see how close that little plane came to the top of the cliff the last day? It is obvious that pictures were being taken, and somebody is reporting back to the bosses."

"I made sure to pull up my hoodie," one of the men said. "They might have got a picture of the machine, but they didn't get me."

Another man tried to inject a bit of humour to the proceedings: "Sure your thick head would look the same with or without the hoodie."

"I was tempted to do a bit of mooning myself," one of the drivers commented, "but I was too slow pulling down my trousers."

"A pity you didn't show them front and back at the same time and you would have been in the running for the selfie of the year."

The next comment drew even more laughter: "That big builder's bum would certainly go viral. What an ass."

The next contribution brought the workmen back down to earth: "Don't forget the way the men from Mayo were treated when they took on the might of the Shell gas and oil barons. It was not just those who went to jail and their families that suffered. There was many a one battered by a baton and it was all swept under the carpet. We should think hard before we try to take on the big buys at their own game."

"I make a solemn promise," Tsunami Tom said, "that I will personally see to it that no man's wife or children will have to suffer because of the stand we are taking on this island to protect our livelihoods and our environment."

A hand was raised, and a man asked: "I am not saying for a moment that you are not sincere, or that you will not stand by what you promise. But have you the backing? Have you the money to do so? Could all of this collapse like a house of cards and leave us all in the shits?"

"There is a simple answer to that," Tom said quietly: "I am in a position to put my money where my mouth is. A lot has been spent, and all of you have helped me to spend it. But there is more where that came from. I can guarantee you that."

"There are rumours that the Government are going to get the RAF to bomb the wall. I don't want to be beside it that day."

"There are all kind of rumours," Tom said, "one more daft than the last one. I don't believe that any Government is stupid enough to risk killing people because of a wall on top of a cliff. It may seem ridiculous now but I can imagine the day that Government ministers will be falling over themselves seeking an invitation to officially open what is now being condemned. Well, not the wall, maybe, but certainly what my wife Róisín is doing. That will make people everywhere sit up and take notice."

"So, we just keep on doing what we are doing?" one of the workmen asked.

"Ok, we are breaking the law, but I will put it like this, we are not flouting the law," Tom said. "We are not trying to rub anyone's nose in the dirt, but we are taking a stand on behalf of the island. So, do everything by the book in so far as you can. In other words, don't give them an excuse to close us down or land us with a fine from the European Commission that is too big for us to pay."

"Any other business?" Tom asked. He left little opportunity to his workmen to reply before continuing. "We have advantages in this and the other islands that people throughout the country do not have. I know we have many disadvantages, but the sea all around us is our biggest plus. It worked for islanders at the time of the evictions long ago. It worked to a large extent for other aspects of the land-war. It worked at the time of The Black and Tans It always gave the people a place to hide, whether it was John Dillon in Inis Meáin or the Playboy of The Western World. It worked for Lynchahaun in Achill even though that island has a bridge to the mainland. It worked for poteen-makers for centuries. We learned at a young age to be cute and to be careful and not to allow anyone to get the better of us."

Clíona and Jacob were delighted that their mother Róisín was at home from the city when Tom dropped them off at their home before heading back to the building work on the clifftop wall. Their mother hugged and kissed them as she wrapped an arm around each of them and carried them squirming and squealing with laughter into the sitting room where she deposited them softly on the big couch: "Tell me every single thing that happened while I was away," she said.

"Jacob was bold," Cliona announced.

"Clíona said a bad word too," Jacob countered, "and she pushed Topsy out of the way when he was knocking the sandcastles."

"And is that all that happened in the three days I was in Dublin?"

"Dado fell asleep today when he was minding us," Jacob said.

"But he told us some lovely stories," said Clíona.

"How could he tell a story if he was asleep?" Róisín asked, laughing, but curious at the same time.

Jacob tried to rescue his grandfather when he realised that what he had said might get the old man into trouble: "Dado fell asleep because he got tired telling stories."

"And Dad came back at just at that minute to help Dado to mind us,"

Clíona said. "We were hunched down hiding behind the big flowers."

Róisín was sounding more serious by the minute: "Do you mean that you were playing away for a while without Dad or Dado keeping an eye on you."

"It was only for a minute," Clíona said.

"Or a second," Jacob said.

"What game were you playing?" their mother asked.

"We were making castles in the sand but Topsy was knocking them one after the other. It was then that Jacob said the bad word. Will I tell you what it was?"

"I have a very good idea," their mother answered.

Jacob pleaded innocent: "I didn't want to say it, but it slipped out of my mouth."

"Another word slipped out after it," said Clíona and she said what it was.

"Never say that word again. Do you hear me?" their mother said crossly. "The other one is bad enough, but that one is horrible. And mean and insulting."

"Sorry Mom," the children said together.

"We will leave it like that," Róisín said: "All I have heard so far is about bad words and bold stories. Did anything nice happen? At home or at school or anywhere else?"

Jacob shrugged: "No."

"Nothing nice happened," Clíona said, "because you were not here."

"Never go away anywhere again," Jacob said.

"Are you telling me that you never want to go away on holidays again in your lives?"

Cliona had a quick answer: "I mean never go away without me or Jacob or Dad"

"You know that I am starting a very big job soon on behalf of everyone on the island, so I will have to go away now and again to arrange things?"

Jacob replied: "Don't we have lots of money now, so you don't need to go anywhere. You can stay at home like other Mums and look after us."

"I hate being idle and having nothing to do," Róisín said: "I hate to have nothing to do while the two of you are at school and Dad at work."

Clíona had her own idea: "You could stay at home and make lovely dinners for the rest of us."

Jacob has his idea as well: "And you could get us other brothers and sisters."

Róisín laughed: "And do I have any say in what I want to do?"

Jacob made a suggestion: "I know that you are going to build a very very big glasshouse to grow lots of fruits and vegetables. Wouldn't it be nice if you had more children so that they could take the weeds out of the turnips like Mamó and Dado did long ago when they were children."

"Whatever else will be in the glasshouse as you call it, I can assure you that it will not be turnips. I like them as a vegetable, but heat does not suit them. Where did you get this idea? Is it from your grandfather?"

Clíona answered: "Dado has been telling us lots of stories about working in the fields and about the time his sister nearly killed him."

"With a bottle," Jacob added.

"Did she hit him with a bottle?" their mother asked,

"She broke it on the floor and he caught the glass and it cut his thumb but his father saved his life with a dirty cobweb from the barn." Jacob said.

Clíona added: "The blood was squirting up to the roof."

Their mother shook her head in amazement: "Tales of blood and accidents, where does he get them?"

"I like stories about blood," Clíona said. "It gives me a shiver in my back." She added: "I only like it in stories, though. I don't like real blood." Jacob asked his mother used she throw bottles out of her cot when she was small: "Like Dado's sister. What is her name?"

"Maggie," Clíona answered. "American Maggie."

"I was never a bold girl," her mother said.

Clíona corrected her: "Didn't you often tell us about the time you went mitching instead of going to school?"

"That only happened once, and it was the longest and the most boring day in my life. Schooldays can make a person fed-up sometimes, but they are not half as bad as trying to pass a cold wet day with nothing to do except to make sure that you are not caught."

"Tell us again what you did all day," Clíona said.

"We were hiding under the trees near the crossroads at first because the morning was nice and sunny. Then there was a shower of rain but that was not too bad because the leaves were sheltering us. When the heavy rain came, we had to run to an old shed in which cattle used to shelter. We enjoyed that for a while, bouncing around on a pile of hay. Then we saw mice or baby rats in the hay. At first, we thought that they were little birds whose feathers had not grown yet, and we thought that they were lovely. That was until we noticed that each of them has four legs and a tail. We didn't know if they were mice or rats, and we did not wait to find out. We ran out of that shed as if the biggest dog in the world was coming after us."

Jacob asked what did they do for the rest of the day.

"The rain had stopped so we went back under the trees, but the rain was dripping down from the leaves and our clothes were wet through. We sat out on the rocks then until the clothes dried. And would you believe what we ended up doing for the rest of the day?"

"You went back to school," Clíona guessed.

"Nearly as bad. We took out our schoolbooks and played school. One of us would be the teacher for a while and the others the pupils. Whatever we did we could not get the little rats or mice out of our minds, and we could not wait to go home at the usual time the school closed every day."

Clíona asked her mother if she still hated rats and mice.

Róisín gave a little shiver: "I'm scared of them more than anything. The little ones I saw that time were too small to harm anyone or anything, but they are dirty and dangerous. They can spread infection and disease."

Jacob had a question for her: "Did Dado ever tell you about the old man from this island who could catch a rat with his hand and shake him until his neck broke and he died?"

The very idea of telling stories about rats disgusted Róisín: "Why is your grandfather constantly telling those stories about blood and guts and rats and spiders? I will have to ask your Dad to have a word with him."

"You don't want to hear the story so?" Jacob asked.

"You are bursting to tell me, and I may as well listen to how bad it is."

Jacob imitated his grandfather's storytelling method as he began: "A man from this island went over to England at the age of sixteen long ago. He stayed in a place that is famous for soccer nowadays. Liverpool is the name of that place. He got work on the docks and he trained to be a ratcatcher. He could kill a rat with a flick of his wrist. He came home to live here on the Western Isle after many years. He was cleaning out a pit of potatoes one day when he saw a rat sitting looking at him. It was as if all the rats he had ever killed had sent one of their own to get him. The old man thought that he was as fit as he ever was. His arm shot out with the speed of a snake. He thought he would catch the rat and shake it to death. He missed. The rat was ready for him, and he bit him on the wrist. The man was found in a heap on top of the potatoes. There was blood everywhere and the black crows were watching to pick the spuds."

"And watching to suck up the blood too," Clíona said, "I heard Dado telling that story and it was as good as Fionn and the Fianna."

Róisín shook her head from side to side in wonder: "How can you love such bloody and such scary stories?"

"Our schoolteacher told us that the older people have the best stories," Jacob said, "because they have the big world walked."

His mother was not convinced: "When I was at school, we had stories about Cuchulainn and Ferdia and Fionn and the Fianna. Heart-warming stories about valour and chivalry."

"And blood," Jacob added. "Do you remember that statue of Cuchulainn we saw in the GPO in Dublin when you and Dad brought us to learn all about the 1916 Rising? Poor Cuchulainn was bleeding to death."

"And Padraig Pearse had a revolver in his hand in one of the pictures," Clíona said, "but I don't think that it was him that shot Cuchulainn."

"Why don't we talk about something other than blood and mice and rats for the rest of the day?" Róisín suggested.

"It was you that started that talk," Clíona reminded her.

"How do you mean?" her mother asked.

"You told us about the little bald ones in the barn the day you were mitching." "I don't want to hear about anything like that as long as I live," Róisín said.

Clíona and Jacob teased her: "Rats, mice, spiders, creepie crawlies."

Róisín dramatically covered her ears with her hands and said she was about to make lunch: "What would you like?"

"A rat sandwich," Clíona laughed,

"Toasted mouse," Jacob said.

"Calm down now, or that is exactly what you will get."

When they were sitting down for lunch, their mother asked: "Did either of you ever go mitching from school?"

Jacob and Clíona looked at each other before shaking their heads, but their giggling soon let them down.

"Guilty," their mother proclaimed: "I know when children are hiding something. What did you get up to?"

Jacob admitted: "We went to Dado's house one day instead of going to school."

Róisín turned to Clíona: "Is this true, or is he making it up to annoy me?"

Clíona hung her head: "It only happened once, and Dado brought us to school at lunchtime."

"But you never told me," Their mother said: "And worse again your grandfather never told me or your father."

"Dado didn't want to get us into trouble," Clíona said meekly.

"What did you do when you were at Dado's house that morning?"

Jacob shrugged his shoulders: "I forget," while Clíona said: "I think that we watched television. Can we go and play with Topsy at Dado's house?"

"You will be going nowhere until I get to the bottom of what happened that morning."

"We had pizza, I think," Jacob said.

"We each had a glass of milk," his sister added: "With the pizza."

"Tell the truth," Her mother said. "You hate milk."

"I like the milk that Dado gets from the cow, but not milk from the shop."

"We help him to milk the cow sometimes," Jacob said. "It is not easy for us because our hands are small, but Dado is deadly.

He can shoot milk directly into the cat's mouth. And Topsy hides in case he would do it to him."

"Milk goes into the cat's eyes sometimes," Cliona said. "It is funny to see that, but the cat loves it. She is wiping her face with her paw and licking it for the rest of the day."

Róisín shook her head and spoke as if to herself: "The two of you have lives of your own that I know very little about. I know that you are very close to your Dado, and that he is very good to you. Does he ever wrestle with you or hug you when he is playing with you?"

"Dado is not a hugger," Clíona said.

"He does not even hug Topsy," Jacob added, "and he is his very own dog."

None of this did much to ease Róisín's worry. Why would children skip school to visit their grandfather? She had heard all the horror stories about child abuse but doubted involvement of that nature: "But you never know," she told herself. "I will have a lot to discuss with Tom when I eventually get him to sit down."

"What makes you love Dado so much?" she asked the children.

"Because he is the best in the world," said Jacob.

Clíona added to that: "Dado is not just the best. He is the very best."

Róisín felt that her questions were not getting her anywhere. She was thinking to herself: "What if the children are right, that their grandfather is great and wonderful and that I am doing him a disservice by even questioning what he does? But if he is as good as they say he is why has his son Tom so little to say about his youth? He hardly ever mentions his youth, good or bad." She tried another tack: "What other kind of stories does your Dado tell you?"

Clíona had a quick answer: "Every kind."

"Nice stories," Jacob answered. "I like listening to him. He tells great stories and some of them are funny. He makes us laugh."

"Tell me one of his stories," his mother said.

"You tell one," Jacob said to Cliona. "You are the best at it."

"He is just saying that" Clíona said, "because he is too lazy to tell you himself, even though he has all the stories off by hear."

Their mother thought of a plan: "Why don't both of you tell a story together? One person will think of something the other one forgets."

Clíona looked at Jacob: "What about the story about the pig?"

"You start," Jacob said.

"Dado and his sister Maggie were on their way to school one day when they came on a pig that was dead at the side of the road."

Jacob corrected her: "It was on their way home from school that it happened. Men from the village were after killing a pig for the dinner."

Clíona cut across her brother to explain: "They were going to put the pig into a barrel that was full of salt and to take out lumps of meat to put into a saucepan to boil for the dinner when they would be hungry."

"It must have been very salty bacon," Róisín said, hoping that her input would encourage the storytellers.

Clíona explained: "There were no fridges or freezers that time, so salt kept the meat from going rotten."

"They put salt on fish as well when they came in from the boats, to keep it from going off."

Clíona laughed: "What do you mean 'going off'? Sure, a dead fish could not go anywhere?"

"Going off means getting smelly," Jacob said.

Róisín said: "Clíona knows that. She is just having a laugh. Everyone must have been very thirsty after all that salt."

Jacob continued with the story: "The pig was squealing when they stuck a knife in its throat. Blood was splashing all over the place. The dogs were barking, and the gooses were screeching. The hens were running all over the place. There was blood on the people's faces and clothes and everywhere."

"What kind of a story is that to be telling children?" his mother asked, as if to herself.

"We will soon be coming to the good bit," Cliona announced.

"You mean there is more?" Róisín asked.

Jacob got on with the story: "The granddad of the house fell down on the ground like a sack of potatoes."

Clíona interrupted to clear up any misunderstanding: "It was not the men that killed the pig that killed the old man. It was his heart that killed him. He fell down dead as a doornail,"

Jacob carried on with the story: "It was just than that Dado and Maggie came along on their way home from school. There was panic everywhere. Blood all over the place. The pig was stretched on a donkey-cart. The old man was stretched on the ground with his bare feet sticking out where the priest had put oil on them. The men were smoking their pipes; The women were crying. They asked our Dado and Maggie to say a prayer for the dead man."

Although in one sense appalled by the story, Róisín was actually enjoying the storytelling ability of her son and daughter. They had not just taken the story word for word from their grandfather but had added their own embellishments along the way: "were your Dado and his sister Maggie scared?" she asked the children.

"It didn't bother them a bit," Jacob said. "They went home and had their tea."

Clíona added her own pieces to the jigsaw: "They did their homework. They did not watch television because they didn't have one. They played a few games. They never even thought of the pig until their mother came in the door with a basin of blood in order to make black pudding for everyone in the village."

Jacob had the last word: "Is it the pig's blood or the old man's blood?" they asked their mother.

"Gross," Róisín said, as if she could not even bear to think about it. "Why is your Dado continually telling you horror stories like that??"

"I love that kind of talk," Jacob said, "blood and guts and ghosts. It never gives me bad dreams at night."

"It is just like watching crazy cartoons on TV," Clíona said. "They are always chasing and killing each other, but we know that it is not real."

"The last thing I would like to think about when I am going to bed at night," their mother said, "is a basin of blood."

The children rubbed it in: "Basin of blood. Bucket of guts. Saucepan of Poo."

"Stop, stop..." Róisín covered her ears "After that story I will never be able to look a rasher or a sausage in the eye again." Children's logic quickly took over: "Rashers don't have eyes," Jacob said.

"Or sausages either," his sister chimed in.

Their mother laughed: "They will have eyes and ears when I am dreaming about them tonight. Are you sure that kind of talk does not give you nightmares?"

"Not me," Jacob answered: "I wished they did because most of my dreams are boring."

"Boring in what way?" Róisín asked.

"Boring about school, and you and Dad and Clíona and things."

"So, you are saying that we are boring?"

"Not really, but I like excitement. Blood and guts and stuff."

"And what about you Clíona?"

49

"My dreams are not boring. They take me out into space and up to the stars and stuff. I love going to bed at night because I don't know where my dreams are going to take me."

Chapter Five

Tsunami Tom was dealing with paperwork in the little cabin that doubled as an office and a canteen when one of his workmen put his head in the doorway and announced: "That new lorry you bought the last day is hanging out over the edge of the cliff between heaven and earth. Between the sea and the land."

Tom thought it was some kind of a joke: "Is it learning to fly?"

"It might be as well if it was. It wouldn't take much to send it crashing down to the foot of the cliff."

"Did it skid or what?" Tom enquired.

"It was deliberately driven there."

"And what are you doing about it? Do you expect me to do everything?"

"We need your input. We were thinking of attaching it to one of the big machines with chains. That could go the other way because the lorry is filled with rocks, and it could drag the machine down after it. A double loss and maybe loss of life involved as well."

"Who would do that with a new lorry?" Tom asked, more to himself than anything.

"A right eejit," the other man said, "because he could have gone down himself with the lorry if he had brought it forward another few feet."

"Come on," Tom said. "This has to be sorted out." They went out to the little jeep that they used to travel the length of the wall and around the island.

"Are the other men still working?" Tom asked as they travelled along.

"They are waiting for you because they don't know what is the right thing to do. Nobody wants to see a good lorry in pieces at the bottom of the cliff. Apart from anything else the footage would be all over the world before the day is done."

"That is exactly what the bloke that set this up wants."

The workmen gathered around when they reached the site and assessed the situation. The rear of the lorry hung over the cliff from which it had been reversed into place. The load of stone which threatened to carry it to the bottom could clearly be seen Tom barked out orders: "Bring up the strongest chains we have and two of the biggest rock breakers. The engine of the lorry should drag it forward when the horsepower of the big machines is attached."

"Who is going to try and drive the lorry?" the man who had called Tom in the first place asked.

"Me, of course," Tom said. "I wouldn't ask anyone to something that I am not prepared to do myself."

Tom had some regrets later in the day that he had been so bullish when the front wheels of the lorry were spinning as they failed to get purchase on the clifftop. The big rock breakers were at full power but seemed unable to shift the lorry forward.

"Could we dump the load?" the man who had called him in the first place shouted to him where he was seated uncomfortably in the cabin as he wondered would he have enough time to jump from the lorry if it was dragged backwards. The lifejacket he was wearing seemed completely inadequate even if he managed to live until the whole shebang landed into the sea.

"If we tip the load now," Tom shouted down to his crew, "it could pull the lorry and the machines backwards. There is great momentum over the cliff in a pile of rock like that sliding backwards."

"We could always let the lorry go. Take the hit," the other man said.

"I wouldn't give them the satisfaction," Tom said.

"There are things more important than pride. Think of Róisín and Jacob and Clíona. Think of your mother and father."

"I am thinking about them all.," Tom answered. "I am thinking of tumbling down there to my death, but I have no earthly intention of doing so. Get those two rock breakers to crawl forward at full power together, and I will put my foot to the board in this yoke."

The power of the big machines brought the lorry forward a matter of inches at first, but they helped the front wheels of the lorry to gain a grip. It seemed to take forever for the rear wheels to reach the cliff edge. They seemed to anchor the lorry there until Tom shouted down: "Let the back wheels go. They will be of no loss compared with the rest of the wagon." A couple of men went to the edge of the cliff and stretched full length to watch the big wheels and the metal which attached them together hit the tide far below. It was as if the sea was angry as the undercarriage of the lorry sank and rose again and again before breaking into separate pieces and disappearing beneath the waves.

Tsunami Tom received a rousing round of applause when he climbed down from the engine section of the lorry. He hid the fact that he was shaking in his skin as the lorry hung "between heaven and hell," as one of the workers put it: "I will see all of you in the public house at five o'clock," he announced. "No more work today, but I have to arrange security for the lorries and machines after what has happened. We have been far too lax up to now. Anyone who wishes to be part of that security group should meet me in the canteen at three o'clock."

"Will security people need guns?" he was asked.

"I haven't thought about that properly yet, but if you have a gun, take it with you. It might help to frighten off those involved in today's episode. I would prefer to do without guns, but if that is the only language they understand, that is the language that we will speak. We faced up to scoundrels in other parts of the world before now, and we will not let something like this get the better of us. Right now, I don't know who the enemy is, but I would like to look into his eyes. And tell him a few home truths."

One of the men stretched out a hobnail boot: "If we catch the devil that did this, he will get a taste of this. Guns are too dangerous. As we often see from America, they cause more trouble than they cure."

"It's not the wheels of a lorry that will be sent swimming," another man said, "but the bloke that did this." He continued: "For the first time in our lives we have work, good work available at home, and someone does this on us. He will have a lot to answer for."

"We will take this evening to think things over and share a drink," Tom said. "The work will go ahead tomorrow." He gave a wry smile: "If we have any lorry or machine that has not been sent for a swim."

Those quiet words drew a nervous laugh, as men wondered were their lives going to be suddenly changed by an enemy they did not know or understand.

It came as a surprise to Tsunami Tom later in the day to find that there were so many men willing and ready to take on security roles. Groups of four were delegated security duties each fortnight, after which they would return to their ordinary work. It was not just the machinery that needed to be cared for, Tom insisted, but the glasshouses that were to be part of Róisín's project.

When all of those arrangements had been finalised, Tom went home to take a shower and have a meal before joining the other men in the bar. Róisín seemed peeved that he had not phoned earlier to tell her what had happened with regards to the lorry on the clifftop. "I felt like a complete fool," she said, "when I went into the shop to get a few groceries on my way home after collecting the kids from school. Everyone was talking about my hero of a husband, and I didn't know a thing about it. Even though I am supposed to be your wife,"

"It was one of the most stressful days of my life," Tom said, "one thing happening after the other. We had to try and save the lorry, and then organise security so that the likes of it could not happen again. I was the man in charge, so I had to take responsibility. Anyway, I am not the kind of man who brings his work home with him. Otherwise, I would be stressing you every evening, coming back like a little pet looking for sympathy."

"What you did was stupid and dangerous," Róisín said. "You didn't just risk your own life. Cliona and Jacob could have been orphans by now, and me a widow."

"But you are not," Tom said. This was not the first day I risked my life and I am sure that it will not be the last. There were times in the tunnels in London and Abu Dabi that it might all have collapsed in on top of us because of brittle rock. We managed to shore it up and get on with it. I didn't come home crying to my wife afterwards. I didn't even tell you because I did not want to worry you. You wouldn't even know about today if you had not gone into the shop. I am in a risky business, but I am still alive."

"If we cannot even talk about things like that," Róisín said, "we might as well give up. They say that lack of communication is the death of marriage, or of any kind of partnership."

"You need to get out more," Tom said. "You are watching too much of that Doctor Phil. The sooner that works starts on those glasshouses, the better it will be for both of us. You will have something to concentrate on. Other than me."

"I have been thinking," Róisín said, "of staying at home altogether until the children are older and going to secondary school. The other project could be put back a few years until they get bigger and will be better able to look after themselves."

"What brought this on?" Tom asked, "on this day of all days?"

"I was talking to Clíona and Jacob when I came back from Dublin, and they were asking me to stay at home with them all of the time."

"They just missed you," Tom said: "You would go crazy if you had nothing else to do except to mind children. You need to get out there. You were full of ideas that last night when you were in the hotel and we had a long chat, do you remember that?" He asked "Communication."

"There are a lot of things we need to talk about."

"What things?" Tom asked: "Does it have to be this evening?"

"Things about those stories your father tells the children. All about blood and guts and people dying."

"I heard all of those when I was a young fellow. They went in one ear and out the other. Did they do me any harm?"

"But Clíona and Jacob are sensitive souls." Their mother said.

"Was I not? Am I not?"

"You are hard and tough. I am not knocking that. You have to be in the job that you are in, but we need to talk about all of these things without having to run out the door to another appointment, another meeting, another job."

Tom looked at his watch: "Do I need to do it at this very minute? I am supposed to meet the men in the pub to try and wind down a bit after all the trauma of this morning."

"A man's solution to men's problems," Róisín said, sarcastically.

"Bear with me on this one," Tom said. "What do they call it nowadays? A debriefing session. It was never needed so badly."

Róisín seemed to ignore what Tom had said, "I tried to talk to you about the children a few times recently and those stories they are hearing from your father. A football match on the television was more important to you the same evening than your children's welfare."

"Why do you always do that?" Tom asked. "Make me feel guilty if I sit down and take things easy for a few minutes. "Take it easy" you are telling me one minute. Do this or that the next minute."

"You never listen to a thing I say."

"I am listening now," he said. "Get on with it."

"Why are you looking at your watch? Is my time measured?"

Tom spoke slowly through his teeth: "It is well you know that I have an appointment with my workmen in less than half an hour. I need to have a shower. I may not have sweated blood when I was up there with the lorry hanging over the edge of the cliff, but by Jesus I sweated. So, I don't smell the best and I need to wash. But go on. Have your say. Get it off your chest. Get rid of the poison. Say what you dislike about my father who has a broken heart because his wife is dying with Alzheimer's disease."

"What is the point of me trying to say anything now?"

"I need to know in what way is my father abusing our children."

"They have names," Róisín said, "Clíona and Jacob."

Tom gave a sarcastic reply: "I thought that Jacob and Clíona were the names of our children, but of course the girls have to come first in this feminist world."

"There is no point in trying to talk to you when you are in this kind of a mood."

"If you had a day like I had," Tom said, "you might understand." He headed for the shower in order to get ready to go to the pub.

Chapter Six

The day's happenings were still being discussed when Tsunami Tom reached the island public house. Men were worried that lorries or other machinery could be blown up, as bombing equipment that had not been decommissioned during the Northern Ireland peace process was still fairly readily available to those in the know. There were other more subtle ways of creating mayhem such as interfering with brake fluid, or that people could be killed in incidents that had unintended consequences.

"I don't expect to see much happening in the short-term," Tom told the men who sat nearest to him. "Those who did the damage today will know that lorries and machinery will be guarded for some time. They will wait for people to get complacent, at Christmas, or when there are tourists around and people are taking things easier, but by then I hope that most of the work will be finished."

"I am surprised that you have not sent for the police," a man said.

"What we were doing is technically illegal," Tom explained, "because we do not have planning permission. You and I think the work is necessary to break the force of any tsunami that might hit us, as happened in Aran years ago. By bringing the police on board the work may have to stop long before the job is completed."

"This island never had a police presence," one of the men said, "by the Garda Siochána or the RIC who came before them in the time of the British."

"The British flag never flew over this island," someone said proudly.

This drew a witty answer: "There are those who would say that the British captured anywhere worth invading, but they didn't bother with us because they thought we were not worth it."

"In fairness to the Brits, they gave plenty of work to our people down through the years."

"They paid well, but they got value for money, in blood, sweat and tears."

One of the men drew attention to the great wave that struck Inis Mór in the Aran Islands more than a century and a half earlier: "How come there is no talk about it, if it actually happened. Did it miss the other islands for some reason? They are actually lower than the big island."

Another made a suggestion: "When something really bad happens, such as The Famine or a big flu, people don't talk much about it. People were just after the Famine then and the loss of fifteen men to a freak wave must have been devastating altogether."

Tsunami Tom gave his own interpretation of events: "There was a great man for drama living on the islands about fifty years after that wave. He is still remembered, especially on the middle island, John Millington Synge. He was the man who wrote that play about the poor widow that lost all of her sons to the sea. 'Riders To The Sea,' they call it."

The oldest man in the company remarked: "The Abbey Theatre came around here with that play onetime and put it on the stage in the old hall. It was one of the saddest plays I ever saw."

Tom continued with the story he had started a few moments earlier: "When Synge looked across from Inis Mór to Inis Meáin, he wrote that the thatched houses in the distance looked like a straw rope thrown across the island. They houses were all in the same line and more or less at the same height above sea-level." He asked the rhetorical question: "Why do you think that was?"

There were a couple of murmurs that his listeners had no idea.

"Because the great tsunami fifty years earlier had stayed in the minds if the islanders. That is the reason. The houses were far enough away from the sea to have shelter from a wave coming from the south. At the same time, they were built high enough above sea-level for the dying waters of a wave to wash past them. People begin to build on the crags later on because of better views and all that, when the folk memory of that wave had died away."

A man rose from his seat to go to the toilet: "If a tsunami hits while I am in the loo, let someone pull up my trousers so that when I am in my coffin people will say that I was caught with my pants down." He pointed at Tom: "Whatever about waves and all that. one thing we have to thank this man for is for bringing steady work and good pay to the island. It beats being out on the water trying to get lobster and crabs and crayfish, and it will give a chance for some of them to grow before we have to face the sea again."

"If you wait much longer before going to the toilet, we may have another tsunami to deal with." His further comment about catching crabs was lost in the laughter that followed.

The mood in the bar changed when one of the men asked bluntly: "Does anyone think that we may have a Judas among us? Is the so and so that caused all the trouble this morning sitting here and having a laugh, not with us, but at us?"

A silence descended and it was as if people were reluctant to look each other in the face in case they would recognise that the culprit was among them.

Men then seemed to get Dutch courage, as if the drink was rising inside them and crudely expressed: "I would like to see the geezer that brought that lorry to the edge of the cliff last night being sent in to swim from the top of the cliff after getting a kick in the arse from my hobnail boot."

Another commented: "I would like to see him hanging from one of the cranes or one of the big buckets on the machines. It would not be half good enough for him."

"Nobody here will be jumping to conclusions or taking the law into their own hands," Tom said. "Revenge is sweet," they say, "but it often picks on the wrong person. There will be no kangaroo court here."

"Didn't you tell us a while ago that you broke the law yourself by not applying for planning permission?" one of the men said.

"That is true, but that is different from picking on someone in the wrong and then finding out that they had nothing to do with it. I have to take responsibility that I allowed myself to slip into a false sense of security. Everything seemed to be going well and there was no evidence that someone was plotting against us."

"But why are they doing that?"

"It is a free country, and nobody has to agree with what we are doing," Tom answered. "We would prefer if they showed a bit of courage and made their points publicly at a meeting instead of doing damage like thieves in the night."

"Where were they," it was asked, "the night of the big meeting when everyone had a chance to express an opinion? That would make a lot more sense than trying to send an expensive lorry to the bottom of the sea."

Another man called the perpetrators some choice names, before announcing: "They are like constipated skeletons. They don't have the guts to shite."

Tom looked everyone that made a comment in the face. He knew from experience that in cases like that the culprit would likely be the loudest in condemnation, in order to cover his own back. He thought of the picture of the twelve apostles his mother had in her kitchen but did not see Judas in any face.

The night finished with a call from Tsunami Tom to be more careful, to report any suspicion, however small to him personally and to take care of themselves: "Let us finish what we have started," he said rousingly, "and let the devil take the hindmost." He had no idea of what that meant, but he had heard it somewhere and it seemed appropriate for the occasion.

He expected to find the bedroom door closed when he got home, and the spare room waiting for him. He got a surprise as he tried to slip in beside Róisín without waking her. She turned her warm body towards him: "Don't try and stop this tsunami," she whispered.

Chapter Seven

The clifftop wall on the Western Isle was raised in the Irish Parliament, Dáil Éireann the following day. Rumours had circulated about the lorry that had been partly reversed across the edge of the cliff and the danger for the workers involved. The local representative spoke of "this beautiful island which had been peaceful for a thousand years or more now plunged into anarchy, not to speak of arrogance." He began his question to the Minister for Transport and Tourism with a flourish: "It was there I was sent as a teenager to brush up on my Irish, and it is the place to which I still go on holiday on a regular basis in summertime, unlike those on the benches opposite who tan their hides in far-off expensive locations."

"That is just fake tan," came a quip from across the chamber, followed by:

"Not to speak of fake news,"

One belly needs more tan than another."

There followed the observation: "There are more Fir Boilg on that side of the house than on this one."

"Some of you think that it was Arthur Guinness who invented the Fir Bolg, and he did a lot to help them to expand in the waistlines, but they were a people that came in from Bulgaria thousands of years ago."

The Ceann Comhairle, or Speaker Of The House rose to his feet: "An answer will be given by the Minister as soon as order is restored. This is a serious question which does not deserve the amount of levity that it has engendered."

The Transport Minister responded when calm was restored: "Reports from the Western Isle are a cause of great concern to the Government. It is clear that a great deal of building work has been done there without planning permission, Officers from my Department will travel to the island without delay to examine what is happening and to report back to me. That information will be shared by the Taoiseach and this house as soon as it is obtained."

The local representative asked: "What does 'without delay' mean in this context. Is it this week, next week or during the Christmas holidays?"

There is no need for the questioner to be facetious. Without delay in an island context includes the proviso: "weather and other circumstances permitting."

"Does the Minister hope this problem will go away, or does he propose to do something practical to relieve a dangerous situation on an island on which he never set foot and is not proposing to set foot in the near future?"

"I am sure that there are places in Ireland on which my questioner has never set foot himself. Everybody cannot be everywhere, as he well knows. But that does not prevent us from providing help and sustenance to the most remote parts of our country."

The representative quoted the words: "the most remote places," back to him. "Are we back to the noble savage image that our conquerors promoted in Punch and other papers in days gone by?"

"The deputy opposite might well revel in the title 'noble savage', but I look on everyone in the State as being of equal importance. I have answered his question and will report back to the house as soon as possible."

The questioner took a different tack: "Your answer reminds me of a question attributed to a former Minister of this house,

James Fitzgerald Kenney, the man who took over Justice after the murder of the late lamented Kevin O'Higgins."

"Does this matter have any relevance to the house?" the Ceann Comhairle asked, but the representative ploughed on: "This actually happened in a court case rather than Dáil Éireann. The relevance will become clearer later."

"Proceed," said the man in the chair.

The matter related to a Mrs Ponsonby and had to do with a signature on a document. Mr Kenney of Clogher House, Co Mayo, asked the immortal question: "Do you make your 'P' with a flourish, Mrs Ponsonby?"

Dáil Éireann was in uproar for a moment. The Minister then stated: "I suggest that it is the representative opposite that is taking the 'P' in this context. What you have said has absolutely nothing to do with the matter in hand. You are just having a laugh and I hope that in the long run the laugh will be on you when your voters see through what you are doing."

"The point I was making is that you were not answering my question properly, or at all, apart from feeding me with parliamentary waffle. It is a scandal that no one from your Department has visited the Western Isle to report to this house on matters there."

"The Minister reiterated that nobody is allowed to take the law into their own hands."

His questioner pointed out: "Is there any party in this chamber whose members did not break the laws of the land with regard to everything from national independence to water charges?"

A shout from Government backbenches said: "There was nothing wrong with breaking British law, because they were our oppressors."

"What about water charges?"

"That was west-Brit law."

The questioner changed his tactics: "It is patently obvious that the population of that island is split with regard to these issues. Something needs to be done urgently before there is a death, accidentally or otherwise."

A woman member of Parliament from Dún Laoghaire asked: "Where are the Gardaí Síochána in all this?"

The member who had raised the matter in the first place explained: "There is very little Garda presence on any island, because for the most part they are among the most peaceful places in the State. Things get out of hand in every area from time to time. What does the Minister propose to do about it?"

"I have given my answer," the Minister said abruptly.

"And a useless meaningless answer it is. Waffle about weather permitting and all of that is not an answer. You gave no indication of when your delegation will be travelling to the Western Isle, how many will be involved, to whom will they make their report to you and to this House."

The Minister began to show signs of frustration: "I have given my answer. You are the person who muddied the waters by dragging the Fir Bolg and Tuatha De Danann and Fionn Mac Cumhaill into the equation. This kind of waffle may impress the listeners to your local radio or those of your voters who can read the local papers. It is past time you allowed long lost heroes to be forgotten and to address the problems of this day and age."

The Leader of the Opposition came to the aid of his own colleague: "It is a great pity that the Minister is unable to give a clear and concise answer without insulting and making little of the questioner."

The Minister started to argue that it was the deputy that raised the question in the first place who had brought the Fir Bolg into the matter. The Ceann Comhairle told him to sit down as the Leader of the Opposition had the floor. He thanked him for his intervention and proceeded: "It is obvious that we do not have the full story of what is happening on the Western Isle. I know the island. It was my privilege to visit there many years ago as a Minister of State to open an extension to the pier. I found it to be a peaceful and welcoming place and I am disappointed to find out that it is now in what the great dramatist, Sean O'Casey would call 'a state of chassis' I think the island community there and the people of Ireland in general deserve clear answers from the Minister to the questions asked by my colleague. Those answers should include where the money involved in this project has come from and why planning permission was not sought or obtained in advance of the work starting."

There were shouts from the benches opposite: "The Lotto. They won the lotto. Lotto, lotto, lotto," they continued to shout until the Ceann Comhairle called a recess.

Chapter Eight

Tsunami Tom seemed to have woken up with a completely different attitude the following morning. "It must have been the drink that did it," his wife Róisín said as they "sat around the breakfast counter with their children, Clíona and Jacob.

"What has the drink done?" Tom asked.

"It has put you into good form, taken away the nerves."

He winked: "It might not be just the drink that did it."

"Will Dado be minding us again today after school?" Cliona asked.

Róisín and Tom looked at each other and they answered "yes," at the same time.

Jacob and Clíona clapped their hands: "Goody. We will have fun," she said.

"And stories," Jacob added. "Dado has great stories."

"Do you really like his stories?" his father asked: "Are they not a bit old-fashioned?"

"What does old-fashioned mean?" Jacob asked.

"About things that happened long ago that nobody really cares about now."

Róisín added: "The world has changed an awful lot since your Dad and I were young, but much more even since your Dado was a boy."

Clíona had an answer at the top of her tongue: "Everything on television is about a different life to what we have here as well. But we prefer Dado's stories to TV any day."

"What is so great about them?" Tom asked.

"They are funny," Jacob answered.

"Funny ha ha?" Tom asked.

"Funny because they happened to Dado or to his sister or someone else like that. They were real things."

"I give up," Tom said.

"If Dado is free, he will pick you up from school," Róisín said. "I have a few other things to do this evening."

"Yes, yes," the children cheered.

"We will give your father one more chance," Róisín said when the children had gone to school. "If we are not happy about his stories or anything else, we will have to get someone else to mind them when I am busy."

"What kind of other things are you talking about with regard to my father?" Tom asked. "Are you worried that something else is going on?"

"If there was, he would never get to see the kids," she answered. "But every time there is a programme on television about abuse, you wonder. People involved in that kind of thing are so cute at grooming youngsters."

"I suppose there is nothing wrong with a few stories, if that is all that it is."

"Sweets and pizzas are not as big of an issue, of course," Róisín said, "but so many children are overweight nowadays."

"There isn't a pick on our two," Tom said.

"It is about bad eating habits more than anything."

"Don't go down that road," Tom said, "or it will only create problems. Anyway, won't you have the healthiest of products growing in your glasshouses?"

"I suppose," Róisín answered. "Why are we all so worried all the time about things that might never happen?"

Tom asked: "What kind of stories did you like yourself when you were a kid?"

"Enid Blython and that kind of thing. Stories about ponies and boys a bit later, of course when the teenage years came along. Imagine we have all of that in front of us yet. What were you into yourself?"

"Spiderman and adventurous things like that, Star Wars."

"Was there stuff like that available on the island?"

"We got a big cardboard parcel from Chicago every couple of months."

"With comics?" Róisín asked.

"With clothes and shoes as well. I remember the smell of camphor as we opened the white twine around the parcel. Of course, we were not allowed to cut that off because use would be found for it as a clothesline or something else. But it all added to the drama of opening the parcel. The comics would be at the bottom, Mickey Mouse and Minnie at the beginning. Then it was like as if they were growing up with us, moving on eventually to Star Wars and stuff like that."

"All from Chicago?" Róisín asked.

"From people we never knew or saw. People who had emigrated fifty years or more before that."

"Did you get to see them when you were bigger?"

"They had died by then. The last of them was a Nun. She made it back to Ireland before she died. A tough cookie. She took up social work when she retired as a teacher. It was said that she could walk any street in the city with an escort or anyone to mind her, because all of the homeless, black white or any other race had such respect for her."

"You never told me you had a nun in the family before?"

"You never asked," Tom said, "I was never into that kind of stuff, but I had respect for her because she was a rebel."

"Like yourself?"

"Maybe that is where I got a taste for taking on the big boys."

It was time to go to work again, Tom to the great wall on the clifftop, and Róisín to a meeting with island women who were free at that time of the day while their children were at school. It was a preliminary meeting to see who might be available the following year to work in the conservatories that were to be built across the island in which to grow exotic fruits and plants.

"Is this cheap labour?" one of the women asked. "Work for women because it is not good enough for men?"

"Not at all," Róisín answered. "Men are welcome, but there are very few unemployed men on the island at the moment. Pay will actually be the same for women as for men. Hours will be flexible to make childminding easier. People can work for three, five or eight hours as they wish so that they will be off if they so choose while their children are home from school."

"When is all of this due to start?"

"We are awaiting planning permission at the moment, and we are in the process of leasing the amount of land that will be needed. That in itself will be an extra income for workers and others willing to lease land to us, so I reckon that it will be a considerable boost to meeting the cost of living."

"Do we have to sign up today?"

"There is a list that people can sign but this is only an expression of interest," Róisín answered. "We cannot expect anyone to sign a contract until everything is worked out and the glass houses built, but it would be a great help to know how many people are interested."

"Those who had attended to meeting seemed very positive about the project as they gathered around to drink tea and coffee when the formalities were over: 'Bring it on,' seemed to be the order of the day."

Chapter Nine

Clíona and Jacob were delighted that their grandfather was waiting for them outside the school. They hugged him and each held on to one of his hands as if they were afraid, he would escape from them before getting them to his house for their regular pizza. He used an old cliché to express their affection for him: "You are as great with me today as a cow with a cock of hay."

"We were not sure if you would be minding us today, Dado," Clíona said.

Her brother agreed: "We thought that Mom might be getting someone else to mind us."

"Why did you think that?"

"We don't know," the children answered together.

The old man was not willing to let go of their simplistic answer. "There must be some reason for you to say that."

Jacob did not like to admit that he has overheard a conversation between his parents: "We were dreaming last night that you might not be waiting for us after school today."

"Both of you had the same dream? I heard about twins who were so close that they had the same thoughts. But a brother and a sister with a year between them? That is remarkable."

Clíona hugged the dog: "Topsy has the same dream as we have sometimes too, because he is very sensible."

"Don't you mean sensitive?"

She shrugged her shoulders as if to say: "It's all the same."

Their grandfather probed further: "Tell me what this great

dream was all about."

"It was about you not being at the school gate today," Jacob said.

"If the two of you are not going to really tell me about your dream, I am not going to tell you about mine," their grandfather said.

Clíona was immediately curious: "Do old people dream too?"

"Of course, we do. We are much longer in the world, so our heads are full of dreams."

"Tell us what you were dreaming about," Jacob said.

"I was dreaming that I had a lovely pizza ready for today's lunch but when young people I know were hiding things from me, I ate it all myself."

"You are joking," Clíona said. "You did not."

The old man rubbed his hand across his stomach: "It was yummy."

"You are fibbing," his granddaughter said. "Old people should not tell lies."

"Why old people?" their Dadó asked.

"Because they are much nearer to going to hell than we are," Clíona said. "You could drop dead just like the old man in the story you told us about the pig."

"Come on," the old man said. "It is time to eat the pizza."

"How can we?" Clíona asked, with a glint in her eye, "when you have eaten it yourself. I know that it is still in the freezer."

"How do you know?"

"I had a peep when I was supposed to be going to the toilet."

"And you always share everything with us anyway," Jacob said. "You are the best Dadó in the world."

"You are just saying that in case I would eat all of the pizza myself," he joked.

"We are saying it because it is true," Clíona said.

There was very little talking while the food was being eaten. As soon as they were finished their grandfather made a big gesture by beating his hand against his chest: "We are after making a huge mistake."

"What is it Dadó?" Clíona asked.

"We did not keep any pizza for poor Topsy."

"Keep your hair on, Dadó," Jacob said: "Topsy is not allowed pizza. The cheese gets stuck in his teeth and his gums, and he twists his mouth from side to side on the grass when he is trying to get rid of it."

"And it gives him bad breath too," Clíona added. "Just like Mom's friend, Gearóidín. She is always washing her teeth when she comes to our house."

"Maybe she has no toothpaste in her own house," her grandfather joked, before turning his attention back to the dog: "What does Topsy like? If he cannot eat pizza?"

"He likes to break the castles we build in the sandpit," was Clíona's answer.

"What does he eat at this time of the day? After school?"

"You are silly, Dadó. You know well that dogs do not go to school."

Jacob added: "Anyway he is your dog most of the time, Dadó. You should know what he likes?"

"I know what Topsy likes best," Clíona said.

"Turnips," her grandfather suggested jokingly.

"Ice-cream," she announced.

Jacob has his own point of view: "Topsy likes ice-cream best when he is sharing it with us. Sharing is caring, as you always say, Dadó."

"I never said that in my life was his reply."

"It might be Mom that says it, or our teacher or someone," Cliona said. "Anyway we know that it is true."

Their grandfather spoke: "If that is the way things are, I suppose I will have to eat the ice-cream along with Topsy."

"Don't worry Dadó. We will help you."

"Off you go then and get it ready."

When had they eaten the old man asked: "Is there anything on TV at this time of the evening that you like? It would be nice to chill out in the house for a while and go out to the sandpit for a while then."

"Cartoons" was their answer to his question about television. The old man was delighted to stretch back in his armchair as crazy looking characters swooped back and over across the screen: All too soon in his mind the children were asking: "What about that story that you were supposed to tell us after school?"

He tried to give himself a bit of time and space by saying that he needed to finish his tea first, before adding: "And I am dying to see that story about the two monkeys in the cartoon ends."

Clíona told him: "You are silly, Dadó. Those are not monkeys. It is a cat and a mouse chasing about."

"I wouldn't like to meet a mouse as big as that."

"The cat will be sad and the mouse is happy at the end," Jacob said. "Most of the stories are all the same."

"They are trying to kill each other one minute," their grandfather said, "but all of them are alive even if they are a bit battered in the end."

"Animals are like people," Jacob said. "They are fighting one minute, and they are the best of friends again the next day."

"Are you talking about yourself and Clíona now?" his grandfather asked.

"Or Mom and Dad." Clíona chimed in.

"Grownups don't fight," their grandfather said jokingly.

Clíona had a different view: "They were the worst of friends two days ago and the best of friends today. I hate it when they are fighting,"

"I hate it too," Jacob added. "They fight more now than when we had no money before the lotto."

Clíona asked her grandfather: "Used you and Mamó be fighting? Before she lost her mind?"

"That is not a nice thing to say," the old man answered.

"But it is true," Jacob said.

"It is not like losing money or losing your watch," their grandfather said, "Your Mamó became ill, and it affected her memory."

"Did something poison her?" Cliona asked: "Or someone?"

Their grandfather tried to answer as best he could: "Diseases come in all sorts of ways. Something in the atmosphere maybe. Something in the food, some kind of a virus. Your Mamó was healthy all of her life. She never drank or smoked but she still got that Alzheimer."

"Maybe she eats too many turnips," Cliona suggested.

"Why do you say that?"

"Because I don't like turnips. Anyway you didn't answer my question."

"What question?"

"Used you and Mamó fight? Like Mom and Dad?"

"Like me and Jacob?"

"Like cats and dogs," he said. "Like cats and mouses on the telly?"

"We had arguments from time to time like everyone else. No two people are the same and they have different opinions, so they can't agree about everything, as you and Jacob know well. To tell you the truth I would give anything if your mother and myself could have a right argument instead of her being the way she is."

"Will Mamó be in hospital forever?" Jacob asked.

"She needs the kind of care that I am not able to give her," the old man answered: "I tried to look after her for a while, but I was not up to it. And she needs medicines and other remedies that are not available here on the island."

"Used you fight with your sister Maggie when you and she were the same ages as Jacob and me?" Clíona asked.

"It was much the same then as it is now. Brothers and sisters don't get on with each other all the time, but they usually make up and are friends again."

"I hate Jacob sometimes when he steals my stuff."

"I don't steal them," he said. "I take a loan of them."

"But you don't put them back again?"

"You know where they are, and you can collect them."

"What about when you steal my collection of model cars that Dad had when he was a boy himself?" Jacob asked.

"They are not just your cars," Clíona said: "Dad gave them to both of us."

"I was watching the two of you playing in the sand the other day," their grandfather said, "and you were getting on very well together."

"But we were not getting on with Topsy," Clíona said, "because he was breaking the castles we made again and again. I would love to murder him sometimes." She wagged her finger at the dog who just wagged his tail.

Jacob promised: "I will kill him myself if he breaks any of our castles again."

"Aaah," said his Dadó pleadingly: "You are not going to murder the poor dog?"

"But he destroyed the lost city."

"Can't you build another one today? You can call it the found city instead of the lost city."

"Don't be stupid, Dadó."

"Don't call Dadó stupid," Clíona said to her brother: "You are stupid."

"And you are stupider, because you are a girl."

77

Their grandfather tried to steady matters: "There is nobody stupid around here."

Jacob did not agree: "Except Topsy because he keeps breaking every castle we build. We should build concrete castles as hard as the wall Dad has built on top of the cliffs. Topsy would not be able to break them with his tail. He would need dynamite to break them."

"He might have dynamite in his tail," Clíona said.

Jacob gave a skit of laughter: "He has dynamite under his tail when he is going to the toilet."

"We don't need that kind of talk," his grandfather said. "If I was the referee in a football match, I would give you a yellow card for saying it."

"What would I need to do to get a red card?"

"If you keep being cheeky, that is exactly what you will be getting." The old man looked out through the window: "It is a lovely evening. Why don't the two of you go out and build up the lost city again?"

"I'm tired after school," was Clíona's excuse while Jacob asked: "What is the point? Topsy will just scatter everything again."

Their grandfather insisted that they get out in the fresh air: "Why don't you put your heads together and think of a plan that will keep Topsy from destroying your castles?"

That stirred the children's interest. Jacob sought an easy way out by asking: "What kind of a plan would you make, Dadó?"

"They are not my castles," he answered, "but yours and Clíona's. If you think up a good plan together, I will help you make it work."

"Why don't we tie Topsy to Dadó's chair? Or to the gate? Or to a big rock?" Clíona asked.

"A good plan," her grandfather said, but you can't leave him tied up day and night. As soon as he would get free, he would scatter sand in all directions."

Jacob suggested leaving him in the house.

"What if he needs to go to the toilet?" his grandfather asked. "You can't put a nappy on him like you would with a baby."

The children got a good laugh out of that. Their grandfather tried to get them thinking: "What about that girl on TV? She is always making plans, and good plans at that."

"She is alright," Jacob conceded, "but I never saw her dog breaking sandcastles."

"What do you think she would do if he was?"

"She would give him a kick in the backside," Jacob suggested.

Clíona put her hand across her mouth and said: "Red card for Jacob. He said a bad word and he has to put more money in the jar."

"All my money is gone in fines already," he answered.

"There will be no fine this time," the old man said, "if you can think of a good plan."

"We could build a wall around the castles," Jacob suggested. Like the knights did in days gone by."

"And they dug a hole and filled it with water," Cliona said: "What did they call it? A mute?"

Her brother corrected her: "A moat."

"Are you talking about a wall of sand or a wall or stones?" their grandfather asked: "Topsy will just scatter the sand or jump over the stones."

Jacob dropped his little shovel in disgust: "I give up. I'm going to watch television, unless you have a great plan yourself Dadó."

"Not really," the old man said, "but it would take a very long time to build a high enough wall around the castles. Sometimes we have to just take things as they are and be patient. So, what if Topsy breaks the sandcastles. Can't they be built again inside half an hour?"

"I like them as they are," Cliona said "And for Topsy not to knock them."

"If the castles were on the beach," her Dadó said, "they would be washed away by the tide anyway. Nothing lasts forever." He took the small shovel that Jacob had discarded and began to fill a bucket with sand: "It is nice to pretend that we are like the man working with your Dad at building a great wall. Clíona went on to her knees next to him and started to fill her own bucket."

"I can do that for you, Dadó," Jacob said, reaching for his own shovel: "Maybe Topsy will grow up and get sense someday, and stop messing with our castles." The children worked steadily side by side for a while. Then Jacob straightened up: "I have a plan," he announced.

The others waited for him to explain. He burst out laughing: "We could kill Topsy."

"We could kill you," Clíona said as she emptied her bucket: "Topsy is my best friend in the world."

Chapter Ten

Self-styled "best newspaper in Ireland" sent young journalist, Annette Nic Airt to the Western Isle to check out and report back on the clifftop wall being built by Tsunami Tom and his crew. Rumours of all kinds were circulating in the capital city about what was happening, and reports from Dáil Éireann, the national parliament only added to the intrigue.

"Retain an open mind, and listen to people on all sides," Annette's editor advised. "I know that is how you operate generally, but in cases like this a journalist can be sucked into siding with the romantic arguments, the little hero against the big bad world, for instance. Having worked in Belfast during the worst of the 'Troubles' many years ago, I know exactly how that feels. People's first instinct is to side with those who challenge the status quo, but it is our duty to present the unvarnished truth." He smiled, before adding: "That is what we are supposed to say, anyway."

"I am on neither one side nor the other," Annette answered, "because I know little enough about any of it. People in the west of the country tend to say that the 'Pale media' as they call those of us who work from Dublin have no interest in them, but I will do my best to present all sides of the argument."

Her editor's question surprised her: "Have you any fears about heading out there on your own?"

Annette raised her eyebrows: "Should I have? We are not talking about armed conflict or anything like that. I hope."

"I don't believe that any physical danger awaits you, but put it like this, you are not going across the sea to interview Peig Sayers."

"I got enough of Peig in my schooldays. It is not that she did not appeal to me as a woman from the amount I learned, but my Irish then was pretty pidgin. I only worked on it properly later for my degree."

"Peig's story, as well as 'The Island man,' and 'Twenty Years a Growing,' a nice glowing picture of most of Ireland's islands life apart from loneliness, emigration and sea tragedies," the editor said: "Liam and Tom O'Flahery in Aran painted a different kind of a picture of islands and islanders, They showed us a picture of an island split from stem to stern by social and class rivalries, as seems to be happening now on the Western Isle. So be careful, and don't take sides."

"It is hard to avoid being seen as on one side or another in that kind of an argument," Annette said, "it is usually a matter of, 'If you are not with me, you are against me,' or which side are you on? I've been there, not on islands, but I remember the water charges and other wars."

"Everyone has their own agenda," her editor said.

"Ourselves included," she said.

"That goes without saying, but in a case like this we have less chance of understanding island people any more than we understand our own people down the road in inner city complexes."

"I will talk to anyone who's willing to talk to me."

"And get the rest of them drunk," he smiled. "It is probably the only way to get them to talk."

"I suppose the rich never understand the poor."

"We are not talking poverty in this case," remarked her editor, "but people with hundreds of millions of euros to spend, even though it is not clear where all of it came from. The lotto story is a bit bizarre."

Annette smiled: "Are you suggesting that they are rich

enough to buy me off?"

"Don't be daft, but I have an instinct that you should concentrate more on the wife than on the husband. From what I understand of their two big projects, hers is the most sensible. At least from an environmental point of view."

"So, you have some of your own study done on them already?"

"There are people in this town from every part of Ireland, and a journalist hears stories floating about, as you well know. The trick is to separate the wheat from the chaff and that is where the old instinct comes in."

"Instinct can be way out," Annette answered.

"But it is always worth a try, and at the very least it eliminates one of the many sides of a story."

"I will do my best," she said, laughing: "Between your instinct and mine, we will probably end up very wide of the mard."

"Or spot on," he said: "It is all a gamble. That is the beauty of it." The editor seemed to go off on a tangent as he mused: "We are often accused of poor journalism, and in this case our critics are correct. As far as I am aware no journalist has travelled to the Western Isle to investigate this story. Not even one of those who constantly claim that we go further west than Kindare. This gives you a unique opportunity to make a real name for yourself. I can see you up there now on stage at the 'Journalist of the year' awards holding up your little trophy."

"Is that more of the journalistic instinct?"

"Of course, so go for it."

"I will do my best," she said. "I will do some more research from now until the end of the day, and I will be on the train west in the morning."

"Good girl yourself," he said, "if a man is allowed to use such language in this day and age. Whatever you do or however you do it, this will not be the end of the world. Win, lose or draw, this will be yesterday's news in a short time. Another day, another story. You will win that gong yet for great journalism."

"In forty years' time, perhaps."

"I will be well burnt in hell by then."

"I thought you didn't believe in any of that stuff?" Annette said.

"Did I say I do?"

"It is often said that people who write for this paper are expected to reject all religious faith. And a lot of them seem to do so."

"People say a lot of things but did any pressure ever come on you to reject anything you believe in?"

"This is the first time ever religion was mentioned, and it was myself that brought it up."

"And that is the way it should be," her editor. "Each to their own, as long as we don't force it down anyone else's throat."

Didn't some great British journalist say: "We don't do God?"

"Alasdair Campbell, an adviser to Tony Blair in his time in Number Ten. A long time ago. It didn't stop Blair joining the Roman church when he left office, and I heard Alasdair say on TV that he was not without faith. Anyway, it is not on some kind of a religious mission I am sending you, even though you are going overseas. Until now I have not heard that particular island tribe have been known to put young journalists in a pot and boil them up for soup, pleasant and all as that might be, given the age and beauty of the product."

"They must not be too terrible so," she said.

"There is no doubt but that they are a stubborn people. I read somewhere that island people are the most political in the country. Not party political, but because of their knowledge of their rights and their knowledge of how to protect and preserve their heritage and places in which they live."

"They are no pushovers so," Annette said.

"They showed how tough they are back in the time of the landlords."

"In what way?"

"They drove the bosses' cattle from the top of the cliffs into the sea."

"Not just tough, but cruel," she said.

"Who are we to judge? We are not in their shoes. Or their pampooties in this case," the editor answered.

"I hope it is not a journalist that they will be throwing over the cliff this time," came Annette's answer.

"Most communities do not see journalists as the enemy. Once they tell it like it is without fear or favour, they are at least tolerated." He shook her hand: "Good luck. Keep safe and I look forward to reading your reports."

Chapter Eleven

"Mind yourself with those letters," his wife Róisín said as Tsunami Tom tore open one envelope after another after returning from his day's work; the post had come late because the ferry had been delayed by a swell in the sea.

"They are hardly going to blow up on me," he answered.

"Don't take any chances. Remember what they did with the lorry.!"

"They are far too light," he said as he shook one. "It is not a stick of dynamite," he said as a short object rolled across the table.

"What is it?" Róisín asked.

Tom looked at it and into it: "It is an empty shotgun cartridge,"

"A warning," she said. "Ring the Guards."

"What is the point? There swell in the sea is getting worse and the forecast is not good. There is no way that any Guard is going to get here tonight."

"They should be told anyway."

"I am ready to take my chances," Tom replied.

"It is not all about you. Jacob and Clíona and myself live here too. It might not be too late to get fingerprints."

"I'm sure it would have been well wiped unless they are completely stupid." He rolled the cartridge around in his hand. "I'm sure it has been well covered in my fingerprints by now."

As he looked inside it again, Róisín said: "Mind would it blow up in your eyes. There could still be gunpowder, or something left inside it,"

"I was wondering could there have been a small warning note inside," he said.

Róisín was distraught: "I'm thinking about the children. Why did we ever start on those stupid projects?"

"Because we wanted to do something good for the people and the place," Tom said. "Ninety-nine percent of the people are behind us."

"What good is that if one percent is trying to blow us up?"

"It is a warning," he said. "If they wanted to really blow us up, that would be a stick of dynamite and we would be dead by now. I wouldn't mind but the work on the wall was never going as well. And you have started the meetings to get the women involved."

"I am not sleeping in this house tonight," Róisín announced. "Or any night until the Gatdaí have been here to check for explosives."

"You are going over the top now," Tom answered. "I know you are worried about the children and ourselves, but the night is bad, and we don't want to put police or anyone else in danger of their lives."

"Our lives are more in danger right now, than anyone," was Róisín's terse reply. "Is there a law in this country or is there not?"

"There is, but we have to be realistic too. You know yourself that the ferry was late, and the weather is getting worse..."

Róisín did not give him time to finish his sentence: "Get a helicopter so. It is not as if we cannot afford it."

Tom turned to sarcasm: "We can't order a helicopter at a moments notice like you would make an order from the chipper, "with French fries and tomato sauce."

"This is no time for joking," Róisín said. "If you don't speak to the Guards, I will. From my own money of course. The safety of our children comes before anything else."

"You are going away over the top now," her husband said. "This could even make the situation worse for all of us."

Róisín called the Garda Superintendant of the nearest district and told him about the cartridge as well as the lorry that had come close to being driven off the top of the cliff: "I am scared for myself and my family," she explained.

"Could I speak to your husband or partner as the case may be" he asked.

This really raised Róisín's hackles: "I rang to look for help," she replied. "I am prepared to and can afford to pay for a helicopter to have this situation investigated. Why do I need my husband's permission to have the matter dealt with? Does a battered wife need her husband's permission to speak to a Garda?"

"Was the cartridge that came in the post addressed to you?" he asked.

"No. As I said it was addressed to my husband."

"That is exactly why I need to speak to him," the Superintendant answered. "Not from any anti-woman or anti-feminist motive."

"I am sorry," Róisín answered: "I will get him for you."

"One moment," he said: "I need to explain. In order to investigate the matter properly I need to speak with the person who received the threat though the post. It is all the same to me if that is a man or a woman. I have to follow correct procedure. In fact, I could speak to both of you together if you have SKYPE, as well as looking at the cartridge at the same time. It will not be the same as close-up scrutiny, but it would help."

"We can get that set up," Róisín said.

The Superintendant explained further; "I would prefer not to send members of the force out to sea in the present stormy conditions, but as soon as there is a break in the weather, I will dispatch a team."

"I am still prepared to pay for a helicopter," Róisín said.

"Given what happened off the Mayo coast some years ago, I would not recommend that at this stage. We need to weigh up each situation differently. This one has fallen on my desk, and I am the person in the eye of the storm, if you pardon the pun, if things do not work out. The buck stops with me."

"And the bullet with us," Róisín said reluctantly, adding in a tired voice: "I suppose an empty cartridge is not a bullet or live ammunition as such."

"Bad weather usually keeps bad people at home," the police officer said. "That is what we find anyway. "Those who use anonymous threats are usually not the bravest of people. That is not to say they will not carry out a threat, but usually not on a wet stormy night."

"That is of very little comfort to us at this moment," Róisín said.

"I understand that, but we have already photographed the envelope in which the cartridge and it will be examined by forensics even before we get the real thing from you. It does seem that it was posted on the mainland rather than the island."

"Local post from the island itself goes out to the mainland and comes back again the following day," Tom said.

"Would the work you are involved in be opposed by people on the mainland?"

"Possibly. Many islanders have brothers and sisters and other relations all over the country and all over the world," Tom said: "When there is a programme about the island on the radio, there are usually more contributions from outside the Western Isle than from within it. Then there are people from all sides of the politics with their own agendas."

"So the enemy within as we might say may actually be the enemy without," the officer said.

"Does it really matter?" Róisín asked, when that enemy is invisible.

The conversation continued in a civilised manner, but it was clear to Róisín and Tom that there was nothing going to happen from a police point of view, at least until the following morning.

"How are we going to stay save?" Róisín asked Tom when they were finished talking to the Superintendent.

"That is exactly why I organised a safety watch the evening the lorry was backed on to the edge of the cliff. It is not machinery they will be protecting tonight, but you and me and the rest of the family."

As sometimes happens in the wake of a short sharp early summer storm, the sun rose on a sunny sea and a warming landscape. The sea may have looked sunny but there was a swell there so sea-sickness was ripe on the ferry as it came ashore beside the island pier. Local islanders had never seen as many police uniforms at the one time as those who came ashore that morning. They did not tell anyone why they were there or who, if anybody had sent for them, but they went from house to house in a very meticulous and professional way.

They told people that their presence was part of their training and that observing the laws of the land was as important on offshore islands as it was in any other part of the country. The kindness and welcome from most of the people impressed them, while those who seemed reluctant to converse explained that they had not slept much during the previous night's poor weather and that they were "a bit under the weather" themselves.

"There is nothing better for you than a bit of sea sickness," many of the islanders told them, "because it cleans out the stomach and gets rid of any bile or sourness. You will be feeling great for months, if not years afterwards."

It is not worrying about the journey that we had on our way here," one young BanGharda said, "but having to face that sea again on our way home. I wish that I could stay here altogether."

"Don't worry about that," she was told, "You will have a

lovely journey back to the mainland with the wind behind you. And sure who knows? You might have a brandy or two in the island bar before you go on board the ferry."

The young man who was with the female policewoman explained: "We are on duty and are not allowed touch a drop of alcohol."

"The law of the land doesn't hold any sway out here on the island," he was told.

"That is precisely why we are here," his companion explained, "that the rule of law reaches every part of the country."

"Does that mean that you are going to knock the big wall at the top of the cliff?" one woman asked.

"That has nothing to do with us. That is a matter for the Government."

"What is the big deal that has you here today besides any other day?"

"We do what we are told. It seems that there was a threat made on someone's life. We don't know who or how, but it is our job to let everyone know that the likes of that will not be tolerated."

"Was it Tsunami Tom that was threatened?"

"We are not allowed to bring personalities into it. That part of it is none of our business."

"Was it Tom and Róisín that paid to bring you out here? Are they trying to bully the community?"

"It is the State that pays our salaries."

One islander said: "I have heard of young Guards being wet behind the ears, but you will certainly be finding salt behind your ears tonight after that storm."

The question was asked if they had ever been on duty before and was the first time, they had even been allowed out of the Training College in Templemore.

One young man admitted that was the case: "We have certainly been thrown in at the deep end. In more ways than one.

We were woken up at four in the morning and were on the ferryboat at seven."

"And seasick at half past seven, I suppose?" one of the islanders said. "It will harden ye up."

"It will, if we survive the journey to the mainland."

"Look at it like this," the man from the island said: "It may be the toughest day of your service to the country. A good start. Enjoy it."

Tsunami Tom and his wife, Róisín invited the young recruits to their house for lunch, to thank them for all that they had done that day: "At least it will show to whoever threatened us, that we will not just lie down and take it," Róisín said.

"What she is really saying," Tom added, "that is was really her that got you out of your beds so early in the morning." He added: "I would love to give each of you a hundred euro for your trouble, but that would probably be seen as bribery by the press and the politicians. We will make a significant contribution to a Garda benevolent fund."

Chapter Twelve

There was relative peace on the Western Isle after the Garda visit. There was no interference with the work on the great wall or anyone involved in its construction. No further threat came through the post or in any other way. Róisín and Tom's children, Jacob and Clíona visited their grandfather, Tadhg Rua most dogs after school unless their mother was free to collect them. Throwaway comments by the children among themselves such as: "It is a pity that we are not going to Dadó's house today" sometimes hurt their mother, but she let them pass. She had work to do.

She did ask one day: "Do you not enjoy the time you spend in your own home with your Mum and Dad?"

"That is where we live," Clíona said. "Going to Dadó's is a bit like going on holidays. We are here the rest of the time."

Jacob corrected her: "We are not. We are at school some of the time."

"So, you don't hate to be at home?" Róisín asked.

"We are only in Dadó's now and then, really," Jacob said.

Clíona added: "Dadó is lonely when we are not there."

"Did he say that to you?" their mother asked.

"Not really," said Jacob, "but we know it."

"Topsy is lonely too," Clíona said, "because we are his very best friends."

"Did he tell you that?" their mother joked.

"You know well, Mom, that Topsy is a dog, not a person."

Jacob answered.

Cliona added: "Maybe he did tell us in a bark, but we do not understand dog-talk except when he barks at the postman." He is saying: "Get out of here and don't be bothering us."

He says sometimes too: "Don't be bringing us bullets and frightening us."

"Where did you hear about that?" their mother asked.

"Everyone at school knows," was Clíona's answer, "and that is why all the Guards were here the last day, but they didn't catch the criminal."

"Will he send us any more bullets?" asked Jacob.

"The Guards are checking the post before they put it on the boat," Róisín told them.

"And Topsy will bark at the postman every time," Cliona said: "Wuff, wuff."

He does not have English or Irish, only dog-talk: "Wuff, wuff."

"Is he a gangster?" Jacob asked.

His mother did not understand wo he was referring to: "Is who a gangster?" she asked.

"The gunman, the bullet man," Jacob said.

"That is all in the past," his mother said. "There has not been trouble of any kind since the day the Guards were here."

"Is the gangster in jail?" Clíona asked.

"There is nobody in jail because of the cartridge," Róisín said, "or the bullet, as you call it. It might all just have been a prank. Somebodies' idea of a joke. So that is the end of the story."

That phrase reminded Clíona of the words with which her grandfather ended many of his own stories: "They put down the kettle and they made the tea, and if they were not happy, that we may be."

After some quiet time, Jacob asked: "Can we go to Dadó's to visit for a while, Mom?"

Clíona supported his request: "just a little while. Please. Pretty please."

Róisín decided to let them be: "Just for a while. A short while, because you know how tired he gets if you are there too long."

"You can talk to him," Jacob said, "and we will play a game outside with Topsy."

"So, it is not Dadó you are going to see at all, but Topsy?"

"We will see Dadó as well," Clíona said, "as we run around and play in the sand. You can keep talking to him so that he won't be lonely."

Róisín seemed nervous: "I am not great talking to older people."

"Don't you like talking to your friend Gearóidín?" Jacob said.

"She is not old."

"She has white hair," was Jacob's answer to that.

Clíona could not contain a sudden fit of laughter; "She is a dyed blonde. She died and her hair went white."

"If you die, you stay dead," Jacob said.

"What about Jesus?" Cliona asked.

"His hair did not turn white," was Jacob's answer.

"Come on," Róisín said: "I don't know which of you is the daftest."

Tadhg Rua, the children's grandfather was surprised and delighted by their visit. He had been lying on his couch for an afternoon nap and he fussed about tidying up the place: "If I knew you were coming, I would have baked a cake," he joked, using a phrase common in rural areas.

"You could bake a pizza instead, Dadó," Cliona suggested.

"Manners, Cliona," Róisín said. "Dadó has enough to do."

"He has plenty of time to have a sleep," Jacob said.

"I don't know how you put up with them," was Róisín's

half embarrassed comment.

"As the old Irish saying has it," he said: "Patience comes with age, but it has not come to all of us yet."

"We are all getting older by the day," she said, "and I am certainly not getting more patient." Róisín always felt a bit of tension between herself and her father-in-law as if he thought that he was over-friendly in some way with her children.

"Only for the children coming to visit, I might as well be dead," he said. "They raise my heart and take away some of the loneliness of life since herself got the Alzheimer and had to go to hospital."

"You must be worn out on the days that you are minding them. I find it hard enough keeping up with myself."

"And you are a bit younger than me," he smiled: "They used to say that it took a village to raise a child. I don't know what about an island. Still, if a family member cannot help now and again." He left his sentence hanging in the air.

Clíona ran in the door almost out of breath: "Where is Topsy, Dadó?"

"I have no idea. I have not seen him since morning."

"Did he eat his dinner?" Jacob asked: "Topsy likes his Pedigree Chum."

Their grandfather did not seem to be in the least bit worried: "He often takes off for a while of the day, after a rabbit or visiting other dogs." He explained to Róisín when the children were going out to search around again: "That old bitch next door has him going around after her every few weeks. I don't know why they can't get her neutered."

Clíona heard the beginning of that sentence and she whispered to Jacob: "Dadó said a bad word – bitch."

"Dadó has lots of bad words," her brother replied, "and he never puts in any money in the curse jar."

It did not take them long to report their grandfather's crime to their mother: "Don't forget the curse jar, Dadó," Jacob said,

"Maybe he has no money," Róisín smiled.

"He is rich," Cliona answered. "I heard money rattling in his pocket. He gets his pension in the Post Office every Friday."

Jacob made his own observation: "Dadó has lots of money, but he does not have as much as Mom and Dad."

"What makes you think that?" his mother asked.

"Everyone at school says that you are rotten with money," was Cliona's answer.

"And who is everyone?" her mother asked.

"All the pupils and Miss, the teacher as well."

"What exactly does Miss say?"

"She is always saying things like: 'It is alright for you two, but not everyone is as well off as you are,'" Cliona answered, imitating her teacher's accent as best she could.

Jacob supported his sister: "And Miss said the last day: 'Not everyone can be a millionaire.'"

"What do you think of that carry-on?" Róisín asked her father-in-law.

"It is the kind of thing I let in one ear and out in the other."

Róisín did not agree with him: "That is what I call bullying. I will be having a word, and not just one word with that Miss. I nearly called her what you called the dog next door."

"I suppose it is true for her in one way," the old man said: "Not everyone is a millionaire."

"But it is not the right thing to say out in front of a classroom of pupils."

"Leave me out of it," he said. "These things are between yourself and your husband to look into. My schooldays and my days on the school Board of Management are long behind me, we only had the one child that lived, so we never had much bother from teachers."

"Your son is the very same kind of parent. He just does not

want to get involved in stuff like that," Róisín said.

Her father-in-law said: "I suppose that he has no time to get involved in anything except building that wall on the cliff."

"That has really gone to his head," Róisín said: "I can't wait until that job is finished and he might have time to listen to what I have to say about school and the kids and everything else."

"Stop fighting you two," Cliona said as she arrived in the back door in a hurry.

"We are not fighting," Róisín assured her. "Just talking. Just having a discussion."

"That is what you say when you and Dad are fighting as well."

"We were just having a chat," Róisín insisted. "Is that not allowed anymore?"

Clíona said: "You and Dad are always fighting, and now you are arguing with Dadó, and it is not fair because he is old."

Róisín shrugged her shoulders: "I give up. We are going home. Get your brother and get into the car."

Jacob heard what his mother said as he came in the door: "How can we go home now? We have not found Topsy yet."

Clíona backed up her brother: "We have to stay here until Topsy comes back."

"What if he does not come back until tomorrow?" her mother asked. "Your Dadó told us that he is out all night sometimes."

"I hope that he is not chasing sheep," Jacob said: "I saw a programme on television about dogs killing sheep. They tear the poor lambs to pieces and they drink their blood and they have to be put down."

"Put down where?" Cliona asked.

"Put down to hell, I think," her brother said, "because they did bad things."

Their grandfather tried to reassure the children: "I don't

think Topsy is fit enough to catch up with any sheep or lamb, and there are not many sheep on this island anyway."

Róisín took out her mobile phone: "I will check with your Dad. Maybe the dog followed him when he was on his way up to the cliff."

"He might have jumped into the jeep," Cliona suggested, more in hope than expectation: "And he fell asleep and dad or the other men did not see him."

Tsunami Tom's answer was blunt: "Do you think I have nothing to do but search for an old dog? We are working flat out here, and we have tons of concrete to pour before the day is out. By the way leave a bit of dinner in the oven, good woman, because I will be late getting home."

Róisín answered him: "You know how much Jacob and Cliona love that dog and it will break their hearts if we can't find him."

"I know. They love him more than they love you or me. But we have a lot of work to get through here yet. But I will keep an eye out for him on the way home."

"Could you ask the other men to be on the lookout a well?"

"You must think that I am going soft in the head. It is only an old dog. It is hardly the right image for a man who is a leader," Tom answered, half mockingly and half serious.

"It is the right image for the father of young children," his wife reminded him. "They would be lost without Topsy."

"There is nothing wrong with learning about how cruel life can be. I remember when a pup we had forty years ago was poisoned. Spot was his name. I cried for three days, but I learned not to become too attached to anything, human or animal."

"Do you mean like your wife or your children for instance?" Róisín asked.

"That is another story, and you know it?"

"I wish I did."

"If you don't, then you don't know me."

"It would be nice to hear about it a bit more often."

"I am shifting a big truck of rocks from one place to another at the top of the cliff at the moment. It is hardly the time or the place for soppy sentimental talk."

Róisín replied: "When we came into the money, I thought we might have a bit more time for each other. If anything, it is worse that things have got. Nothing but work, work, work from morning till night."

"That is what is called real life, and it is getting worse it will be when your own project gets underway. At least you might get to understand what real work is about then."

"I was thinking of postponing that until you finish the wall. You could mind the children yourself then for a while."

"Do you think I could sit down and do nothing?" Tom asked.

"If that is what you think minding children is like, just ask your father."

"That is a different story. He is a lot older than I am."

"Why don't you try childminding for a while when you finish on the cliff and see how easy it is?"

"I will be finished on the cliff and everywhere else if I don't get a move on," Tom answered. "The concrete in the mixer will be getting too hard to pour if I delay things any longer."

"Do what you have to do, but don't forget the children and Topsy."

Róisín arranged to leave Cliona and Jacob with their grandfather for a while. That would give her an opportunity to get a stew going in the slow cooker for dinner later. She called her friend Gearóidín and ask would she be free to join her to keep a watch out for Topsy as they drove around the narrow island roads: "It will not take very long," she said as there are less than ten miles of road on the island.

Jacob and Clíona were out in the sandpit at the same time rebuilding castles that Topsy had destroyed the previous evening. Their logic was that their dog would return to the place he loved most, and do what he loved best, which was scattering sand with his big tail.

"Do you remember what we said once?" Clíona asked, "that Topsy has dynamite in his tail?"

"Keep it clean," her brother told her. "Do not say anything bold like I said that time, or Topsy might never come back. He does not like bold talk."

"I am never going to be bold again," Cliona promised, "especially if he does come back, and I hope he does."

"Close your eyes for a minute and see will he be here like magic when we open them again," Jacob suggested. They counted out the sixty seconds.

"No dog. No good," was Jacob's verdict when he looked around.

"We will have to start again," Cliona told him, "Because I peeped after thirty. I'm sorry."

"Don't give up yet," Clíona said when there was no dog to be seen. "He might be hiding under Dadó's bed, like he does sometimes."

That brought no joy either. They searched the sheds and the henhouse and beneath the flowers, but there was no Topsy. "Why don't we do a moat around the castles," Jacob suggested, "and that might bring him back?"

Clíona filled the buckets. Jacob turned them upside down after pressing tight the sand so that the castles would be strong. The wall of the moat was made with a line of castles standing shoulder to shoulder as they did not have any other kind of a mould to shape them. They stopped eventually and Jacob said to his grandfather. "The lost city is back again better than it ever was."

"Well done," he said as he tried to hide his own worry that

Topsy would ever be seen again. Given the threat posed by the empty cartridge shell some weeks earlier, he feared that Topsy's dead body might be thrown across the wall at his or his son's house as a way to try and intimidate those building the wall. He stretched on the long seat outside while the children worked away in the sand. He was tired and he tried to force himself to stay awake by thinking of the worst-case scenario with regard to the missing dog.

"There were worse things in life." he told himself, and he thought of his wife Nora in her bed in the Nursing Home beside the old lady that used to tell him he got prettier by the day. That thought brought a smile to his lips for a moment, but the sadness that the loss of their pet would bring to the children soon took that away. He thought of where in the garden would they bury Topsy. Should they do it at their own house or at his? The children might want him buried near the sandpit where they played with him almost every day, but how long would that house even be in the family? It would surely be sold when he and his wife died, and would they family want their pet's grave in some tourist's garden? Sensitive issues that would have to be thought about.

"Children are adaptable," Tadhg Rua told himself, "And they deal with death in a different way to adults." Would Jacob and Clíona take it in their stride? He remembers hearing them talk of other dogs and other pets with simple but imaginative faith, thinking of them on the fluffy clouds in the sky. It was the initial shock and surge of grief that he feared for them most, especially if Topsy had killed sheep or had to be put down. After that burial ritual and goodbyes would probably take over. He hoped against hope at the same time that they would be spared all that for now.

Their grandfather straightened himself up to check on the children. They were sitting quietly side by side, seemingly lost in their own thoughts. He loved them. He knew that they were too much for him most of the time, but he would find life very difficult without their laughter. It was the non-stop questioning that got to him most or was it his almost panic as he searched for answers that had a bit of reason to them. Their most difficult questions related to things he knew nothing about, electronic things, new-fangled things that were so far from the way in which he was reared. He knew that the children liked his stories, even if they drove their mother mad. But he was running out of stories, running out of answers. "I'm like an old banger of a car running out of petrol or diesel," he told himself aloud.

"What did you say Dadó?" Clíona asked.

"I was just talking to myself," he answered, "and of course I could not be talking to a nicer man."

"Are you going daft like Mamó?" Jacob asked.

"Your Mamó did not go daft. She has an illness, a disease, something that is not her fault in any way."

"Did she work too hard when she was young?" Cliona asked.

"Maybe she did. Most people did back then, but they were healthy for the most part."

"Didn't she work as hard as a man, out fishing, on the bog, saving hay as you often told us?" Jacob said.

"Dadó used to work hard too," Clíona chimed in.

Her grandfather made light of what he did. "I did my bit, I suppose. In the boat and the bog and gathering sea rods for kelp. I suppose I never really thought of how much a woman had to do at home. Men took those things for granted. In the back of our minds, I suppose we felt that someone at home could sit down any time she wanted, or if she felt tired."

"Did you do some of the cooking?" Clíona asked, "or was it only Mom?"

"She was left to do everything in the house, as well as to look after the hens and the ducks, to milk the cow and other jobs like that."

Jacob suggested that his grandfather must have learned to

cook some place, "because you are great at making pizzas."

The old man laughed: "There was no talk of pizza in Ireland at that time. We had never heard of it. Even now there is no cooking involved unless you are making it from scratch. All I do is to put the readymade pizza into the oven," He paused for a moment, before asking: "Did I ever tell you about the first time I cooked a bit of bacon?"

"Was it the day you killed the pig and the man died?" Clíona asked.

"Oh no. This was only a couple of years ago when your Mamó went into the Nursing Home, and I was on my own trying to look after myself."

"That is funny," Jacob said. "Looking after yourself. He twisted his head around as far as he could and tried to look down his back: Look me. I am looking after myself."

"Let Dadó talk," Clíona said impatiently. Her grandfather continued: "I lit the gas and put down the bacon and said to myself 'I will be back in an hour and a half at the latest and the meat will be nearly cooked by then. I will drop in a few potatoes and a piece of cabbage.' The lazy man's dinner I call it, but it is as nice a dinner as a man can make for himself. I went out to check on a few cattle. I was putting a few stones up on the wall when one of the neighbours was passing. He invited me to the pub for a couple of pints of porter. 'That is grand,' I said to myself 'The bacon will be all the sweeter after that.' One pint led to another and when I was walking home, I got a lovely smell of bacon. 'It is a strange time for someone to be having the dinner,' I said to myself. It was then I realised that the smell was coming from my own house. I hurried home. The saucepan and the meat were burned to cinders. There was a strong smell of gas because the boiling water had put out the flame. I was the lucky man that the house had not been burnt as well as the dinner. The one piece of meat that hadn't gone black was the sweetest piece of bacon I have ever tasted."

"Did you give some of it to Topsy?" Jacob asked.

Suddenly all of their minds were on their dog. He had slipped from their minds as they listened to the story. Jacob and Cliona went out quietly to check the sheds and henhouse before it would get dark. They hoped against hope that Topsy might have wandered into one of them and the door had closed behind him. They knew in the back of their minds that he would be barking furiously if that had happened.

"I wonder did someone steal him," Jacob said.

"I doubt it," his grandfather answered. "What good would he be to anyone?" He hastened to correct himself: "I mean he is not a sheepdog or a gundog or anything like that."

"But he is our dog," Cliona said, "and we love him."

"Topsy will come back when he is finished courting," their grandfather said, more in hope than expectation. "It is not the first time he wandered off for a few days, but he came back again as happy as Larry."

"But there were no bad people around that time," Cliona said. "People who send bullets to Mom and Dad."

"I don't think that whoever did that would bother with a dog," the old man said. "Why don't we just give Topsy a chance to find his own way home."

"What age is Topsy now, Dadó??" Cliona asked.

"I suppose he is about ten years old. We had him a good while before the two of you were born."

"That is just dog years," she said. Turning to Jacob, she asked: "What is that in people years?"

Cliona asked her grandfather what the date of Topsy's birthday was.

"To tell you the truth," he answered: "I have no idea. I don't even remember if we ever celebrated his birthday."

"Topsy is one of the family," she said. "You must know. You have to know."

"Your grandmother would be better at remembering that kind of stuff, but unfortunately she cannot remember anything now."

"Would it be written on your calendar?" Clíona enquired: "Mom is always writing dates on her calendar."

Her grandfather thought that it might be time for a white lie to satisfy her curiosity and keep he mind off the probable loss of the dog for another while: "I think it is coming to me now," he said. "As far as I can remember it was on Christmas Eve that Topsy was born."

"The same day as baby Jesus," she said, "Was it on Christmas Day or the night beforehand that he was born?" he asked Jacob.

"I think it was the nighttime," he answered, "but I never remember seeing a dog in the stable along with the cow and the donkey."

"It doesn't matter because our Topsy was not even born until ten years ago, and Jesus must have been at least twenty years before that."

Jacob had an idea; "Couldn't we pretend that today is Topsy's birthday and have a party ready for him when he comes back?"

Clíona dismissed the idea out of hand: "You can't put someone's birthday on any day except the day that they were born."

Jacob had his answer: "Didn't we often have a party on a day other than the exact birthday because that fell on a school day?"

Clíona was not too sure: "I suppose we do not have to call it a birthday, just a 'welcome home' party. What do you think, Dadó?"

At this stage he was having serious doubts that they would ever see Topsy again; "Whatever you think yourselves," he answered.

Róisín returned after a meeting she had with other parents in the Community Hall. She was excited because of the general welcome that women especially had for the environmental project she had outlined. She was to be part of a factfinding mission to the Kew Gardens in London in which one thousand five hundred plants were growing under glass. Then there was Thanet Earth in which there was room for the equivalent of twenty-five football pitches covered in the same way. There was also the Eden Project near St Anstill which had a huge roof that resembled a collection of umbrellas.

As soon as she entered her father-in-law's house, Róisín opened up her electronic device to show Jacob and Cliona: "These are the wonderful places your Mom will be going to look at in the South of England in the next few weeks."

Cliona pushed the device out of the way; "Sorry Mom, but we have a party to organise, so we will look at your stuff tomorrow."

"What kind of a party?" Róisín asked.

"A welcome home party for Topsy."

"Has he not come back yet?" The children's mother looked as if the wind had suddenly been taken out of her sails. She was on a work-high, and now she would have to deal with the probable loss of the dog they loved. The only thing to do was to make the best of it.: "Who are invited to this party?"

"You and Dad and Dadó, and us two." Jacob said.

"And Topsy of course will be the guest of honour when he arrives," Cliona added.

"And what will be served at the party?"

"Pizza," Jacob said. "And milk, and more pizza for dessert."

"We should really have something healthy as well," their mother said.

Cliona suggested; "Can't you bring me to the shop, and we can buy some healthy ice-cream. Jacob can ring Dad and ask him to stop here on his way back from work. Dadó can blow up the balloons."

Jacob helped his grandfather with the balloons, after which the old man put the pizza in the oven: "I went a bit heavy with the grated cheese," he said. "Your Mom may not like it."

"If it is cooked, she will eat it," Jacob said matter of fact. "She is always going on about healthy stuff, but she is fond of real food as well."

"Dad will be here before long," Jacob explained after phoning him. "He is covered with muck and cement, he said, but it would take too long to go home to have a wash."

They managed to enjoy some at least of the party, even though guest of honour, Topsy was missing. Tom referred to the dog as "the ghost at the feast," and despite the children's enthusiasm, it was obvious that the grown-ups had little hope the dog would return.

"Don't worry," Tom said. "We will get another dog, if he does not come back."

Cliona tried to hide her tears: "But it would not be Topsy."

When "the feast" as the children called it, was over, Róisín and Tom arranged with the grandfather that Cliona and Jacob would stay in his house for the night. There were beds ready there at all times in case their parents were away or one or both of them might be tired and need a nap after school.

"Alright," the old man said, "but I hope that it is not a dog's wake that is facing us tomorrow. Would you mind getting them ready for bed before you go home, they are so wound up at the moment that I may find it hard to get them down."

It was a kind of keening outside that awoke Jacob some hours later. He ran in to wake up Cliona. "I think the banshee has come to take away Topsy. Listen. Do you hear it? We will have to wake up Dadó." They ran into his room and shook him by the shoulder; "Do you hear the banshee, Dadó?"

"Will one of you run down and let in the dog?" he said, before going back to sleep.

Chapter Thirteen

"The bully's big wall!" Was the term used by an Opposition member of the Irish Parliament, Dail Éireann to describe the ongoing work in the Western Isle. "I know this country already has a place called Bully's Acre, but we now have Bully's Island as well. He was addressing the Minister for Justice who was standing in for the Taoiseach who was attending a European Leaders meeting in Brussels. The Opposition felt the Minister would be a fairly easy target and they tried to put him under severe pressure."

He was asked: "Who was it that paid for the phalanx of Gardaí that were dispatched to the island to intimidate the natives?"

The question had to be rephrased as the Speaker objected to what he described as the loaded language in the question. "'Natives' especially could be seen as a derogatory term," he said, "as it has echoes of colonialism."

The question was rephrased; "Is it true that the owner of the machinery used to build the offending wall without planning machinery paid for the Garda recruits to be sent out in mountainous seas on what was basically a public relations exercise?"

"The answer came back across the chamber: "The recruits in question were renumerated in the same way and with the same amount of money as if they had spent the day marching around the square in Templemore. No more, no less." The Minister went on to thank the young officers, as he described them for their service that day, and he wished them well for the future.

"Is it true," the Minister was asked, "that those young men

and women had to put to sea in a small boat on one of the worst days seen in the Atlantic Ocean this year? I am told that each and every one of them suffered from seasickness on the occasion. While we commend their bravery, we are appalled by the way they were treated by those in authority."

The Minister opened a file on the bench in front of him with a certain amount of dramatic effect, before outlining the wind direction and speed recorded that morning on the west coast of Ireland. "While there had been a mild weather warning for small craft the previous evening, the ferryboat in which the Garda recruits travelled was anything but a small craft. That boat would have put to sea that morning with Gardaí or without."

"Is that boat really fit for purpose in this day and age?" the Minister was asked.

He replied with a certain amount of relish; "The leader of your party and respected leader of the Opposition had the honour of launching that ferryboat four years ago when he was Taoiseach. He described it at the time as a 'floating bridge for the inhabitants of the Western Isle.' It has since journeyed more than three hundred times between the mainland and the island without a problem of any kind. I would recommend to members of the Party opposite to sail in it at any time."

"You want to see us drowned," shouted a TD across the chamber.

"I have no such desire, sir," came the Minister's reply, "just to see you retired by your constituents."

The Leader of the Opposition indicated his desire to speak, and the Ceann Chomhairle gave him the go-ahead: He swiftly came to the point; "Is the work on that offending wall proceeding, or is it not? And if not, when will it be?"

The Minister stood back a little and joined his hands together, before answering: "The Gardaí who visited the island were not there to knock the wall but to ensure that there would be peace on the island."

The Opposition Leader spoke with great patience; "You have not answered my question. I will restate it: "When and how is that wall going to be removed?"

"This matter is being looked into at the moment, and matters are at a delicate stage, so I am not in a position to comment for fear of upsetting delicate negotiations."

"I am long enough in politics to recognise waffle when I hear it," the Leader of the Opposition replied, "All I want to know is whether work on that illegal wall has been stopped, with a view to it being eventually removed."

The Minister did not answer his question, fully aware that the time allowed was running short: "I would like to put on record," he said, "mine and the Government's gratitude to the people of the Western Isle for the welcome that they gave to the visiting Garda recruits, and the refreshments that they gave them."

"Could that be construed as bribery?" interjected a backbench TD.

"The people of this country, and of its islands in particular have always been renowned for their hospitality," the Minister answered, "and that is the kind of reception the young Gardaí got. No more. No less."

The Opposition Leader was getting upset at the way question time was being frittered away. He addressed the Ceann Chomhairle in a voice louder than that he usually used; "Please tell the Minister to answer my questions."

With almost a sigh, he called on the Minister: "Please answer."

The Minister feigned ignorance: "What question is in question?" This raised a giggle in the chamber and took from the seriousness of the question; "Is work continuing on that illegal wall on the Western Isle?"

"It depends on what you mean by illegal," the Minister for

Justice answered, "if you mean has planning permission been obtained, it has not. Yet."

"That is what I wanted to know," the Opposition Leader said. "There is no permission. What are you and your Government doing about it?"

Shouts of: "Nothing, nothing," echoed across the chamber.

The Minister spoke directly to the Chair: "With your permission, and I know that time for questions is running out. I had not quite finished my reply when the deputy opposite interrupted; 'There is illegal, and then there is legal, and I fear my questioner does not quite understand the finer points of the law;' If there is a threat to life or limb, such as fire, for instance, or flood in this case because of a tsunami, people have a right to protect themselves, and seek protection from the law of the land later. It is obvious that a person, or persons in this case feel a danger from the sea because of an historic precedent. I believe that they would have a case in the European Court of Justice. The cost of such legal action would of course be exorbitant, unless of course they won it."

"Let them spend the lotto on that," came a shout.

The Leader of The Opposition had not given up yet: "There was not a tsunami in the Atlantic for a century and a half. Your argument is ridiculous."

"A tsunami that we are aware of," answered the Minister. "It is easy for us to pontificate from inside this cocoon," He looked up at the ceiling of the Dáil. "It is a different story for people living on the edge of the world, on the edge of the sea."

The Leader of The Opposition said: "We have all heard the mythical stories of heroes trying to turn back the tide with a hayfork or some instrument like that. What difference is ten metres at the top of a two hundred foot cliff going to make?"

"It could be the straw that broke the camel's back," shouted a deputy.

The Ceann Chomhairle announced that question Time had

run out, but he would take one more query from a member who had been waiting patiently for a long time.

She asked: "Is it true that an ancient fort or Dún has been covered in concrete as part of the so-called Great Wall? It this is true it is a great scandal and would not be unlike Brú na Bóinne or some such part of our heritage to be destroyed. On an international level it would as serious as one of the tombs of the kings in Egypt being wrecked."

"It was the Brits that did that," a Republican member shouted. "They shifted half of the treasures of Egypt to London. There was hardly a mummy to be seen in the land of the pyramids by the time that they were finished."

"I would say you are a bit of a mommy's boy yourself," was shouted from across the Dáil chamber."

It took the Ceann Chomhairle some time to restore order after that. Long standing deputies often referred to the rise in the level of banter, most of it good natured as lunchtime approached. Eventually the Minister got an opportunity to answer the question that he had been asked; "This Department has no reason to believe that any such damage was inflicted on any national monument in the Western Isle. In fact, we are reliably informed that no such Dún had ever been built on that island, unlike similar erections in the Aran islands and the Burren."

"Could the Minister clarify that what he is really saying is that no such Dún was ever built on that island 'from erection to resurrection' as one of our greatest writers Brendan Behan was wont to say?"

"I will not ask you to withdraw that remark," the Ceann Chomhairle said, "simply to observe that it is not worthy of this parliament."

A final question was asked: "Is it true that the Red Bull company has obtained permission to organise a high-diving competition from the top of the cliffs on the Western Isle. If so, will the divers have adequate insurance in the light of possible accidents affecting either competitors or onlookers?"

The Minister seemed to be tiring, particularly with answering irrelevant questions; "I suggest that the deputy in question drinks a can of that companies' product. He will then be able to fly from the top of the cliff instead of asking ridiculous questions."

Chapter Fourteen

One of the hottest days of the year brought a group of divers to the Western Isle for a cliff-diving competition. Similar competitions were already quite common at Poll na Beist in Inis Mór in in the Aran Islands and at various locations throughout the world. It was Tsunami Tom who invited them in an effort to obtain positive publicity for the work that he and his crew were doing by building their now infamous wall to break the potential power of freak waves.

There was no deep natural pool on the island similar to Poll na bPeist in Aran.

So they compromised by creating a round pool between rubber pontoons which actually made for a safer landing than island rock for anyone who might miss the pool as they dived. There was a safety aspect involved in these as younger divers rather than those at the top of their game were taking part almost as apprentices. If that years project was successful it was hoped that top-notch divers would be made available the following year.

Tsunami Tom spent quite a bit of money and time to make sure that the wooden diving structure was safely attached to the top of the cliff. He was well aware that an accident would make his project even more unpalatable to the media and politicians. It was bad enough that parliamentary questions were being asked each week in Dublin, but there seemed to be a campaign of hatred in the social media to blacken his and Róisín's names. The urban media, as opposed to the local radio stations and newspapers were constantly questioning where their money was coming from. Local outlets belonged for the most part to the "us against the world" mentality and they constantly praised the fact that there was virtually no unemployment on the Western Isle.

Boats of every kind headed for the island that morning. Galway hookers with their great big rust-coloured sails had appeared on the horizon from early morning, as were the gleotoges and half-boats which looked like chickens of the larger boats and had similar type sails. Skiffs, yachts fishing boats, wooden and canvas curraches gathered in the calm waters close to the cliffs which for once seemed completely free of any swell. Some of the sailboats took the opportunity to sail around the island as they waited for the diving to start.

"There will be more photographs from here online than ever before," Róisín said to her father-in-law Tadhg Rua as they stepped carefully from one limestone slab to the next. They took turns to carry the picnic basket as they continually advised Jacob and Clíona to slow down and look where they were going. Clíona had already skinned her shin against a rock, while Jacob was complaining of a sore ankle.

"Take it easy on the excitement," their mother said. "We will get there long before the action starts."

"I can't wait to see the divers," Jacob said.

"I can't wait to see is it boys or girls," his sister added.

"Did you ever see so many people on the cliffs, or boats on the sea?" They had paused for a moment to allow the children to catch up and to take in the view.

"A pity she is not here to see it," Tadhg Rua said.

"Even if she was not in the Nursing Home, it would be too much for her to walk up here," Róisín replied and immediately thought of what an inadequate answer that was for a man who was grieving for his wife who was ill. She tried to rescue the situation: "Sure you can bring her in some of the photographs the next time you visit?"

"You might as well be showing her a picture of a wall," her father-in –law answered. "Sure, the poor woman hasn't a clue at all."

The diving platform had been erected at one of the breaks in the newly built clifftop wall that was meant to break the force of a wave by allowing some water through here and there. Some of the crowd decided to take their picnics to the top of the wall as there was protection for children there rather than allowing them close to the edge of the cliff. Others spread blankets on slabs of limestone as close as they were allowed to go to the big drop. Let's anyone would miss any of the action, a large screen such as one of those used in football stadia had been erected. Cameras were concentrated especially on the divers as they jumped and as they hit the water.

Some people complained that there was a shine on the big screen that acted more as a mirror than a display unit. Others were anxious for the diving to start so that their children might settle down and not be so impatient. Most complaints were about the searing heat, not just from the sun but from the limestone rocks which were almost too hot to touch. Parents rooted in their handbags for suncream which they spread generously on their children's faces and bodies as they threw off most of their clothes. Little flies and creepie crawlies began to appear from beneath the rocks and stick to the suntan lotion on people's bodies.

"Can we go home now?" Cliona asked as she shattered a horsefly with a slap of her hand. "I don't like it here anymore."

"Don't be a sissy," Jacob told her.

"I'm not a sissy. You are a sissy."

Their grandfather tied a knotted handkerchief around his head: "Look at me," he said: "I am the sassiest of all."

The children laughed at him, and all was well for a while; The diving started, and people were able to concentrate on that.

Each had their favourites.

"The girl in the pink swimsuit is mine," Clíona said, as the young woman made a spectacular somersault as she launched herself from the diving platform, straightened her body and entered the sea as directly as any gannet, Clíona covered her eyes: "Did she hit the rocks under the water?" she asked.

"She bounced up like a mackerel," her mother told her, and Clíona allowed herself to look. "Who is your favourite?" she asked her brother.

"That boy in the black shiny thing," he said. He asked his mother: "How come they don't wear ordinary swimming togs?"

"Because the sea would wash them off them as they hit the water so fast," Róisín answered as the young man launched himself feet first with arms outstretched before bringing himself to a diving position just before entering the water.

"I think my man won," Jacob proclaimed.

"He was not half as good as my pinky," Clíona said.

"Always the competitors," said their mother as she reached for the picnic bag.

"The coca cola is hot," Jacob complained: "I thought that was supposed to be a cool bag."

"Right now, it is the only drink we have," his mother answered: "Just make the best of it."

He poured out his drink which sizzled on the rock: "I don't want to make the best of it. It tastes like piss."

Clíona giggled as she asked: "How do you know?"

Their mother groaned in frustration as she said: "I can't take the two of you anywhere. Typical. Let me down in front of the whole world." There was silence from their little group for quite a long time after that.

A whisper went through the crowd that wondered would the tide turn at all that day. People knew in their heart of hearts that the tide always turned. It had to or it would be the end of the world.

There was a sense of impatience because the tide was remaining so low. Fish could be seen here and there fighting for their lives as the lack of water left them stranded. Some of the bigger buats seemed to be grounded on the underwater rocks.

Someone put words on the fear that many were feeling: "Are we going to have that tsunami that Tom Thadhg Rua is always talking about?" They looked out towards the horizon. Little woolly clouds, like a small flock of sheep could be seen.

"People can get hallucinations in this kind of weather," someone said.

"Next thing will be talk of oasis, and I don't mean that English band."

Someone went off on a tangent: "Wasn't their mother from Mayo? They are an Irish band really."

"With English accents?"

"What is wrong with that? Look at Kevin Kilbane."

"Sure half of England is from Mayo?"

People began to stand up and gradually move away from the top of the cliff, or at least to the other side of the recently built wall where they could still watch the diving on the big screen. Most people at this stage seemed to have lost interest in the diving and the getting anxious for those out in the boats and particularly the sailboats which had no engines with which to face a possible freak wave. Were the boats going to be smashed against the cliffs. People were reluctant to even think of such things, not to speak of saying them out loud.

There seemed to be a collective sigh of relief as trickles of water began to appear on the exposed sea-bottom. The tide had started to turn. An answer to prayer, some thought. Nature taking its natural course in the minds of others. But nature was sometimes unnatural. Volcanoes and earthquakes proved that, as did tsunamis. Eyes still combed the horizon. Would it be like Our Lady's Day long ago when men on the clifftop were easy targets just like the diving watchers were now? Would they have enough time to get to the concrete bunkers Tsunami Tom had built, like bomb shelters, to save people from the power of the wave? If the great wall and the bunkers were seen as a luxury up to now, they no longer seemed to be. They were necessary if only to provide peace of mind.

Róisín and her children, Cliona and Jacob still sat with their grandfather on the site of their picnic, a certain tension between them because the row caused by a comment Jacob had made. Tsunami Tom himself was speaking from the microphone on the diving platform that reached out across the clifftop as he thanked the divers, the boats and their crews as well as the viewing audience for their participation. "See you all again next year," he finished.

Cliona suddenly stood up from the picnic blanket and ran in the direction of her father, shouting: "Dad, Dad" as she headed towards the diving platform. Her mother, Róisín felt for a moment as if she was stuck to the ground, and one of her legs was stiff from the way she was sitting on it. She stood up and told his grandfather to: "hold on to Jacob." She stood and called after Clíona to "come back," but she did not seem to hear her. She shouted again and again as she forced herself to run through the ragged rocks even with a dead leg.

Clíona was coming close to the edge of the cliff at this stage, and she seemed to suddenly realise the danger. She just stopped in her tracks. There seemed to be a warm breeze rising from the sea below which seemed to be drawing her towards the edge. She just plonked herself down on the rock and waited for Róisín to pick her up and carry her away from the danger.

"Let us get to hell out of this damned place," Róisín said to Jacob and his grandfather when she carried Cliona back to the place in which they were seated. "Can you bring Jacob and the picnic basket?" she asked her father-in-law. "I need to carry Cliona for a bit after the fright she had."

She started to run, Clíona calling to let her down but Róisín did not relent: "None of us is ever going to go near that bloody cliff again," she said. "We could have lost you."

"Dad will have to go to the cliff every day," Clíona said, "because that is where he works."

Róisín squeezed her to herself: "I was so afraid my little angel was going to end up at the bottom of the cliff."

"No way was I going to jump down there," Clíona said: "And anyway I don't have wings like an angel, or I would have flown down."

"That is what I was afraid of."

Jacob was just catching up with them: "If you drank Red Bull, you would have wings."

"God between us and advertising," his mother said.

Chapter Fifteen

Róisín and he friend Gearóidín flew to Holland to check out the large plants that grew under glass or plastic. They also used the opportunity to visit art galleries in Amsterdam, and especially those which contained works by Vincent Van Gogh. They travelled by boat on some of the canals, sometimes having lunch while drifting slowly along. They took pictures of beautiful bridges and architecturally unusual houses and other buildings. Their main focus of attention was The Hague because of what they had heard and read about Fachtjan Plandai which supplied large exotic plants to hotels, banks and houses of Parliament, as well as Cathedrals and other large buildings. Some of the plants were up to ten metres in height. They looked more like trees and weighed up to three thousand kilograms.

"How would get one of those into the Western Isle?" Gearóidín wondered. "One or two of those could sink the ferry."

Róisín had the answer; "We would just buy seeds and grow them on the island."

"You would need a conservatory with a very high roof."

"That is partly what we are looking for," Róisín said. "We are not just looking for the kind of glasshouses we saw as we flew out of Dublin Airport. They are fine for fruit, and we need lots of those as well, but not for what we are talking about here."

Gearóidín looked at the label on one of the plants: "Barringtonia, a plant of Burmese extraction." She moved on to another: "Caryota, from Malaysia originally. Are those really what we are looking for? They would literally raise the roof."

"We are just checking things out," Róisín said, "window shopping, if you like."

"Window shopping with very big windows," her friend answered. "How are we to remember the names? We should write them down. Caryota was the last one."

"Just think of carrots and parsnips," Róisín joked. "I am sure that there is a list and pictures someplace that they can let us have."

"The staff in the building were polite and helpful, while keeping a certain distance so as not to appear pushy." As soon as she was asked, one of the women gave them a lot of information about the plants and the kind of glass or other cover they would need, especially in winter. "But none of these plants comes cheap," she explained.

"Don't worry about that," Gearóidín said. "You are talking to a millionaire here."

"Really?" The woman looked at her as if she thought there was some kind of a scam involved: "I have never actually met a millionaire." She still looked a bit doubtful as she reached out her hand.

Gearóidín shook her hand before explaining: "And you have not met one yet either. My friend here and her husband are not just lucky in love, but lucky in lotto also. Money will actually be no object."

Róisín cringed with embarrassment: "Lucky is the word, I suppose. It was just a chance really. We were in the right place at the right time and are trying to make good use of it now."

"A pity we can't all be as lucky as that," the Dutch woman said.

"What goes around comes around" was Gearóidín's answer to that. The other woman looked at her as if she did not understand,

"What I mean is that if we do business with your company,

you will be gaining from my friend here's win as well."

Róisín explained her and Tom's plans to not only make their offshore island self-sufficient, but to export produce as well. "I do hope to be back to do business with you later in the year."

"Gearóidín and Róisín went to a restaurant for lunch. They sat quietly for some time, Róisín pushing around pieces of meat on the plate with her fork but eating very little."

"Do you not like the beef?" Gearóidín asked.

"Do they eat anything in this country except meat from Argentina? I thought this place had a reputation for good food."

"For me it a change from the green rabbit food I have at home most of the time." Gearóidín smiled: "I don't mean by that that I eat green rabbits."

Róisín pushed her plate across the table: "You can have my meat as well if you want."

Gearóidín looked her in the eye and asked: "Is there something that you would like to tell me? You are not expecting?"

"I wish,"

"I thought you were happy enough with Jacob and Cliona?"

"Of course, I am," Róisín answered. "But the years are going by. I would prefer another baby to money any day."

"Has Tom been shooting blanks or what?"

"If he is, he is shooting them into a condom. He doesn't want another baby and is even talking about the snip at the moment. The big wall is his wife at the moment, apart from the odd lapse."

"What do you mean – lapse," Gearóidín asked.

"We do have the odd roll in the hay, but it is nothing like it used to be."

"I thought you meant he was having it off with someone else when you said lapse. You don't doubt him, do you?"

"His interests may lie elsewhere, but I don't think it is in another woman. Anyway, any bit of fluff, as they used to say, has taken off to the mainland. It is nearly all married women we have, except for yourself. And you say you couldn't be bothered with a man anymore."

"They are more trouble than they are worth," Gearóidín said.

"Still, if a bit of alright came along?"

"Like a big Dutchman?" Gearóidin laughed: "After a good feed of Argentinian steak. I think they have horny buffalo out there."

"I shouldn't even mention children," Róisín said. "I know things did not work our well for yourself."

"The past is the past," she said quietly.

"They say we should be careful of what we wish for," Róisín said, thinking out loud: "We could have lost Cliona the last day from the top of the cliff. There are more important things in life than plants and glasshouses. Enough should be enough but are we ever satisfied?"

"That is the nature of the beast, I suppose," Gearóidín replied: "Was Tom upset about Cliona?"

"Do you know what he said?" "She is safe, what else matters? When she could have been dead and buried by now. It is as if nothing in the world matters but that bloody wall. There is not a day I don't regret that we came into money. We were a lot happier without it."

It is easy to say that when you have it in your pocket, and no money worries to bother you for the rest of your lives.

"But there are other worries. Will the children's lives be too soft? Will people treat them as they are, rather than spoiled well-off kids? We have tied a millstone around their necks."

"Your kids are the best-balanced young ones I know, for their age." Gearóidín said. "I think their grandfather is doing a lot to keep them grounded."

"That is another worry," Róisín answered. "You should hear some of the stories he tells them. Blood and guts. Killing pigs in the old days and that kind of stuff."

"That was life. That is good for them." Was Gearóidín's answer to that: "I wouldn't trade a bit of comfort and fun for poverty any day."

"Don't take this the wrong way," Róisín said, "but I was very embarrassed when you told that woman in the plant house that we had won the lotto."

"I did think you were a bit peeved when we came in here," her friend answered. "I knew something put you off your food."

"That is nobody's business but our own, as the song says."

Gearóidín put a finger to her lips: "I will keep them from now on. But think of the good you can do. Think of the people who will have work. Think of the environment that you are always talking about. You would have given anything a year or two ago to be where you are now."

"I understand all of that, but is it needed? A vanity project is what it was called in one of the good papers as they call themselves. Should what I am trying to do not be a job for the Government rather than a random woman who has come in for a bit of money?"

"This is a chance that you have got," Gearóidín said: "Could this have been written in the stars or someplace millions of years ago? How am I to tell? But it is your chance. Grab it with both hands."

Róisín looked across the table, looked her friend in the eyes and said: "Thank you. It would be lovely if that was true, and surely it may be some day."

Gearóidín asked: "Are you ever going to eat that piece of meat? Or do you intend to bring it back to Topsy?"

"I don't know why I am so hungry."

Róisín smiled: "Is there something that you are not telling

me?"

"That I am eating for two? I don't think that they do immaculate conceptions anymore."

"Do you not miss it?"

"You mean having a man? Or a woman for that matter? What do they say about an overrated pastime? I think that ship has sailed as far as I am concerned. Too much bloody bother."

"You are still in your prime."

"It is not that I am not asked from time to time."

"Why are you so coy?" Róisín asked.

"Who said I am?"

"You have more or less said it yourself."

"Married men," Gearóidín replied and shook her head.

"They have the same equipment."

"They should have it chopped off if they wander."

"I am with you there," Róisín nodded.

Neither of them said anything for some time, Gearóidín sipping her wine, Róisín checking her phone: She surprised her friend when she asked: "I wonder where Greta Thunberg lives? I would love to live to meet her and hook up to discuss the matters we have in mind."

"Is she from here?" Gearóidín asked: "I thought that she is from Sweden."

"I would love to get the opinions of someone so young, so inspiring."

"Google her. I am sure that she has the same phones or tablets as all of the young people. And I am sure that all of her opinions are available online."

Róisín gave a nervous laugh: "I would be nervous about even sending a text or an e-mail. What if she was to ring back? What would I say? It would be like a call from the Pope or the King of England. I would probably just end up saying: 'Wrong number. Sorry about that.'"

"You are no shrinking violet," Gearóidín assured her, "or you would not be involved in a major project like this. You would just say out what you are planning on behalf of the environment. That is, of course, after congratulating her for all that she has done herself to raise awareness."

"I would run out of talk straight away," Róisín told her. "And then I would hand the phone straight over to you."

"You better do nothing of the sort, or I will be the one to say she dialled the wrong number. Anyway, don't ring until you have written the main points of your plans on a piece of paper."

Róisín fumbled in her handbag: "Have I got a piece of paper handy?"

"This is the kind of time you would miss cigarettes," her friend said. "There were more important notes written on cigarette packets than on anything else in the world."

"I wonder would she come if I invited her to the official opening when the main work is done, and the green shoots are appearing?"

"That is a wonderful idea," Gearóidín assured her. "It would certainly lead to having an international audience."

"All that is a long way away at present. Greta would be a year older and might be away at college or something."

Gearóidín joked that they could arrange a place for her at the local Irish language college. "And anyway, she might have a completely different attitude at that stage of her growth.," she added.

"They say that a leopard does not change its spots, and if anything, I reckon that our Greta will have an even deeper knowledge of environmental matters then than she has now."

"She is one formidable lady," Gearóidín said.

"Not a word to anyone about this,"

"Who would I be talking to?"

"I don't want even Tom to know," Róisín said.

"What would I be talking to him about? He doesn't even like me."

"He fancies you," her friend answered. "If he wasn't married... She did not finish her sentence."

Chapter Sixteen

Island life continued as normal, as did the daily rhythm of the seasons on coast and inlets of the sea nearby. Hardly a week went by that there was not a Regatta or other festival in the area, with sailboat and canvas currach racing high on the various agendas. There were horse shows and fairs, pony shows and donkey derbies to be attended, buying and selling, sport and fun for old and young. There were hurling and football matches for men and women. There were faith festivals too, in Mám Éan and St MacDara's island patterns at holy wells or slightly further away on St Patrick's triangular mountain, Cruach Phadraig.

Other people of religion and some of none walked the Spanish camino, while other pilgrimages took off for Lourdes, Fatima, Mejogore or to the Saint Padre Pio shrine in San Ciovanni in Southern Italy. But whoever asked: "Where would we be without festivals?" seemed to have got it right. It was what killed off communism in the end. The people were left without their opium, fun and games. China is another question altogether, of course. It was capitalism that killed communism there.

The population of the Western Isle had their own festival. Like many such traditions it seemed to have originated in pagan times and obtained a cloak of Christianity with the passing years. "Gregory's Bone" was the most common name given to the festival, though it was often called the "feast of the holy relic" or some such name as well. The Gregory in question was the Pope after whom the stretch of water or Sound between the islands of

Inis Mór and Inis Meáin was named. As he approached death, Gregory the Great as he is officially referred to in church documents, asked that his body be placed in a coffin on the river Tiber when he died.

He prayed that the ocean would carry him to the holiest place on earth, which as you might expect, turned out to be Aran of the Saints, Aran a Naomh. For some reason never properly explained, the saint's coffin came ashore on the Western Isle on its voyage, and by the time it reached its destination, a hand was missing. This bone was treasured on the island, and it was passed from generation to generation to be cared for, as well as being especially revered on the saint's feast day. Which family were custodians of the bone and why they were chosen was a mystery lost in the mists of time. The present custodian was the wife of Tadhg Rua and mother of Tsunami Tom who was being cared for in a Nursing Home on the mainland due to having contracted Alzheimer's disease.

There were those who would swear that it was through the saint's intercession that Tsunami Tom and his wife, Róisín came to win the lotto, or at least come into money. This seemed strange, since Tom was a confessed atheist and Róisín did not seem to be dripping with holiness either. But then "God works in mysterious ways." Tom claimed he "did not believe in religion or superstition of any kind." He had no problem with his children attending Catholic school because there was no other alternative on the island, and because "they would grow out of it eventually as with every kind of fairy tale."

Some people wondered about where the bone would go next, as it was on the female line it was passed from one generation to another, and Tom had no siblings. Would Cliona be the heir to the mystery? Or could it be Tom's aunt Maggie in the United States? All of this was mere speculation, of course. The real question was where was the bone being kept at present. Nora, its keeper had lost her memory, and her husband Tadhg Rua said that she had never told him where it was. "Matters like that were what he called: "Women/s business, like having babies and that kind of thing."

There had never been a resident Roman Catholic priest on the Western Isle in people's memory, although a Church of Ireland Minister had lived there for a time during the Famine and its aftermath when there was a great deal of proselytization in the Gaeltacht areas and on the islands. He was one of those clergymen of different faiths who succumbed to cholera and died in the service of the people. He was still remembered with some affection one hundred and seventy years because it was his 'soup' that had saved so many lives at the time. He had never been replaced and the small church he had built had been transferred to Catholicism as a place of worship for the islanders and for whenever a priest could attend for religious ceremonies.

A rumour had been spread on social media some time before the festival that Tsunami Tom had thrown the blessed bone to Topsy, his father's dog. This he had strenuously denied and threatened a lawsuit on the electronic site involved, after which it was quickly removed. The "no smoke without fire" school of rumour were quick to ask where exactly was the bone if not eaten or buried by the dog. Some called for a DNA test on the bone in case something new was presented, which to them would be close to sacrilege. Others, of course, had a laugh, saying that Topsy had never looked so good.

"Maybe he caught up with a sheep or two," someone suggested. "A drop of blood might explain why he is looking so good;"

"Didn't he go missing the last day and nobody seems to know where he was."

"He was riding the bitch next door and the two of them got locked in overnight," was eventually accepted as the explanation.

Mass was said in the open air of the cemetery surrounding the little church. The visiting priest spoke of the faith tradition that had lived on in the islands off the west coast of Ireland: "from Sceilig to Tory as he put it, naming many of the islands in between, many of which were not lived on anymore. There are very few islands that monks had not left a trace of their hands on. They had picked the stones, not just to build walls but to clear the fields and grow their crops, lands used by other residents in subsequent years, land which saved many from Famine because the potato blight did not reach them, and there were fish all around them."

He went on to say that it was the people's faith above all else that had stood the test of time, "faith that had lived for a thousand years and more." He was getting into his stride: "Faith that will outlive the computer, the tablet, the mobile phone, the social and unsocial media, the natural and the unnatural. They don't call what we preach supernatural for nothing." After a pause, he continued: "Is there any Patrick here, or Bríd, or Gregory for that matter who wishes to abandon a faith that has lasted a thousand, five hundred years for some unsubstantial nonsense that happens to be fashionable at present? Are we the generation that will give up the real for the fantasy?" He finished with a story about Saint Ciaráin who studied in Aran before moving on the Cill Chiaráin and eventually to Clonmacnoise. "When he moved from Aran people feared that he would take his blessings with him and that his followers would be abandoned. But we know now that they were not abandoned, because we have the ruins and the stone icons which helped the faith to survive hunger, fire and sword."

His powerplay over, the priest spoke more easily, more conversationally: "I hear that you have a sacred bone here associated with Saint Gregory the Great, a saint who is commemorated in Rome quite close to where I did my studies. It would raise my heart and soul to touch and to kiss that historic relic."

There was a silence, such a deep silence that even the little children playing among the tombstones stopped running about. Some of the church committee went and whispered in the priest's ear. He cleared his throat before saying: "I am told that the person tasked with minding the sacred relic is in a Nursing Home at present. May the Lord look after her and may she be among us alive and well next year."

When the church ceremonies were completed, most of the community sat around on the dry grass or the old rocks that marked graves from older times. Picnic baskets or just carrier baskets were opened. Teenagers supplied music, which was far too loud for the older population, but they tolerated it for the sake of encouragement to the younger generation. Clíona and Jacob were there with their grandfather, Tadhg Rua because Róisín and Tom had other commitments. Róisín was on the mainland with her friend Gearóidín. They were meeting contractors who had forwarded estimates for the cost of glass covering for the growth of vegetables and fruits. Tom had to deal with paperwork for his own project, he said. He had given the day off to his workers, but he didn't really want to partake in a religious ceremony himself.

Jacob asked his grandfather: "Was it about our Mamó that the priest was talking when he said a prayer for a woman who was sick in a Nursing Home on the mainland."

"Isn't it you that was listening carefully," his Dadó answered: "What makes you think it was your Mamó he spoke about?"

"I don't know of any other Mamó that is in hospital at the moment."

Clíona interrupted their conversation: "Tell us about the holy bone that Mamó is supposed to be minding."

"I would say that you know as much about it as I do."

"Did Topsy eat the blessed bone?" Jacob asked directly.

His grandfather replied: "Topsy has eaten or buried many a

bone but there was no talk of any of them until this false rumour started. Topsy couldn't have eaten it, because no more than myself he doesn't know where it is."

"But our Mamó knows?" Cliona suggested.

"I don't know whether she knows or not. You know yourselves that she is not in the best of health. She can think of something today and completely forget about it tomorrow."

Jacob asked: "Do you think the holy bone might be in the old, ruined church near the back of the graveyard?"

"It could be behind one of the rocks or under one of the gravestones in there, but I don't know. Your Mamó never told me where it is."

Jacob stood up: "I will find it," he said, and he started to run towards the ruin of the church.

"I will help you." Cliona ran after him, fallowed slowly by their grandfather. The children looked between and under rocks and stones. They got stung on nettles and scraped by briars. They hoped to find a magic stone that would open some kind of space or passage like they had seen in some film. Jacob went on his kneed to look under gravestones. Clíona did the same at the other side of the old building, but there was no holy bone or any other kind of a bone to be found anywhere.

Clíona had no doubt in her mind: "Topsy has definitely eaten the bone."

Jacob asked his grandfather: "Could the vet operate to find out if the bone is in Topsy's tummy?"

"I thought Topsy had got fatter when he came home after being missing," Cliona said. "I'll bet the bone is inside him."

"Or it might be puppies?" Jacob suggested.

"Are you stupid or what?" his sister said. "Boy dogs do not have pups."

"I forgot that" was Jacob's reply, "so it must be the bone that made him fat." He asked his grandfather: "Was there meat on the holy bone, Dadó, like you would see on a leg of lamb?"

"Or a pig?" Cliona asked, "when you used to kill a pig long ago?"

"We are talking of a bone," the old man answered, "that is a thousand five hundred years old, or near enough to it. Whatever meat was on it would have rotted a very long time ago."

Jacob sounded worried: "What are we going to do so? Is there any other place we should search?"

"It could be anywhere in the house at home," her grandfather said: "It is not that I have not looked, but your grandmother had her own hiding places in case things that were important got lost. I am talking about bills and receipts and things like birth certificates. The bone could be in with them in a biscuit box, but where she left it, I don't have a clue."

"I hope you find it," Cliona said, "because there could be nice biscuits in it. Mamó liked those furry kind of ones with pink stuff on the top of them."

"Mikado," Jacob said. "I love them too."

The old man's mind seemed to be elsewhere: "I will just have to ask her straight up where the saint's bone is."

"But she might not know what you are talking about," Clíona left her hand on his to show her compassion.

He mused aloud: "Maybe she will, maybe she won't. Things come back to her now and again. Important things. It might help if the two of you were with me. You would know from her eyes when you are with me that she comes out of herself in some kind of a way. She looks as if she is alive again. But don't take too much notice. She might mistake you for your Dad and Mom for instance, but for sure she is nearer to being the woman she was when you are in the room."

"Will the priest be mad if we don't find the holy bone?" Clíona asked.

"He can't expect us to find what seems to be completely

lost."

"Lost like the lamb in the story we had at school," Jacob said.

"The one the shepherd found, and they had a party?" Cliona asked.

Jacob had a suggestion: "We could get a bone from the butcher and show it to the priest."

His grandfather could not help laughing: "If they did a DNA test, they might think Saint Gregory was a sheep."

"Or the lamb of God," Jacob replied.

Chapter Seventeen

The journalist, Annette Nic Airt met Róisín and Gearóidín in Dublin to interview them about their plans for an environmental project on the Western Isle. They did not want to have to deal with the controversy about the wall on the clifftop, they said, or there might be confusion about what exactly they themselves were planning: "I agree with you fully," the journalist told them. "Your plans are if anything more important than the work on the cliff, and certainly more appealing to the readers of our magazine section, most of whom are women."

"We have no argument about that," Róisín said. "As we see it there should be room for both projects." She smiled: "And of course ours is the more important in the long term, unless of course they arrange a tsunami to contradict us."

I can see both sides of the coin, I think, Annette said. "What the men are doing is in a way a statement written in stone, a kind of a metaphor to do with the environment that shows the importance of protecting what you have. And the creation of walls to hold back tides will probably be seen in the future as a very important development if sea levels continue to rise. But right now, I see yours as the more important project."

"Don't tell that to my husband," Róisín said with a smile.

"What you are doing, or at least planning," Annette continued can show the world what can be done environmentally on a small remote island, "if you will forgive me for using that description. It seems to be a unique project in worldwide terms."

"It will not be done without money," Gearóidín said, "says the one who is not contributing a cent to the work."

"Without you I wouldn't be taking it on," Reassured her.

"OK," Annette said, almost dismissively: "You are proposing to put up a huge amount of money, and if I understand it correctly, are asking for a similar amount from the State. This, of course, is very welcome from a Governmental point of view, but it also raises serious questions about where the money has come from. It is no way an attack on your integrity, but I am sure you understand that questions will need to be asked by journalist as well as by Revenue and other bodies. Money laundering, tax evasion and tax clearance are some of the issues that will have to be examined, as you well know, but I am sure you would not be here if your hands are not clean."

Gearóidín held up her hands and joked: "I wash mine every week."

Róisín reasoned: "We would not be approaching the Department if we had anything to hide. She went on to explain the research they had done in the south of England as well as Holland, as well as plans to visit sites in Seattle and California before long."

"And we hope to get Greta Thumberg on board in the near future, as well as asking her to officially open the project," Gearóidín interjected.

Róisín gave her a withering look: "That is more of a pipedream than anything else at the moment."

"But we have discussed it. And didn't you call someone?"

"I Googled her address. That is all. There is no point in getting too far ahead of ourselves until we have the finances in place."

Annette asked: "Have you seen what has been done at Singapore Airport, with beautiful gardens that have a huge covering of glass? I was thinking about your project when I read about it."

Róisín admitted that she had heard nothing about it and added: "But Geuróidín might have. She is way ahead of me in some of those matters."

"I can't see why they would need glass cover in Singapore," Gearóidín said: "Isn't it roasting hot out there?"

Annette answered: "I have only seen pictures of it. It is a full tropical forest under glass. You should research it or fly out to see it."

"It is not easy with children," Róisín said. "There are those who think we are away from home too often already."

"That raises a question I would not ask a man," Annette said: "How is all of this impinging on your lives as young women living on a small island off the west coast of Ireland?"

"It is a long time since I was called a young woman," Gearóidín answered, before she explained that she did not have children, so she welcomed any kind of travel as a small holiday.

Róisín thought carefully before answering: "It is a question that I hope you put to men as well as women. It should be asked too of single women who are high up in business, politics and the Banks. I have no problem with a woman making that choice, but it should not be a matter of either/or. Otherwise, we would be as well to go back to the marriage ban, they had years ago, and nobody wants that."

"The truth is," Gearóidín interjected, "that both men and women want it all, if they can get it."

Annette probed: "But it does have an effect on family life?"

"We actually have bigger problems than those," Róisín said. "Not because we are women, but because we live on islands. We have a shaky enough broadband service, and we are stranded either on or off the island from time to time. As we sit here, we just don't know will be able to get home tomorrow or the next day. I am constantly using the word 'probably' to clients or businesspeople."

"Not to speak of "weather and other circumstances permitting," Gearóidín said. "Someone even called me 'Ms Probably' the other day because I was not able to give a direct answer to when something could be delivered."

Róisín spoke of the storm the night before the Gardaí were sent to the island, and of the fear generated by the empty cartridge shell: "A person feels very much hung out to dry when you don't have access to the most basic services." She went on to draw attention to what she considered the lack of understanding most journalists had about island life. "And it is not just the islands," she added, "but any place in the country outside Dublin."

Annette seemed to dismiss that argument: "The same is said of the inner city and the suburbs and anywhere except 'Dublin 4.' But is that all just an urban or a rural myth? Depending on where you come from."

"There are, of course, advantages to island life," Róisín said, "and Gearóidín will fill you in on those."

"What are they?" she asked bluntly, neither Annette nor Róisín understanding quite what she meant.

Róisín tried to rectify the situation: "You know well what they are, the beauty of the island and of the sea, the freedom children have to run around, the way people come together in times of crisis, no matter what other issues they have at the time. I intend myself to take things easy when this project is finished and just enjoy island life with the children."

"And your man?" Annette asked: "Isn't Tom his name?"

"Of course," Róisín laughed, "but that is another story. Tom is a workaholic. You would need to tie him up to make him take a break."

Annette smiled: "They say that some people enjoy that kind of thing." turning to Gearóidín she asked: "Have you to tie down your man?"

"I don't have a man at the moment," was her answer. She

seemed embarrassed, but quickly recovered: "But I will buy the handcuffs in case I ever fall for someone again."

Annette asked her: "You seem less enamoured by island life than Róisín is?"

"I was not born on the island, and some of the difficulties outlined earlier really get to me, but what life is perfect? But I do miss my extended family and friends, and just the bright lights sometimes. A person can only admire so many stars in the shy on a winter's night."

"But you do get in and out to the mainland a little more these days," Róisín said, "since you began to help me with this project?"

"If anything that leaves me less time with my relatives, because we have so much to do when we come ashore."

Annette looked Gearóidín in the eyes and asked: "Do you feel that you are the poor relation in this partnership?"

"I don't quite understand your question."

Annette explained: "I understand that Róisín here is actually a millionaire, and let me put it like this, you are not quite as rich. Does this come between you?"

"We are friends," Róisín said: "We do not see things in that way."

"Are you happy to be just friends, or do you want more from the relationship?" Annette asked Gearóidín.

"You are beginning to sound like you think we are a couple?"

"There just seems to be a huge disparity and you seem to be at an unfair advantage?"

Gearóidín tried to explain her side of the story: "Róisín obviously has advantages that I do not have. She and Tom have money. Good luck to them. I have no problem with that. I am not jealous. I don't cry into my pillow every night thinking about it. They are rich. I am not. So what?"

"We will have to deal with those matters," Róisín said quietly. "Right now, we are trying to get things up and running."

"Are you talking about legal advice?" Annette asked her.

"All kinds of advice. I have to discuss matters also with my husband about our children and those looking after them. We were not down this road before, so everything is very new. We are all learning as we go along."

"Don't get things wrong," Gearóidín said to Annette: "It is not for money that I am helping Róisín, "but for the sake of the environment and the future of the Western Isle, whether I will be resident there or not. I have learned a lot about life there, and those are valuable lessons."

Annette sounded realistically cynical: "I love to meet a person who is so innocent, but if I was in your shoes, I would be inclined to look out for myself as well as the future of the world."

"There is more to life than money," Róisín remarked.

Easy to say when you have plenty of it," was the journalist's comment.

"I could lose it all in this gamble," was Róisín's reply, "but I would at least have tried something that means a lot to me. At least I would not die wondering."

Gearóidín laughed: "If she wanted, Róisín could buy out your esteemed newspaper and give all of you the sack;"

Annette showed her self-confidence: "I would have as good a job or a better one the following day. It would not be the first threat made to me by the rich or famous, and I am still standing."

"Keep your knickers on," Gearóidín said: "I was joking."

Róisín added: "We came here today to explain our project and to get some publicity for the Western Isle. We did not really expect the cross-questioning, or the enmity shown towards the end of the interview."

Annette had her answer: "As the late lamented Seamus Brennan once said: "You are playing senior hurling now. In other words, you will get as good or bad as you give. Or is it the other way around? We deal with rich and poor in the same way but do try to balance our approach."

"Bloody bitch," was Gearóidín's comment about Annette as she and Róisín left the building. "She will hang us out to dry in that rag of a newspaper tomorrow morning."

"She can say what she likes," Róisín answered: "Neither she nor anyone else can stop what we are trying to do. I have learned that much from Tom: get down to work and neither Government or media whether radio, television or newspaper can stop us."

"Why did we bother talking to her at all?" Gearóidín asked.

"All publicity is good publicity, they say, so long as our names are spelt correctly. The newspapers will be wrapping fish and chips tomorrow night, as they used to say in England. We will be ploughing ahead with our plans."

Chapter Eighteen

Tadhg Rua, the father if Tsunami Tom went to the mainland to visit his wife, Nora in the Nursing Home in which she had spent the previous three years. It was then that Alzheimer's disease had got to the stage that it was no longer possible to care for her in her own home.

Tadhg felt a certain amount of shame when he counted the number of weeks that had slipped by since he last visited Nora. He tried to salve his conscience by asking: "What is the point of trying to talk to someone who does not understand you or even recognise you?" But things were not always like that. When he had taken Cliona and Jacob to visit their grandmother during the Easter holidays, she had seemed to recognise them. She had hugged and kissed them, but he asked himself: "Had she really recognised them, or would she have been the same with children other than her grandchildren? How was he to know? Anyway, he could not bring the children with him that day, because they had school.

Tadhg was glad that the children were not with him that day for another reason. He had questions to ask about the blessed bone that his wife had cared for down through the years, but nobody knew where she had left it before she got ill. "Typical," he told himself with a smile: "She would find a place that nobody would know about but herself. That was her legacy to the world, "he thought, "to leave everyone guessing."

Tadgh knew the moment that he saw his wife that she would not be telling him anything about the holy relic that day. Or maybe any other day. She had deteriorated a lot since he had seen her last. She lay back in a large leather chair looking as if she had lost all feeling.

"How are you?" he asked.

Nora looked at him as if she had never seen him before. Tadhg felt ashamed that so much time had passed since his last visit. When he remembered that Cliona and Jacob had been with him, he realised that it was five or six weeks since he had been there. "Where did the time go?" he asked himself as he wondered was he getting forgetful in the way his wife had been when affected by the disease at first.

There was silence between them for a moment and Tadhg looked on that in itself as something to be ashamed of. There was nothing worse than silence, he felt:

"The grandchildren are great," he said and then he realised that he should mention their names. Nora would recognise 'Cliona' and 'Jacob,' while general talk about children or grandparents might not mean anything to her.

He just needed to keep talking, more for her sake than for his own. Silence was their enemy. He spoke of how Tom's work was progressing on the wall on top of the cliff, and how Róisín's plans to cover the island in glass, as he put it, were getting on. He talked of the recent storm, of the children playing in the sandpit and the way Topsy scattered their castles. He seemed to just run out of something to say then.

He got a bit of a start when his wife spoke. It became obvious that the disease was affecting her speech much more than when he had seen her last. She found it difficult to even say: "Who...you?"

Those words went like a knife through his heart. His wife of almost half a century was asking who he was. He took her hand and kissed it tenderly: "You know very well who I am."

Nora moved her head slowly from side to side:

"Who...you?" she asked again.

Tadhg smiled and pointed to himself: "I am me. And you are you. I am Tadhg and you are Nora. I am your husband, and you are my wife," he said as he took her hands in his and kissed them.

That little bit of activity seemed to stir something in Nora's eyes. She lifted their joint hands for a second as if wishing to kiss them, but they fell back on the bed again. For a second Tadhg saw a look of Cliona's face and he remembered how beautiful she had been in her youth.

"Do you remember the day we got married?" he asked. "You were the most beautiful woman in the world."

Nora gave him a doubtful look: "Who...you?"

Her answer pained him, but he knew that it was the disease rather than the woman he had loved for most of their lives that asked that awful question. He decided to talk about something else entirely, so he switched to the subject which was one of the main reasons he was there on that day: "Have you any idea Nora, where the blessed bone is at present?"

Her body began to shake so much that he had to call the nurse. She was a young Filipino woman with no understanding of the Irish language in which Tadhg and his wife had been speaking, but she managed to calm Nora by singing a little lullaby in her own language. The nurse explained that shaking like that was part of a turn for the worse Nora had suffered in recent weeks. It was a natural part of a process in which the brain no longer controlled parts of the body.

Tadhg was asked to spoon-feed Nora so that she and her husband could share the evening meal together. It seemed to take an eternity to get though the food, one spoonful at a time because Nora found it so difficult to swallow. Again, this was explained as part of the progression of the disease.

"I could understand about the speech and the mind," Tadhg said to the nurse, "but I did not realise that every part of her body was giving in."

The woman shrugged her shoulders as if to say that is the way with Alzheimer.

Tadhg stayed in a bed and breakfast down near the Docks as it was too late for the ferry back to the island that evening. He would have liked to go to a public house for a couple of pints of porter but would have felt strange to be "out on the town," while his wife was so ill. He stretched himself on the bed without even changing his clothes, pulled a blanket across his body and slept until a call of nature got him up at five o'clock in the morning. He remembered this might have something to do with the letter he had got from his doctor about a check-up on his prostate, but that was something for another day, he told himself. "My little problem is nothing compared with Nora's."

He did not sleep again after that as the previous day's happenings came through his mind. It was clear now that his wife was far closer to death now than he had imagined. He would have to come to the mainland more often to visit. He wondered was there any chance that he could bring her home and mind her on the island in her final days. But was that not the reason she had been brought to the Nursing Home in the first place? Because he was unable to care for her in her home.

Tadhg wondered was his love for his wife fading. What a difference there was between the relationship they used to have down through the decades and her "Who...you?" the previous day. In another way he felt he loved Nora more now than ever. Or was it pity? "Are her feelings being killed by that dreaded disease as well as everything else?"

Tadhg went back to the Nursing Home the following day after his breakfast.

The staff were going about their business, readying beds and some of those who were unable to get up. Most of the residents were gathered around the tables in the canteen. Although he had already eaten, Tadhg was put sitting opposite Nora with a table to themselves. The chair on which she had lain back the previous day had been straightened up and she looked better because of it. Tadhg tried to lay his hand on hers, but she quickly pulled her hand away and looked at him as if he had done something untoward. She did accept half spoonful of boiled egg that he reached across the table, even though it took her a long time to swallow.

Ah image of a priest with holy communion occurred to Tadhg as he fed boiled egg to Nora. There seemed to be something intimate and spiritual about it that made him wonder might it be the last time that they would share anything. A traditional phrase used at Easter more by people than by priests came to his mind: "The son of the virgin has risen," about Jesus's bursting from the tomb, the bird from the egg, the butterfly from the cocoon. "Pull yourself together," he told himself: "You are going soft in the head altogether."

Nora and Tadhg remained at that table long after residents of the Nursing home had scattered, some to their rooms, others to walk the corridors or sit in the big dayrooms. Tadhg raised the question of the sacred bone one more time. For some reason Nora put a thumb in her mouth. Her husband wondered was she trying to tell him something, that the dog had eaten the bone, maybe, or did she want some more of the boiled egg. When he looked at his watch, he realised that he needed to hurry, or he might miss the ferryboat.

"It is not that I want to go," he said, as he gave her an awkward kiss on the forehead, but you know yourself: "Time or tide waits for no man, as they used to say in the old days. It does not wait for man or woman."

Chapter Nineteen

Many residents of the Western Isle wondered was it thunder. Many others thought it might be a distant earthquake. All of the island seemed to shake a little even though no cup fell from a table, or no crack appeared in a wall. Tom Thaidhg Rua's first thought was of a tsunami. He remembered that his father was on the mainland and was due to return that evening, He called him on his mobile phone.

"Were you out on the tear last night?" Tom asked, thinking that his father's voice sounded strange.

"It is far from drink I was, unfortunately."

"How is she?" Tom enquired.

"Not good. You should go to see her. It looks like she is not long for this life. It is not just me that is saying it, but the nurses as well."

"I will go to see her one of the days."

"Don't leave it too long," his father said. "How are things there?"

"That is why I am calling. There was a strange noise here a while ago It was as if the island just shook. Not too badly, but enough to cause a swell maybe. Don't come home on today's ferry. That is what I rang to tell you."

"Thanks, but I am already on the sea."

"Watch out for big waves. It might be nothing, but it sounded like thunder or something."

"Yourself and your tsunamis," his son said, half joking, half serious: "You are obsessed with them. You can't wait until one of them washes across us. Your mother is more important to me this minute than the tsunami."

"I know, but I didn't want you to get drowned either."

"Thanks, but see your mother soon."

"See you. I have to go to the big wall now."

"Maybe it is that that has fallen into the water and made the loud noise," his father joked.

"It could be a big whale letting off steam or anything."

"Don't worry about me," Tadhg sail. "The sea is as calm this morning as a bucket of buttermilk."

When Tsunami Tom reached the top of the cliff it looked as if there was some kind of smoke or dust rising from the waters below. For a moment he felt the wall had been bombed because it was obvious that part of the wall had sunk and the ground beneath it partially disappeared.

"I will hang the fucker that set this explosion," Tom said angrily as his workmen gathered around him.

"It is not an explosion, but a slippage," one of the men said. "Part of the cliff has collapsed and fallen into the sea. The steel that ran through the wall had kept it from falling although it dipped in the middle."

"Thanks be to God that nobody was killed" the foreman said.

"I hope you can get God to build it again," Tom said angrily.

The supervisor ignored that comment: "There was too much weight on top. That part of the cliff was always fragile. You can see from the shape of the rocks that it is not like the rest of the cliff."

"Now you are telling me," Tom muttered.

"I thought the steel and the concrete would actually hold it together," the supervisor said. "And it did. It held the wall together."

"We can't leave it like that," Tom said, "hanging out over an empty space. We will have to concrete up the cliff."

"Let it go," the other man said. "It would be like plastering over a crumbling piece of masonry."

"How come the wall stayed and the rest went?" Tom asked. "You would thing a cliff that lasted thousands of years would survive longer than a wall built the day before yesterday."

"Because there was a million euros worth of concrete in the wall."

"Is it all going to go now?" Tom asked despairingly.

"The rest will be alright, or most of it anyway," the supervisor said. "There may be another few weak points here and there, but there is nothing that can't be fixed."

"What will we do now?" one of the men asked.

Tom seemed to be getting back to himself: "We will drink tea and eat our sandwiches. We will think things through and come up with a plan."

There was such a deep silence during teatime that you could almost hear men chewing. Then Tsunami Tom spoke: "If there is anything about this on social media, then the man who posts it will be out of a job tomorrow."

The supervisor asked: "What will we do about the wall? It will be seen from the sky and from space and on Google maps?"

"It can be seen already, I'm sure," one of the men said.

Tom had his answer to that: "That will just look like a trick of the light because it will have disappeared between now and evening."

"Are you going to blast it?" was the next question.

"The rock breaker on the big machine should be able to do it for us. We can't chance a blast or more of the cliff might go down."

"There will be a big gap in the wall, even if we manage to

break the piece that is sagging."

"There won't be," Tom answered "because we will build a wall like the letter 'U' around it. It will look like the concrete Dún they were complaining about in Dail Éireann."

The supervisor shook his head: "How will we be able to bring the big machine close enough? The slippage is from a long way behind the wall. There is a lot of danger involved. I would not loke to be sitting in the cabin of that machine."

"You won't either," Tom said. "I would not ask anyone to do anything I would not be prepared to do myself. I will be in that cabin," he said quietly.

The usual machine driver spoke: "I am prepared to smash the piece that is hanging loose."

Tom thanked him and asked: "Would you mind driving the machine to within fifty metres of the wall? I will take it from there. Back to work with the rest of you. We have wasted enough time."

The other workers found it difficult to take their eyes off Tom and what he was trying to do. They understood now why he was such a fearless leader of a working group. Whether it was in tunnels far from home or on the clifftop of his native island, he had no equal. That was why men trusted him and followed him even when what he was going looked foolish.

While his workmen contemplated the danger that surrounded him, Tom was thinking about what his father had said on the phone about his wife and Tom's mother's condition in the Nursing Home. Although not a religious man, he asked her to look out for him and mind him so that he could see her alive one more time.

Despite how powerful the big rock breaker was and the way it could smash through rock, the supervisor had an image in his mind of a seagull picking at a piece of granite. That in a sense was a tribute to the quality of the steel and concrete with which the wall had been built. Much had been learned about concrete mixing as they worked for an architect on an all-concrete house he was building near the Thames in London. "Unbreakable" was the word that came to his mind as the point of the rock breaker bounced off the top of the concrete wall. "This was built to last," he thought to himself, but then he noticed that the constant hammering, the non-stop picking at the concrete was having an effect. It had barely broken away a foot of concrete in an hour, but Tsunami Tom was succeeding in what he had set out to do one more time.

Tom's rock breaker was about halfway down through the wall when the other men's day's work came to an end. He stopped for a few moments to ask one of the men to bring him a sandwich from his lunchbox to eat as her worked. The usual machine driver offered to take things from there and to let him have a real break for a while.

"Half an hour," Tom agreed. Ok? He felt that the ground beneath the machine would not collapse at this stage. He had managed to reverse the machine further away from the wall so that its long arm would have even more power.

"That pick is like a bloody crow on drugs," the driver said.

Tom told him to keep the pressure on: "You can take all the credit when it collapses."

"I am not pushed about credit, just to get the work done." He urged Tom to go home for an hour and have his dinner. They would call him if there was any problem.

Róisín was not very happy when Tom told her he would have to eat a quick dinner and go back to the top of the cliff again. It was also possible that he would have to work through the night if he did not get what he had to do finished.

"It would be bad enough to be in competition with another woman," she complained, "but to be in competition with a JCB. That is something else altogether."

"If it is of any help," he said jokingly: "You are not in competition with a JCB but with a machine a hundred times more powerful. A JCB would be loke one of Jacob's toys compared with the big rock breaker. It is a giant among machines."

"Why is there always some kind of a crisis going on in your life?" his wife asked. "You are not alive unless there is a crisis or a problem to solve."

"Says the woman who has walked England and Holland in recent weeks. You have your work to do. I have mine."

"I wouldn't mind," Róisín said, "but I have prepared your favourite dinner with wine and lobster and all kinds of sauces. I did not have time to do a dinner like that last night when Gearóidín and myself came home tired. I thought we would have tonight to ourselves. The children are with your Dad. We could have a lovely time if it was not for that bitch of a JCB."

"There will be other nights," Tom said, "but I can't leave things as they are on the cliff until tomorrow or the news media and the politicians will be on our backs." Róisín had served dinner at this stage, with a glass of milk for Tom and a glass of wine for herself.

"Speaking about journalists," she said: "have you seen what Annette Nic Airt wrote about Gearóidín and myself in today's paper?"

"I barely had time to use a piece of toilet paper, not to speak of reading a newspaper," Tom said.

"Trouble in paradise," was the headline. "She was trying to show that Gearóidín and myself have an unequal relationship because we have more money than she does. She is the one with the poor mouth and I am the one with the pockets stuffed with money according to her."

"Paper never refused ink," Tom answered lightly. "Don't take any heed of the likes of her. That crowd have to be always pulling someone down. Look what you are planning for the island in comparison with her. I wouldn't give the satisfaction to that paper that I would wipe my arse with it."

"Do you have to be so crude?"

"I do actually," Tom said. "What I am saying needs to be said. What did any of that crowd ever do for us?"

"It is publicity, I suppose," Róisín said, "even if it not the best publicity in the world. We were on the front page."

"Was there a picture?"

Róisín showed him the newspaper: "I don't like my hair like that."

"I like it that way," he said. "It was like that when we got married."

"That style does not suit a woman getting on in age," she said.

"You are still a young one, and a fine looking one at that," he said. "If your husband likes your style, how can you go wrong? You look so much better than your friend Gearóidín. She is just skin and bone in that picture. Was she drinking that day, or what?"

"I do look so fat compared with her."

"What are you talking about?" Tom asked. "You look better now than you ever did, but your mate would need to start eating all those healthy vegetables that she is always talking about."

"When did you hear her talking about vegetables?" his wife asked.

"To tell you the truth," he said, "I don't listen to half of what she has to say."

"Why do you never have a good word to say about her?" Róisín asked. "But without her, I would not be able to survive here."

"She doesn't bother me one way or another," Tom answered, "as long as she stays out of my way."

Róisín laughed: "Are you trying to say she fancies you?"

"What woman doesn't."

"A pity every other part of you is not as big as your head," she joked... She was soon to get back to talking about the journalist, Annette. "Do you know what I think? I think that one looks on Gearóidín and myself as two idiots up from the bog. We can hardly wear our best clothes on the ferry. If we were dressed like those newsreaders and the ones that present the fashion programmes, they might take notice of us."

"It is not all bout fashion," Tom said.

"That is where you are wrong. If you are not fashionable, you are nothing in this day and age."

"What is to stop you from that stuff they make in Westport pumped into your forehead like mass concrete?" he joked. "Or getting your face lifted or your ears shortened? You have the money to renew any feature you want from top to bottom. That is not to say that your bottom is not fine as it is."

Róisín put her fingers to her ears: "Are they really long?" She went across to the mirror: "Have I aged that much in a short time?"

"I hope that it is joking you are," he answered, "because it is joking I am. You are the best-looking woman I have ever seen. Now, did I say the right thing?"

"Flattery will get you nowhere. If I look that good, why are you looking at your watch every second minute?"

"Because I promised to be at the clifftop inside the hour to finish the day's work before coming home for my reward."

"It will take more than that to claim your reward. Off you go. We might get five minutes together sometime."

"Do you think five minutes is long enough?"

Róisín threw a table napkin in his direction: "Get out of here. The sooner you go, the sooner you can be back."

"I may be in time to slide in beside you if nothing else goes wrong."

"Promises, promises."

"Thanks for the dinner," he said, and he was off.

Tsunami Tom began to curse between his teeth as his little

jeep came closer to the circle of light that surrounded the machinery, the supervisor and the other couple of men who had remained to continue the work while he was gone for his dinner. The most noticeable fact was that the work had stopped.

"Technical problems," he was told. "Followed by the throwaway phrase: 'Why do they always happen at the wrong time?'"

It turned out that things were not as bad as they had looked at first. The stand-in driver told Tom that the teeth of the bucket with which the broken concrete was being cleared away were catching in the broken steel. "I was afraid the wall would break in the middle and if the machine was being caught by the stell rods it could be dragged down after it to the bottom of the sea."

"With you inside it?" Tom's question sounded more like someone thinking out loud. "What are we going to do now?"

The supervisor suggested: "Just keep smashing away with the rock breaker. We can clear the rubble afterwards, or just leave it where it is. The sea clears off the top of the cliff in nearly every storm anyway."

"There is your answer," Tom said: "That is the kind of input I like to hear from men who are working with me."

"What is rare is wonderful," the supervisor said: "What Bank can praise like that be lodged in?"

"Let's get on with the work and get out of here," Tsunami Tom said.

Chapter Twenty

Tadhg Rua visited his wife, Nora in the Nursing Home on the mainland almost every week since he became aware that she would not live much longer. His grandchildren, Cliona and Jacob did not get to see him as often as they would have liked, but they understood the reason why. They painted pictures and sent get-well cards to their grandmother every time that Tadhg was going to visit Nora.

"Is Mamó really dying?" Cliona asked her mother, Róisín one evening. "We have no fun anymore without Dadó."

"Dadó and his stories," she answered a little wearily. "You will just have to listen to my boring stories. I will not be travelling abroad for a few weeks, so I will be doing most of the minding after school."

"Your stories are not boring, Mom." Clíona told her. "They are just not as exciting as Dado's ones."

Jacob contradicted his sister: "Mom's stories are boring. They are all about vegetables and glasshouses and not eating too much fat stuff or sweets."

Cliona tried to keep the peace: "Your stories are nice, Mom, but Dadó's are the best. The very best in the world. Nobody could be as good as he is."

"I am putting it up to the two of you now to think up your own stories. You have been listening to the master storyteller, Dadó for years now, so you must have learned a lot. We will have a competition: 'Think up a story each between now and dinnertime and your Dad and myself will put up a prize, and the stories will be told during dinnertime.'"

"What is the prize?" the children asked together. "I will get first prize," Jacob declared.

"And I will get the very first prize," Cliona said.

"I have an even better idea,"

"Spit it out, Jacob."

"But Mom, you said not to spit in the kitchen."

"I mean tell us your idea?"

"You and Dad will have to tell stories too."

Their mother tried to get out of that: "We are too old, and you said that my stories are boring, and I don't know if your Dad has any story." Eventually she agreed to the children's request.

"I am going to talk about killing the pig and the basin of blood," Cliona volunteered.

Her brother dismissed her suggestion immediately: "You will not, because that is my story."

Their mother Róisín disagreed: "That is your Dadó's story. Every story has to be completely new that nobody in the family has ever heard before."

Cliona laid down her own rule: "We don't need stories about the big glasshouse or about the wall on the cliff."

Jacob chimed in: "Boring, boring. Stories about interesting things are what we want. Not stupid things."

"Stories about homework are what I want to hear first of all," Róisín insisted, "or nobody will be getting a prize for anything."

Jacob did not like to hear that: "But you have no homework, Mom. You will have lots of time to make up your story."

"I have a dinner to ready: That is my homework."

"There is no reading or writing or sums to getting a dinner," Cliona told her.

"I will have to count the potatoes and carrots and parsnips and guess how long should I leave the meat in the oven, there are lots of sums in that." Róisín added as the children reluctantly brought their schoolbags to the kitchen table: "And lots of concentration in what I am doing. I have a knife in my hand, so I have to make sure that I do not cut off one of my fingers:"

"Do, do, the children chorused." Clíona added: "There will be lots of blood. You can make black pudding like they did with the pig's blood."

Jacob introduced his own joke: "If you want to kill the potatoes or the carrots, Mom, just stick a knife in them."

"Homework now," their mother ordered, "or there will be no dinner or sums done before your dad gets home."

"He never gets home in time," Jacob said. "We are often in bed by the time he gets home from work."

"He promised to be in time this evening because he was out late last night because of some problem with the wall."

"They had to put some of it into the sea," Cliona said.

"How do you know that?"

"Everyone at school knows everything that happens," she told her mother: "Because most of the Dads work with our dad."

"There was a big splash when it all fell into the water," Jacob said, "as he threw himself on the floor in imitation of the falling wall as he made a sound like water splashing."

"Our teacher said at prayer time that nobody got hurt or killed in the accident," Clíona added, as she looked up momentarily from her homework.

Jacob interjected: "It was not an accident. Dad and the other men wanted to knock that part of the wall because there was nothing really holding it up because the ground had slipped away in an earthquake or something."

"Maybe there was a volcano," Cliona said.

"If there was a volcano we would see the fire from here,"

her brother said.

"Do you remember when we were in Lanzerotte and they were cooking chickens on the hot lava?" Róisín asked: Suddenly her children could not control their laughter: "What is so funny?"

"You said something about hot chickens cooking in the lavatory," Jacob told her: "It just sounded funny."

"Do you not remember anything about it?" their mother asked: "You were very small at the time, I suppose."

All this was quickly forgotten when Tom came home earlier than they had expected. Cliona wrapped her arms around one of his legs, Jacob the other: "Welcome home, Dad. Long time no see."

He laughed: "It is not that long. I was late last night but I was not far away. I was not on the moon or anything, just up at the cliff."

"We would love if you were home early every day," Cliona said.

"As soon as the job on the wall is finished, you will be fed up looking at me."

"Don't make promised you can't deliver on," his wife Róisín said, as she handed him his dinner.

"What do you mean by that?"

"Haven't you in mind to go off to save some island in the Maldives when the wall here is finished?"

"That is just a vague idea. Could you put the dinner in the oven for a few minutes? I need a shower, or I will stink you all out of it with sweat."

"Stay where you are," Róisín told him. "Or the children will think that you have abandoned them again. Tomorrow is a school day and they need to be in bed early. You can wash yourself all night after that."

"When will the stories be starting?" Clíona asked.

Tom wondered: "What stories?"

"Everybody has to tell a story," Jacob told him, "and I have the best story of them all."

"It is the first that I have heard of it," his father said, "and I am a bit thick. It will take me a while to make up a story."

"We will let you go last," Cliona told him. "It will give you time to think of something. You are the oldest, so we will start with the youngest, and that is me."

Tom put on a mock dramatic voice: "Hear ye, hear ye. The stories are about to start. Let the games begin: 'Speak Cliona:'"

"Long, long ago," she started: "There was a fairy, and she had a holy bone that was hiding in the graveyard."

"Are you talking about our Mamó?" Jacob asked.

"Mamó is not a fairy," Cliona answered.

"But she had a holy bone," Jacob reminded her, "and Topsy ate it."

"What are you talking about?" his father asked.

"The bone the priest was talking about in the cemetery," Cliona said: "The one that is lost and nobody knows where it is."

Tom asked: "What is this all about? I was working away and heard nothing about it from anyone. Another bloody Pishrogues. More superstition."

Róisín explained that Tom's mother was the keeper of the bone.

"I know all that old shite," her husband answered.

"Róisín stared at him and said: "The children."

"You will have to put money in the curse jar, Dad," Jacob said triumphantly, "because you said a bad word."

His father put up his hands and apologised: "I'm sorry. Get the jar, Jacob and I will pay up." He realised that he was causing too much aggravation about a child's story: "Tell your story, Cliona," he said quietly. "Good girl,"

"The holy bone was actually a magic rod, and you could do anything you liked with it," she said: "She built a big wall at the top of the cliffs without using any machine or even putting cement in it. She built it to keep out all of the sea monsters because she was afraid, they would eat all of the lovely fruit in the glasshouse she had made with her wand as well." She bowed like an actor on stage: "That is my story," she said, "and a good story it is."

"Is that all?" Tom asked: "I would like to find out what happened next."

"I did not have time to think of anything else," Cliona replied: "I will finish it again tonight or tomorrow."

"Well done, Cliona," Róisín said, as she led the applause: "It is your turn next, Jacob."

He gave a nervous laugh as if he had not the confidence to compete with is sister who had spoken so clearly and well: "There was a king in Ireland once who had a tail on his bum like Topsy." He burst out laughing before adding: "That is my story and a good story it is. Mom next."

"Come on, Jacob," Róisín said: "You have more than that scribbled on the page in front of you. Don't be shy."

He continued reluctantly: "There was a king in Ireland once who had a tail, but the people or animals in his kingdom did not mind because they liked dogs. The king's name was 'King Topsy. There were no people in the world that time, only animals which came out of the Ark when a big flood dried up and the Ark came to rest on a heap of sand in the Western Isle. All of the animals spoke the same language, barking language, so they all understood Topsy when he was talking. I mean barking. A white horse told Topsy that he saw a red dragon when he looked out one of the windows. Topsy jumped out and chased the dragon away to the Antarctic where he turned into a penguin" He bowed: "That is the end of my story and a good story it is."

"A very sudden end," his mother said as she led the applause: "You should work a bit more on the end and on what happened next."

"Nothing happened next except 'the end.' That is how

every story finishes: THE END."

"You are both very good at starting stories," their mother said, "but you are inclined to finish too quickly. You should listen to your Dadó and watch out for the way he tells the end of a story."

Clíona had enough of that advice, so she tried to move things along: "Mom's story now, she announced. And you be ready, Dad."

"I will let Dad go before me," Róisín said.

Tom made a grand gesture with his hand: "No escape. Ladies first."

She began: "There was a queen on this island once called Melissa. People gave her that name because she was as sweet as honey and the Irish for honey is mil. Melissa had no problem in the world except that swarms of bees used to follow her everywhere because she smelt like honey. They would never sting her, but they stung anybody that might seem like a threat to her. All of the bees loved her, and they would make a crown around her head sometimes like you would see in pictures of the Blessed Virgin. The ladies in waiting in the palace were afraid that the bees would eat Melissa alive someday, but she was never afraid. The other ladies used to keep out of her way when there was a game of camogie because they were afraid of the bees. Melissa was delighted, of course because she would get more scores and win the match.

Clíona was becoming impatient: "Did she marry a prince? Or were the princess themselves afraid of the bees?"

"Melissa did not marry a prince but an ordinary man who went around the country selling honey to the kings and princes who were very fond of a drink called mead that was made from mixing wine and honey. Melissa's bees made so much honey that herself and her husband became the richest people in the country."

"Just like us," Jacob said, "because Man and Dad won the lotto."

"I hope you don't be boasting about that at school," their father, Tom, said.

"We don't," Clíona said, "except now and again when people are teasing us."

"Teasing you in what way?" Róisín asked.

Jacob blurted out: "Sometimes they say that Dad is crazy, that building the wall is a waste of time and money."

"They say what they are hearing at home," Tom said to Róisín. He spoke directly to his children: "What do you say?"

"We tell them to fuck off," Jacob answered straight out.

His mother and father tried to correct or even discipline him, but they could not help but laugh. They just let the matter drop as they continued with the story competition. Jacob said to his mother: "That was a lovely story, Mom. Now Dad."

"There was a young man on this island once," he began, "It was not that long ago. A young man as fit as the best athlete in the Olympics."

"Was he a prince?" Clíona enquired.

"Not a prince in a palace," her father answered, "but a prince among men. A film company came to the island to film the way in which young men used to climb down the cliffs on ropes to collect the eggs of seagulls and other birds. They used to do the very same thing in the Aran Islands and the Cliffs of Moher."

"Did they suck the eggs?" Jacob asked.

"Or did they make omelettes?"

"I don't know if they made omelettes or not, Clíona, but eggs of any kind are healthy when people are poor and the potatoes are rotten. There came a time when people had enough to eat, and they do not need to collect birds' eggs anymore. The film makers had read about it in a book, and they thought it was a very brave thing to do, to climb down a rope for eggs. They wanted to find a man who would act it out in their film. They had said nothing about money, but this young man stepped forward and said: "I will do it for a hundred pounds." That was a lot of money at the time.

"As much as the lotto?" Jacob asked.

"Not that much, but it could buy a second-hand car."

"Did the prince slide down the rope?" Cliona asked.

"As I said," his father answered, "he was not a prince but even braver than one. He did not slide down the rope because it might have cut his hands. He went down hand over hand, letting the rope slip slowly between his feet so that he could trap it and use it like a brake anytime he wanted. He had a bag tied to his belt in order to collect the eggs."

"A plastic bag?" Jacob asked.

"Plastic was not even invented that time, or at least it had not come as far as this island. He put the eggs into the bag carefully so and not to break them."

"Were the hens picking at his hands, the way Dadó's hens pick at us when we are collecting eggs for him?" Cliona wondered.

Jacob corrected her: "It was not hens. It was seagulls."

"The seagulls scattered when they saw him coming, but they flew in circles above him making an almighty racket. He wondered were they going to pick at his hands or even at his eyes, but he had to just get on with the job."

"Did any egg fall down into the water?"

"No, Jacob, but the man nearly did. He was hanging from an old hemp rope, and they were not as good as those kind of blue ropes you would see down at the pier nowadays. When the young man was climbing back up to the top of the cliff he noticed the rope was unravelling because the sharp edge of the rock was cutting through it. He shouted to the men with the camera to grab his hand, but they seemed more interested in getting their picture than in saving a man's life. The rope broke and he fell about a hundred feet."

"Was he killed stone dead?" Jacob asked.

"Hadn't they fixed a net down below to catch him that they did not even tell him about. I think they wanted to get the fear in his eyes on their film."

The children's mother, Róisín asked: "And do you know the name of the young man who climbed down that rope?" She laid the flattery on with a trowel: "That hero, that prince, that man among men?"

"Cúchulainn," Clíona answered.

Jacob tried: "Fionn mac Cumhaill, or was it Oisín?" It was then that he noticed the smile on his mother's face as she looked across the room.

"Dad. The hero."

"Our Dad, the prince," Clíona answered as she hugged him: "Prince Dad."

"That was the best night ever," was Jacob's comment "We will have to have a story competition every night."

His father replied: "We would soon run out of stories. Once a year, maybe."

Jacob had one more question: "What happened to the eggs?"

"They were so smashed. I had to leave the bag at the bottom of the cliff."

"Pollution," Clíona said.

"The seagulls soon cleared up the mess."

Clíona was not letting the matter go: "But the bag was still there."

"It sank like a stone and was never seen again," was her father's reply.

"The best night ever, bag or no bag," was Jacob's continued verdict.

His father asked: "What about the lovely nights we had in Italy, in Spain, in Portugal or in Greece? Not to speak of Lanzarotte when you were both very small and you talked about it for years."

"We were not making up new stories off the top of our heads.

Róisín laughed: "It was not all creativity. Some people had stories in which they themselves were the heroes. The bit of bravado was never lost on anyone."

Tom's mind was elsewhere: "I wonder is there a copy of that film about gathering the eggs on the cliff anywhere?"

"If you could find out who made it," Róisín said with a shrug.

Some crowd from Italy, I think. Their embassy might know. It would be a great attraction in the island museum."

"We don't have a museum," his wife reminded him.

"Wouldn't it be a good idea to build one? On top of the cliff with a ninety-degree view of the sea. It could be part of the big wall and a museum at the same time." He was still thinking out loud. "With bullet-proof glass to keep out the elements."

"And to keep the cartridge crowd away," Róisín said cynically "Let us not lose the run of ourselves."

"It could not be too close to the edge," Róisín said, "in case of a collapse like you had the last day. There is not always a net at the bottom to catch who or what is falling."

"Some people have more luck than others," was Tom's answer to that.

"You are inclined to go too close to the edge in more ways than one," Róisín said. "That is what worries me. I do not want our lovely little family destroyed by grief because of an accident."

"I don't either," he answered. "Ok, I take risks from time to time, but they are always calculated risks."

Róisín told him that she never believed in the phrase: "A man has to do what a man has to do. Even a calculated risk is a risk."

"Have I got it wrong yet?"

"If they were ever famous last words, you have just said

them."

Tom shrugged his shoulders and called to the children: "Look at the clock. It says bedtime. Tomorrow is a school day."

"I didn't hear it saying anything. Except tick tock."

"Don't be too smart," his father said lightly."

Clíona chimed in: "All I heard it saying was 'bong, bong,' at nine o'clock. It didn't say bedtime."

"Nine bongs are bedtime," her father said.

"But I would love to hear another story," Clíona pleaded.

"Into your pyjamas first," Róisín said, and your Dad will read a story for you, seeing that he is actually at home tonight." She added as an afterthought: "And don't forget to wash."

Jacob saw the contradiction in that: "If we put on our pyjamas first and wash then, they will be all wet, so we will have to change them again."

"Don't push me," Róisín said. "I am out on my feet tired after a long day."

"Tom was in a bit of a sulk about her previous comment: You never lose a chance to have a go at me."

"I didn't have a go at anyone. What are you talking about?"

"Saying I am never here for the children's bedtime. You are not always here yourself. Who was here when you were away with Gearóidín last week?"

"So, and even if I was, it was not you that minded them most of the time but your father. You are not the only one that has a job. And we need to talk about what to do now that your mother is seriously ill, and your father will not be able to mind the children as often as he did."

Tom answered: "We will discuss that when the children are in bed, and I have my once-a-year job done."

"What does that mean?"

"You would think that I never read them a story. The night was nice up to now, so don't destroy it for the kids."

Tom read a story from an old book he had himself in the National school, a story about Diarmuid and Gráinne on the run around the country because of a disagreement with her father.

"Read it again, Dad," said Clíona as she tried to stretch out the bedtime ritual.

"I will read it again, but not tonight. Bed now, story tomorrow."

Róisín was sitting on the couch with her legs pulled up beneath her and a glass of wine in her hand when Tom returned.

"There was no need to fill the dishwasher," he said. "I would have done that."

"You got the children to bed, that is enough. As long as the work is shared, I am happy."

Tom agreed that they could not expect too much from his father, now that his wife was very ill in the Nursing Home: "But it is handy to have him as a kind of insurance when both of us are busy."

He poured himself a drink and they sat back in a relaxed way without speaking for quite a while. It was Tom who broke the silence.

"That was a good night: I enjoyed the way everyone tried hard with their own story. There was a fair bit of imagination there."

"Look at the difference between that and the kind of stories that your father usually tells them, full of blood and guts and violence," Róisín commented "That kind of thing was alright for his day and age, but people are a bit more sophisticated nowadays."

"Tell that to our Cliona and Jacob," Tom laughed. "The more blood and guts the better most of the time. But kids like that. What is your man's name that was popular when we were growing up? He was big into the scary stories himself."

"Are you talking about Roald Dahl?" Róisín asked.

"The very man. I used to like his stories. They reminded me

of the cartoons on television, but not quite as crazy. Still, I don't think they did anyone any harm. Look at us," Tom joked, "how sensible and balanced we are."

"Oh, yes," Róisín said. "But there is a difference between stories about things that are imagined, no matter how bloodthirsty they are and actual basins of blood after stabbing a poor pig in the throat that your father tells them about."

"But do these things come between them and their night's sleep?"

"Why do they end up in our bed so often?" Róisín asked.

"Comfort," he said, "and the lovely smells. We have discussed this a hundred times. I have seen no evidence that the stories told by my father have an adverse effect on them. In fact, they love him, and they love his stories. In fact, I wish they loved me as much as they love him."

"Don't tell me that you are jealous of your own father. We have no way of knowing how the stories have affected the children. We hear and read a lot about grooming before children are abused."

"So that is what you are accusing him of now? Child abuse?"

"That is not what I said. We need to keep a close eye on this. A man might not set out to do anything, but when his wife is away ill in a Nursing Home? You wouldn't know. Hands could wander and there is no going back. I am not comfortable with having him minding my children," Róisín said definitively.

"Well, I am happy to have him minding mine, and I have not thanked him enough, if I have thanked him at all."

"We need to do something about it", Róisín insisted. "We have to get rid of him. Sooner rather than later."

Clíona had slept for a while when she was awakened by the sound of her mother and father arguing downstairs. "They are fighting again," was her first thought, and from her point of view arguing was fighting. They would say something like "We were having a discussion," when she or Jacob would demand: "Stop fighting. What is it about now?" she wondered, as she tiptoed to the top of the stairs.

The first thing she heard was her mother saying: "We have to get rid of him." Her father's voice was lower, so she did not hear what he had replied. Alarm bells were sounding in her head. She wondered was it their dog, Topsy that was being discussed. "Had he been chasing sheep? Maybe he was, maybe he wasn't," she thought. They had never really found up to what he was at that time that he had gone missing.

Then Clíona wondered was it about the dog continually destroying their sandcastles and what Jacob called the lost city. No big deal, she thought. They had always managed to rebuild the castles again. After all he was only a dog and that was what dogs did in their spare time. "I will have to tell Jacob," Cliona told herself, and then the two of them together would do something about it.

She went to the door of Jacob's room and tried to open it in a way that would not cause a squeak. Her Dad was always going to oil the hinge, but he never did because he had too much else to do. It was at that moment as she waited for the squeak that Clíona realised that it was not Topsy that was in trouble, but her grandfather. She overheard her mother say to her father that his father, her Dadó would have to be got rid of. It may not have been completely clear, but that is what she heard. So, she thought. So, she was sure, or was she, she asked herself. But they could not take a chance.

Clíona went into her brother's room and caught him by the shoulder and shook him.

"Wake up," she whispered. "We have to warn Dadó."

"I was having a lovely dream," Jacob groaned. "Why did you wake me up. Will I tell you the dream?"

"Never mind about that," Cliona said gruffly. "I heard Mom and Dad arguing in the sitting room. I thought they were talking about Topsy when they said they were going to get rid of something. Or somebody. I found out after a while that it is Dadó that they want to get rid of."

"Are they going to stick a knife in him? Like Dadó's friends did with the pig?"

"They just said: 'Get rid,' They did not say 'kill' but that could be what they meant either."

Jacob gave rein to his vivid imagination: "They might cover him in concrete and drop him down from the cliff into the sea. That is what they do in America. Is it the sea or the river? he wondered. I know that it is water anyway."

Clíona had a less spectacular idea: "Maybe they are going to put him into that hospital place Mamó is since she lost her mind."

"Lost her mind, that is funny," Jacob said, as he pretended the brain was falling out of his head.

"That is bold," Clíona said, "when we are talking about Mamó."

"She would have a laugh too," Jacob answered. "She was always making fun until she got sick. Or is it 'ill' I should say?"

"It would not be as bad to be put into the Nursing Home," Cliona mused, "as to be thrown off a cliff."

"Poor Dadó," Jacob said, as he stretched out on the bed and seemed to be falling asleep again.

Cliona dragged the covers from his bed and threw them on the floor. "Get up out of that. We need to save Dadó. I have a plan."

"What plan?" her brother yawned.

"We will go to his house and break the bad news to him. Be ready to come with me when I come back. I have to check on Mom and Dad. We cannot go anywhere until they are sound asleep."

"High five?" Jacob said as they slapped hands together. He regained his bedclothes and cuddled beneath them, hoping that all the talk about his grandfather was a nightmare, and that he would have a lovely dream instead.

Clíona returned to her room and climbed into bed. She tossed and turned nervously in her efforts to keep awake. She pretended to be snoring when her parents came in to kiss her goodnight and pull the covers up to her shoulders. She knew she would need to stay awake until her mother and father were asleep in their room. She fought sleep as hard as she could by walking around her bed again and again, getting tired of that, she stretched out on her bed above the covers. Sleep just seemed to gently close her eyes despite all her efforts.

"What time is it?" Clíona felt that it must be morning when Jacob shook her awake: "Where were you?" he demanded to know. "I was waiting and waiting, and you never called me."

"I tried to stay awake, but I must have dozed off."

"I was asleep alright, but I had to get up to go to the toilet," her brother told her. "But I am ready to go now."

Cliona asked: "Are Mom and Dad asleep?"

"There was not a sound out of them when I listened at their door."

"Let's go so." Cliona tied her dressing gown around and put her school coat on over that in case it was raining. They went slowly down the stairs in case there would be a squeak from the timber. It was when they reached the ground floor that they met their first hurdle. The doors were locked front and back with the keys hanging up out of their reach.

"Get up on my back," Jacob said, "and see if you can reach them."

He bent down, but every time she tried to climb on his back Cliona slipped off his shiny raincoat.

"Where is the sweeping brush?" Cliona asked.

"What do you want to go sweeping now?"

"We might be able to knock the keys with it."

They tried that and were successful in that they knocked down the keys, but they clattered on the floor tiles. The children stood as if they were frozen to the floor, waiting to hear their father or mother get up. The next problem was working out which of the bunch of keys would open the back door. Topsy, their dog was staying there that night because the children's grandfather had planned to go to visit his wife, Nora in the mainland Nursing Home the following day. He was excited and anxious as the children fumbled with the keys as they tried to open the back door. They managed to open it at last, let out the dog and took their mother's mobile phone to shine a light on the road.

Their grandfather's house was not far away, but the children were excited and nervous as they walked the road, Topsy running from side to side as if every smell that wafted about needed to be investigated.

"I think he might smell a rabbit or a hare," Jacob suggested.

"Or it could be a fox," Clíona said. "I hope that it is not a lamb or a sheep. Or a ghost."

That thought gave Jacob the shivers: "Hurry up and don't be dawdling about. We are on an important mission. To save Topsy and Dadó."

"I hope Dad and Mom won't miss us too much," Clíona said.

"Won't they see us tomorrow?"

"They will be cross."

"Dad and Mom often say that you need to do what you have to do no matter what other people say," was Jacob's answer to that. "We just want to save the people that we love."

"Topsy is not people," his sister told him.

"He is nicer than people. He is our best friend. My best friend anyway."

"Mine too," Cliona added. "My very best friend."

When they reached their grandfather's house, Jacob shone the light around the yard: "I never saw the lost city in the middle of the night before now."

"Hurry up and wake up Dadó, and tell him that we are here," Cliona told him. "Forget about the lost city until we have done what we came to do."

Jacob knocked at the door as hard as he could, and whispered "Dadó?"

"Why are you whispering?" Cliona asked him.

"Because it is nighttime."

"But there is nobody else to hear us: 'Shout it out.'"

"You shout it out," he said.

Clíona shouted at the top of her voice, but there was no answer. "Maybe he is dead," she said, "but I hope not."

"We could throw a stone at his bedroom window," Jacob suggested.

"The window might break, and the glass would cut him."

Jacob was thinking out loud: "We could throw sand from the lost city at his window."

"That would not waken a fly," his sister assured him.

Jacob looked at his mother's mobile phone: "we could throw this, but we would have no light then."

Clíona had a better plan: "Why don't we ring him on Mom's phone?"

The ringtone awakened their father and he recognised that it was from his daughter-in-law's phone: "Róisín," he asked: "Is something wrong?"

He was answered by a childish giggle and a "Hi Dadó."

"Is that you, Jacob? Or is it Cliona?"

"It is me," Cliona answered. "You know well."

"Is it April Fool's Day or someone's birthday? Why are you ringing me in the middle of the night?"

"Mom and Dad are trying to get rid of you. And Topsy too."

"I don't understand," her grandfather answered: "I am just trying to wake up at the moment. It takes an old man a while to get the cobwebs out of his mind and out of his head. What is that you said about your Mom and Dad?"

"Jacob and I heard them talking. We thought at first that they wanted to get rid of Topsy. But then we heard them say something about getting rid of you."

The old man was finding it all very difficult to understand: "Maybe Jacob would be a bit clearer," he thought, "because he is a bit older: "Is Jacob there with you?" he asked.

"He is. Do you wish to speak to him? Will I give him the phone?"

"Do, please. Good girl."

"Hi Dadó," Jacob said.

"Hello Jacob. I am just after waking up and I do not quite understand what is going on. Something about me and Topsy, is it?"

"Could you let us into the house, Dadó?" Jacob said. "It is very cold out here."

"Out where?" his grandfather asked, wonder in his voice.

"Outside your back door."

"You should have told me that."

"We thought you knew."

"I am going down now to open the door. Don't stir until you see me." When Tadhg Rua opened the door, the children stood there almost like statues: "What is wrong?" he asked.

"You said not to stir until you opened the door."

"Come in quickly out of the cold. Wait until I turn on the heat." Their grandfather felt it was better not to ask any questions until they were settled down and comfortable. He had many strange stories about all kinds of abuse on the radio and he felt it was better to take things slowly. He got each of them a blanket to keep them warm until the central heating was up and running and the house warm. At the same time, he realised that there was not a sign on either of them that they were in any way traumatised.

When they were nice and cosy in their blankets, Jacob said: "Topsy is cold as well, Dadó."

"Topsy would not like any of the other dogs see him wrapped in a blanket. It would shame him for seventy dog years. He has a fine coat of hair from top to bottom. The only time he gets cold is when he is wet. Then he wets everyone else by shaking himself."

Dadó said 'bottom,' Jacob whispered skittishly to Clíona, but she pretended not to hear him in case in case it upset her grandfather in any way. He let it all pass. There were more important things in life than making mountains out of molehills. He sat between the children on the couch: "Now I would like you to tell me what brought you here. But before that I am going to call your father and mother to let them know that you are here safe and well along with me."

Clíona answered first: "You might not like it Dadó, when we tell you why we came here to warn you. Mom and Dad were talking about getting rid of you."

"And getting rid of Topsy as well, we think."

"I would say that there is a misunderstanding somewhere. Anything your Mom and Dad do is for your good."

Jacob interrupted: "But they might think it is for our good to get rid of you?"

"This is the way I see it," the old man said. "They think that I am too old to be looking after you, and they are right. It is not that I do not love it when you are with me, but it is getting too much for me because your Mamó is very ill, and I have to go out often to the mainland to see her. You would still visit me here even if someone else was minding you now and again. We would have even more fun because I would not be so tired, dozing off in my chair while you two are having hide and seek."

"And burning the bacon sometimes," Clíona reminded him.

"You are always telling us that story," Jacob added.

"Can't you see what I mean? I am getting more and more forgetful, and I am afraid I will do something really careless someday."

"Like cooking Topsy instead of a chicken," Jacob suggested.

Clíona tried to be even more outrageous: "Like boiling a basin of blood and giving it to us as soup."

Their grandfather laughed: "It is talk like that I would really miss if you were not coming here regularly. But, as I said, we would still have great fun together."

"You are the best Dadó ever," Jacob said.

Clíona gave him a hug: "And the nicest and the very very best."

"You won't mind now if I ring your Mom and Dad? They would be devastated if they were to wake up and find that you were not in the house."

It was Tom that answered the phone. He spoke in a muffled voice between waking and sleeping: "What is it?" he asked bluntly.

"Everything is alright," his father answered, "but Clíona and Jacob are here." He explained what time and what way in which they had arrived and that it was clear that they had taken up wrong something that they had overheard.

"Was it some shit that was said to them at school?"

"The way that they put it was that yourself and Róisín wanted to get rid of me and of Topsy. They thought they should let me know what you had planned, even though I'm sure it was something that they took up wrong."

"It is the daftest thing I ever heard in my life."

The older man did not hear anything else on the phone, as

his son, Tom was telling Róisín about what had happened and why the children had left the house. When he came back on the phone, he said: "We will be there as soon as we get dressed."

"Take your time. Nobody here will be going anywhere."

Clíona and Jacob expected that their parents would be cross with them, but the opposite was the case. They hugged and kissed them, and it was perfectly clear how worried they were. They asked the children to promise not to leave their own house again, no matter what they heard or thought they heard. "If there is a problem to be sorted, just tell us," Róisín said.

"But you and Dad were the problem," Cliona said. "What good was it to tell you? You were the ones that were going to get rid of Dadó."

"And Topsy," Jacob added.

Róisín looked at Tom: "Did either of us ever say to the other one that we were going to get rid of anyone?"

"No, but I can see how something could be taken up wrong by children with vivid imaginations."

Róisín gave a nervous kind of laugh: "At least I am glad that you had not ran off to Van Diemen's land or somewhere else at the other side of the world."

"Is that a land full of demons?" Jacob asked.

"There are no such things as demons," their father told them.

"That is not what the TV says," Cliona said.

"We won't argue about it," their mother promised. The main thing is that you are alive and well. Just tell us if anything is wrong or if you are angry at what you hear somebody saying, even if you don't understand it fully." Tom and Róisín spent a long time cuddling their children until they drifted off to sleep and had to be carried into the beds they slept in in their grandfather's house.

Their parents sat for a long time with Tom's father at the kitchen table in his house. "Don't think you are insulting me in any way," the older man said, "if you get someone else to mind Clíona and Jacob. I would enjoy an odd day with them, but I find I am too tired in myself to continue as things were. Since I started travelling more often to visit Nora, I am just not able to keep minding the kids."

"We will sort things out in a few days," his son Tom promised.

Things got back to the way they were for a while because Tom was working and Róisín was finding it difficult to get a carer for the children when planning and organising her own project. Clíona and Jacob were still going to their grandfather after school and building and rebuilding their castles in the lost city. Topsy lay quietly in a spot sheltered from the sun beneath the bushes. He emerged now and again to do what a dog had to do, scatter sand in his case. When Jacob and Clíona tired from their play they went over to where their grandfather sat on his armchair reading a newspaper: "tell us a story, Dadó."

"You have heard all of my stories many times. It is your turn now to tell me a story."

"There was a man once," Clíona began: "He was not a king or anything, just an ordinary man. "One day he bought a piece of bacon for his dinner.

Jacob took up the tale: He went home, and he put the meat in a saucepan.

"They filled the saucepan with the blood of a pig." Both children laughed so much that they could not finish their story.

183

Chapter Twenty-One

A big ship that had sailed from Amsterdam lay off the coast of the Western Isle because there was not enough water even in the highest of tides for it to approach the pier. It had been arranged that great wooden boxes of glass would be floated in on pontoons from which it would be transported to fit the wooden frames already built in readiness. This was considered the safest way to bring the glass ashore as boxes of glass swaying on a crane above a fishing boat could be a recipe for major breakages.

Tsunami Tom moved all of his workforce from the wall at the clifftop to getting the glass ashore and into place so that seed could be set, and plants sown as part of his wife's Róisín's project. A number of workers from Holland had travelled to organise the island men and direct them during operations. Some of the big machines that had cranes and lifting equipment were moved from the wall to help get the glass jigsaw into place.

The crew of the boat itself did not partake in the work onshore because they were not skilled in building, so they had a certain amount of free time to walk about the island and mix with the local people not involved in the building work. Many of them were from Africa, from Liberia, Senegal and Nigeria and they soon created a great rapport with the local people and with the children especially. Some of them were invited to the local school to speak to the pupils about their countries and their cultures, not to speak of all they had seen on their voyages throughout the world. Some had little drums and they performed music and dance acts. Teachers and their students were delighted with this new and vibrant addition to island life, even if it was only for a while. The children asked their visitors to put on a concert in the local hall before they left. "We will do the Irish dances and songs," they promised, "if you do the African drumming and dancing."

The crew of the ship got the captain's permission to bring children, parents and teachers on board on a sunny Sunday afternoon to see it all from stem to stern. The captain explained the many television or computer-like screens in his area of operation and fielded questions about radar, engine strength and safety procedures. He was questioned more about the Titanic than about his own ship. "What would happen if this hit an iceberg?" was one of the first questions asked.

"Nothing," was his answer, "because we have equipment now that would not just see the iceberg in front of us, but to avoid it."

"So, is this a better ship than the Titanic?" Jacob asked bluntly.

"I will say this much in answer to that," the captain replied. "This is a better boat at present, because this is the top of the sea and the Titanic is at the bottom."

Tsunami Tom had his own personal tactics in moving his men from the clifftop wall to help build the glasshouses. It was not just to help Róisín in her project, but to soothe the hackles of those politicians and civil servants who were annoyed at the way he started building without planning permission. He had now applied for delayed planning with the excuse that he had taken emergency measures to stop possible tsunamis and was now willing to have his wall legalised. The fact that his workers and their machines were no longer on site should help him, he felt, to get in the good books of officials. He even offered to pay an ex-gratia fine of a million euro for breaking the law. He was well aware that it would be considered a bribe, but money was no object, and he knew that official coffers were at a low ebb.

Tom was coming under pressure from some of his workmen to get them back the wall as they found dealing with sheets of glass needed much more skill than sand, cement and steel. "Bring in a crowd of Eastern Europeans," they urged him. "They will be a lot cheaper, and they have much more practice in dealing with fruit and vegetables. Only for the likes of them, there would not be a strawberry picked in Wexford or in North Dublin."

"I don't agree with cheap labour of that kind," he answered bluntly. "And there is something racist about it."

"That crowd are thankful for small mercies," he was assured. "They would bite the hand off you to earn a few euros for the rest of the year. It is the very same as our people going to England on the beat or to Scotland for the tatie hoking in days gone by. Most people are glad to get a bit of work."

"Maybe I should put them working on the wall so," was Tom's reply.

"They would be grand for soft kind of work," he was told. "Picking fruit and that kind of thing. There is an element of "The Pole for plucking the pears, the Paddy for the plastering."

Tom had his answer to that too: "From what I have seen of the workers you have mentioned whether it is from Poland or Brazil, they are the finest, as good as any Paddy if it comes to that. We will be working on the glasshouses until they are up and running, the seeds set, and the plants planted. For anyone who does not want to be part of that there are plenty of crabs and crayfish out there under the sea." He left it like that, knowing that his message would reach all who worked for him.

Residents of the Western Isle were heard to say that life had never been as good. Tourists were arriving in their droves because of all the publicity the island was generating, both positive and negative. Even the caustic reports on some of the newspapers, radio and television were nor scoring off visitors. "I have often heard,"

Róisín said to her closest friend one evening that good publicity is any publicity people can get. I did not believe it at the time, but it does seem to be true.

As for Gearóidín herself she seemed to be very taken by a tall seaman from Senegal. Since the break-up of her marriage, she had steered clear of men for the most part. She had an occasional date that was arranged online, but most of them had tended to be more trouble than they were worth. "Old codgers" was how she described some of them to Róisín: "They look so young in the pictures they show you that you would think they are in their confirmation suits, but when you see them in practice, they look more like you would see someone in a habit in the coffin. She had met a couple of nice gentlemanly types as well, but the logistics of island life had let to any real hope of romance petering out."

The tall athletic man from Senegal appealed greatly to her. It was difficult to work out what age he was, because as she put it to Róisín: "it is hard to see wrinkles in a face as black as ebony." But his age did not bother her. He was civil. He was mannerly and well spoken. He had the finest of English, teeth as white as an iceberg in his mouth: "I have never met anyone like him," she told Róisín "What am I going to do when he sails away?"

"There might be a spare bunk in the boat."

"The same bunk would do both of us fine," she laughed.

"Be careful," Róisín told her, as she asked bluntly: "Are you ready for a black baby? I know that is not a politically correct thing to say. It is ok if you are happy with it, but it needs to be thought through."

"He is not like that at all. He treats me like a lady."

Róisín laughed: "I hope the does not kiss or do anything else like a lady."

"We have not got around to anything like that yet, we are taking things slowly, He is a complete gentleman. He is kind and considerate."

"And gay, I would say from what you are telling me. I am not homophobic or anything, but it sounds strange to me in this day and age. What will you do if he does 'have a go' for want of better words?"

Gearóidín laughed: "I will jump all over him and give both of us the time of our lives."

Be careful," was Róisín's warning.

"Next thing you will be slipping condoms into my handbag like my mother used to do back in the day."

"A sensible Mom. Imagine I have to face all of that with my two in ten years' time or so."

"They say that good sense comes with age," Gearóidín said with a smile. "In my mother's case it came from having a houseful of children Welcome be the will of God, she used to say every time she got pregnant, but as life changed that is not what she willed for us. She didn't want to have us burdened down with children. The ironic thing is that I have ended up with none at all."

"It is not too late yet."

"It's a long way from romance I have been in recent years."

"What is it they say?" Róisín joked. "Tonight, might be the night. Or tomorrow, or Sunday at the latest. I am sure you will not be saying: "That boat has sailed," when the big ship eventually leaves the bay."

Gearóidín admitted: "He is attractive. Everyone on board looks attractive when a person has been starved for so long. Big black athletic handsome men. There might not be a woman married or single left on the island when the ship does eventually sail away."

"And what will our poor men do then?" Róisín joked.

"They probably wouldn't even notice because they are so obsessed with the wall on top of the cliff."

"My Tom certainly is," his wife said. "He is married to his wall more than he is to me at the moment."

"So, you are not getting your oats either?"

Róisín answered with mock wonder: "Gearóidín! What an awful thing to say. But you are right, of course. Still, he has other things on his mind with his mother so ill and everything."

"It would be a good day for them all if she passed away."

"Your mother is your mother all the same, no matter how ill or old she is."

Gearóidín remarked: "I was visiting in a Nursing Home once and it put me off forever. A lot of them are like the living dead. I certainly don't want to end up like that. From now on my motto will be: 'Take your pleasure where you can get it'. Do you not think that sometimes?"

"Mind would my husband hear you."

"You are a one-man woman," Gearóidín said: "You wouldn't go with another man even if you were paid."

Róisín laughed: "Now that you mention getting paid for it! That's another story altogether." She paused for a little while before answering: "Who knows what a person might do if the temptation was strong enough and if you were horny enough? But things are different for you at the moment. You have that big strong thin hunk of a man out there waiting for you."

"Wouldn't it be nice for once to go from night until morning in the arms of a good big handsome hulk? It would certainly raise my heart."

"Only to be broken when the ship sails?" Róisín reminded her.

"I would have the memory forever. The memory of lying in his arms, his lips on mine, his kisses on my neck and my shoulders."

"You certainly do have it bad. Slow down girl or you will drive me out of my mind. Tom won't know what hit him when I get home. By the way what is this lovely handsome man's name?"

"Patrick. Would you believe it? Now that the Irish are

turning their backs on their own saint's names, we find a Patrick arriving here from Senegal. It seems that there was an Irish nun in the hospital in which he was born, and she filled the place with Patrick, Bridget and Colmcilles. She had gone to the other side of the world but had taken her Irish heritage with her."

"And scattered it like snow in the wind." Róisín smiled: "So long as she does not leave you carrying a little Paddy?"

"Without being racist, wouldn't it be lovely to have a little black Paddy living on the island?"

"There would be nothing wrong with it at all, so long as it was welcomed and loved, and that it was what a person wanted," was Róisín's opinion.

"All I want right now is that lovely long night of love that will remain in my mind and heart forever." Gearóidín said.

Chapter Twenty-Two

Tadhg Rua's next visit to the Nursing Home in which his wife resided lifted his heart in a way that he had not expected. Nora sat upright in an armchair and said him warmly.

"Do you know who I am?" he asked her.

"Of course, I know who you are," she answered. Her speech was slow and weak, but the words were coming out correctly in a way he had not heard her speak for a long time.

"So, who am I?" he asked, eager to find out did she really recognise him, or was she covering up her illness.

"If you don't know who you are, I am not going to tell you," Nora answered with a little smile that reminded him of the way she would give a witty answer when she was much younger and in her health.

"Everyone on the island has been asking for you," he said, "Tom and Róisín and the children, Jacob and Clíona." Tadhg hoped that by naming names the people in question would be more real to his wife. He added: "And of course Topsy the dog and the cat in the barn and the ducks and the hens are all in fine fettle too."

Nora startled him when she announced: "I will be going home this evening."

"It is the first that I have heard of it," he said. "I will have to talk with the manager about the arrangements."

Nora put her head as close to his as she could: "I will be travelling in my own way. Don't tell anyone."

"And what way is that?" he asked.

His wife sat up in her chair: "I am going home to my own house to see my mother and father and brothers and sisters."

Tadhg understood then that while Nora seemed to have improved physically, Alzheimer still held her in its firm grip. He said in his own mind: "They must have changed her tablets again." At that stage he had got used to her improving for a while before falling back again.

Róisín had printed out pictures of Tom, herself, and the children to show to Nora. There were pictures of them at home, of Clíona and Jacob playing in the sand and of both of them hugging Topsy in between them, there were pictures too of the big ship in the harbour and of the machinery at building the wall on top of the cliff.

She looked long and hard at a photo of her son Tom standing on top of the wall and asked: "Who is that idiot? He would need to be careful, or he will fall down in a heap."

"That is your son, Tom. And my son too, of course."

Nora looked him in the face for a while before saying: "You are far too old to have a son, you old devil. Who are you trying to fool? You are not my son or my daughter or any relation of mine. You are just a dirty old devil." She repeated that again and again, each time louder than the next until a nurse came to rub her hand gently and soothe her.

Tadhg enquired about what might have caused the sudden change in Nora's attitude. It turned out that he had been correct about the change of tablets, but it was explained that patients improved or more often got worse as the disease took its toll. By the time he was preparing to go home, Nora was back to much the way she had been when he had first arrived. As the days had got longer, he took daytrips on the ferry in order not to have to stay in tourist accommodation and so that he would get to sleep in his own bed at night.

Before leaving Tadhg took the opportunity to visit the doctor and discuss Nora and her illness. He learned little except d been told already by other members of staff. When he returned to say goodbye to his wife, she was in bed at one side of a double room with another woman of much the same age at the other.

"I know who you are," was again Nora's greeting. "You are the very man. That is what you are, the very man."

The other woman asked: "Who is this fine cut of a man? Did I meet you before? You are getting prettier every time I see you."

"Don't say that too loudly," Tadhg said, "because that is my wife there in the next bed to you."

The woman gave a burst of raucous laughter: "Why don't you get into bed and have the craic with her so?" She shook her head and said to herself: "A man has to do what a man has to do."

"I need to go now," Tadhg said to Nora as he said goodbye. "I have to catch the boat."

"To catch the boat," the other woman mused: "Did it fly away on you?"

Tadhg Rua found himself standing inside the front door of the Nursing Home for a while, waiting to get out. He had forgotten the code that would open the doors. The office staff seemed to have gone for their tea. He began to worry that he might miss the boat. He took some consolation from the fact that while Nora was still and probably would be in a confused state for the rest of her life, she did not seem to be in danger of death.

It was at that moment he remembered Pope Saint Gregory's sacred bone. "Would I have enough time to go back and see if Nora did remember anything," he asked himself.

Just as a young woman was arriving to open the door for him, Tadhg excused himself: "I am sorry, I have forgotten something." He headed back down the corridor towards his wife's room.

"Where did this fine man come from?" the woman in the other bed asked: "And a fine handsome man he is, even if I say so myself."

"I know well who you are," Nora said. "You don't have to tell me. I saw you someplace before."

"If she does not recognise her own husband," Tadhg said to himself, "there is not much hope that she will remember anything about the sacred bone." Because he had turned back and would now miss that day's ferry, he thought he would be as well to ask a question even though he had little hope of an answer: "Do you remember that we were talking about Saint Gregory's relic the last day that I was here?"

"I know who you are," Nora answered, the same thing she seemed to say to everyone. Tadhg realised that there was no point in pursuing that matter with her anymore. He gave her a kiss on the cheek and left the Nursing Room hurriedly. He hoped he might still catch the ferry, if it had been delayed for any reason. Too late. It was out in the middle of the bay already. He went to the Bed and Breakfast he usually stayed in when on the mainland. He felt awkward asking for a room when he had neither bag nor baggage, but he was immediately accommodated. The staff were well used to people missing the ferry. It was more often than not because of drink or bad weather, but they asked no questions.

Tadhg strolled down to the chipshop near the pier. He sat on a wooden seat nearby to eat cod and chips which were hot, salty and delicious. He went to a public house then and slowly drank a couple of pints of porter, savouring every mouthful. He thought that he had almost forgotten how to relax. There was a soccer match on television. He sat on one of the leather armchairs and sat back to enjoy it. He knew little of the teams that were playing, one from France and the other from Italy, but there were great moments of skill being displayed from time to time.

A man sat into the seat beside him. He seemed to recognise all of the players. Some he obviously loved and others he hated and told them so in a loud voice even though the match was a couple of thousand miles away. He jumped to his feet excitedly to urge on players he liked and cursed loudly at those he did not.

"You are the best man to curse that I ever heard in my life," Tadhg told him. "I thought that some of the players you were cursing were actually playing very well."

"But they are playing for the wrong side," the man answered.

Tom laughed: "I am glad that they can't hear you, or your curses might set fire to them."

"Sure, it is only a bit of fun," the other man said easily.

The game ended but they carried on their conversation. When the other man found out that Tadhg was from the Western Isle, he said: "I hear that some eejit is building a big wall on the cliff out there. From what I hear he has more money than sense."

"Were you ever on the island yourself?" Tadhg asked him.

"I was not, and I never will be," the man said. "Everyone out there is stranger than the next. I'm told that the wife of the man that is building the wall is going to put a glass roof on the island in order to grow grapes and sell wine. I would be prepared to drink the wine alright, if it is not piss altogether."

"Isn't it you that knows a lot about a place that you never set foot in," Tadhg said. There was irony in his tone as he asked: "Where do you get all of your information?"

"I like to keep up with the news," the other man answered: "I can tell you that I know more about England than Englishmen, because I buy one of their newspapers every day."

"Those tabloids seem to have plenty of pictures of women without a stitch in them," Tadhg said.

"Some of the Irish papers are even better in that way. They know how to get a man going, if you know what I mean." He added: "But they have interesting enough things to read as well."

Tadhg dug deeper: "What kind of things do you mean?"

"Exposés," came the reply. "Someone should do an exposé on that fool that is building the wall on that island. And on his wife as well. They would not get away with the likes of that in England."

Tadhg had enough: "I would say that you know as little about England as you do about our little island which is less than ten miles from you, even though you feel free to make a mockery of it." The strength of his anger surprised him: "It might be drink that caused it, he thought, but he needed to teach some kind of a lesson to this know-all."

"Do you know that fellow that is building the wall on the Western Isle?"

"I don't know him but I know all about him."

"That fool, that eejit as you call him, is my son."

"I didn't know. To tell you the God's honest truth I didn't have a clue."

Tadhg was not finished yet: "And the woman he is married to, and the mother of my grandchildren is his wife."

"I was not finding fault with either of them. It is just that what they are getting up to seems very strange to me."

"If you can drag yourself away from your topless tabloids," Tadhg told him, "You should spend a couple of days on that island. Everybody there that wants to work, and that is most of the people, has a job. There is a big ship anchored beside the island that us unloading acres of glass under which organic food is to be grown. That will create even more jobs. So, if you ever feel like having a job yourself, you could think of moving in there."

"That kind of work would not suit me. And anyway, there is no way that I could live on an island."

"How do you know unless you try it out?"

"I have a very good idea that it might not work out."

Tadhg was still angry: "What you are is a bloody know-all that knows nothing." He stalked out of the public house and then took a walk so that he would cool down before returning to his Bed and Breakfast.

Chapter Twenty-Three

The Western Isle appeared again on the parliamentary agenda the week in which the big ship from Amsterdam was anchored off its coast. The question was put: "Will the Taoiseach offer his congratulations to the people of the Western Isle because there is no longer anyone on the island in receipt of social welfare payments other than pensions for the elderly and children's allowances?" The questioner reached back fifty years to the time when "full employment in the seventies" was a slogan used by the Taoiseach of the time, Jack Lynch TD. "There was ninety-five percent unemployment on that and every other island at the time and full employment was nothing more than a pie in the sky aspiration. Some political parties' day might have not yet come, but the Western Isle's certainly has. The people of the island deserve all of our congratulations."

The Taoiseach raised a small laugh when he congratulated the islanders for what they had achieved, before adding: "It would be of great help to Government if more islands and other communities were to also win the lotto. That said, the family in question have shown great generosity by sharing their winnings with their neighbours for the good of all."

There was an immediate rush of members seeking permission to speak, and they were dealt with one after the other. Some agreed with the Taoiseach and offered their congratulations. Others spoke of the need for accountability and clarity, of the delay in seeking planning permission, not to speak of the actual need for a wall to slow down a possible tsunami. One of the more blunt questions asked: "How can our Taoiseach praise people who drove a coach and four through our planning regulations?"

"As I understand it," the Taoiseach answered carefully: "Talks are ongoing to iron out difficulties. It has to be understood that islands have difficulties not to be found in other parts of the State."

The question was put by the Opposition Leader: "Is it the Taoiseach's policy to allow the law to be broken first and pick up the pieces afterwards?" It smacks of confession: "Sin all you like and then ask forgiveness?"

There was an immediate surge of accusation that religion was being treated frivolously. "How can someone who continuously goes on about separating church and State try and make a mockery of religion in this fashion?" The Taoiseach of course revelled in this distraction.

He stated: "Life is not as simple as the Leader of the Opposition thinks, which may explain why he is still Leader of the Opposition. I acknowledge that the law was broken on the Western Isle, but it was done because of an emergency. In other words the real fear of a reoccurrence of a tsunami that led to the deaths of fifteen fishermen in the past."

"A hundred and seventy years or so ago," was shouted across the chamber.

The Taoiseach continued as if he had not heard the interruption: "Now that a safety wall has been provided or in the process of being built, the danger to life and limb on the island has been lessened. I assure the House that planning permission has been applied for and that in the meantime work has been suspended. Planning permission has also been granted for an environmental project that it is hoped will leave the Western Island self-sufficient as far as food is concerned and will also preclude the importation of exotic fruits from far-off places and the airmiles involved in transporting them."

Something unusual happened then in that most of the Members of Parliament stood and applauded, but not everyone was satisfied. The next questioner asked:

"Is it true that a million-euro bribe was offered to the relevant authorities to have the planning process speeded up and passed immediately?"

"This brought a gasp from the benches," but the Taoiseach took it in his stride: "I have heard that rumour too."

"No smoke without fire," was shouted across the chamber.

The Taoiseach continued: "I also know how much money has been paid out by the newspaper in question in compensation for false allegations. There will, of course be an enquiry into what has been alleged, but the boat seems to have sailed in so far as the credibility of that newspaper is concerned."

His socialist questioner did not agree: "If it was not for newspapers like that, many of the scandals that occurred in this country would not have been brought to light. It is easy for the likes of you to denigrate the past, but without journalism of that kind, this country would be destroyed altogether."

"All that I am saying," the Taoiseach answered testily, "is not to believe everything that is said in the papers or any other media outlet for that matter."

"Are you or your office denying the rumour that a million-euro bribe was offered to a planning official or possibly to more than one of the same to break the law and look the other way?"

"I have already told you that I deny that categorically. Apart from anything I do not believe that the man in question would be stupid enough to make such an offer, other than in jest. The man accused is certainly not stupid, unlike some other people that I know." His barb hit the target and there was uproar in the chamber for a short period. When business proceeded, the previous questioner still had the floor:

"You talk about stupid, Taoiseach! Could anyone be so stupid as to build a wall on top of a cliff that nobody wants or needs, and then is an eyesore? If it was a white elephant itself, it might have some artistic merit. But that wall is nothing more than a dirty grey elephant."

One of the smart-Alec's shouted: "So that is why you want to have it truncated?"

The question of whether or not an historic Dún had been covered in concrete and used as part of the wall was raised again. A deputy held up pictures which were purported to be of the offending work, but they were too small to be seen clearly from the other side of the Dail chamber. "Put them up a Facebook for everyone to see," the questioner said, only to be told by a member opposite to put his own posterior up on "Arsebook." The resulting chaos led to the proceedings being suspended for fifteen minutes, as well as a warning from the Ceann Chomhairle that such indecorous behaviour would not be allowed, particularly when there were women and children in the public gallery.

The Taoiseach was asked if it was his attention to travel to the Western Isle to officially open the clifftop wall and the glass covered grow houses when they were completed.

"I have always heard that it is manners to wait until you are asked," he quipped, "or as some would say, To wait until you are axed."

His previous questioner could not resist the temptation to answer: "The axe might fall sooner than you think." This was followed by a blunt: "Answer the question."

"As you are all well aware I am not one to believe in rumour," he answered, "but I have reason to believe that someone much younger and better looking than me," He stopped for a second before saying: "Yes that is possible." Before continuing: "A well-known personality in the environmental world may be asked to perform the ceremony, and if so, she will be very welcome to

Ireland and to the Western Isle to perform the ceremony."

"Is it the Pope?" someone who had not heard his statement clearly asked.

"Has a woman Pope been elected?" the Taoiseach asked.

"Greta," was the name on most lips.

"As I have said on many occasions," the Taoiseach answered. "I am not one for rumours."

"Will you accept an invitation to travel the Western Isle on that occasion if you are asked? Or will you remain at home sulking?"

The Taoiseach answered: "It is manners to wait. Ask me first. Who am I to try and dodge a question?"

This was received with loud guffaws.

"You don't know how to give a straight answer."

"What is wrong with that?" came the surprising reply.

"I would ask those of you who claim to be Christians," the Taoiseach said: "Did Jesus Christ ever give a straight answer?"

"He did and he was crucified for it."

"My answer exactly. He would have been crucified even earlier if he had not dodged questions. Take 'Render to Caesar the things that are Caesar's and to God the things that are Gods.' Almost never a straight answer."

"Do you need to denigrate religion as well as everything else?" the Taoiseach was asked.

"I am not denigrating anything, just demonstrating that I know what I am talking about."

"Can we return to the point?" the Ceann Comhairle said: "A question remains unanswered: "Will the Taoiseach visit the Western Isle for the official opening of projects there, despite planning laws having been broken in the building of one of those projects?"

"Yes, is the answer. Is that clear enough," the Taoiseach answered.

"What about allegations of wrongdoing?"

"All will be properly investigated. Thoroughly."

As the debate neared its end, the Leader of the Opposition made a strong attack on the morality of those on the benches opposite who refused to condemn those who were accused of offering a bribe to planning officials with regard to planning permission. "But that is not all," he stated: "You have bribed International Companies to come here who continue to pay a fraction of the Income or Corporation Tax due to the State. This leniency is in itself a form of bribery. You are now accepting a similar sort of bribery from lotto winners who have come into easy money, all of which is tax-free, while children starve. The Government across from me, and I include its backbenchers in that, has been bought lock stock and barrel by the rich. You should be ashamed of yourselves, and the quicker the voters get rid of you, the better."

The Taoiseach looked as if he needed to be tied. He denied that anyone on his side of the House had ever accepted a bribe or a favour. "If there is specific evidence, show it to me or tell it to the Dáil, whether it involves this office or local government. If such evidence is shown, I will immediately appoint a retired Judge to investigate it without fear or favour. It is one thing to offer incentives to companies to set up in isolated rural areas. It is something else completely to offer bribes to those interested in foreign direct investment."

"Put your money where your mouth is so," the Leader of the Opposition told him bluntly.

"What do you mean by that? I need specifics, not wild allegations."

"Support a Private Members Bill that a member of my party is putting forward to tax all but ten percent of lotto winnings over ten million euro. The remainder should be ring-fenced for the building of proper accommodation for the homeless."

"That would amount to larceny," the Taoiseach answered: "The biggest incentive that the lotto can offer is that its winnings are tax-free."

"Tan million tax-free from winnings of one or two hundred million should be enough of a tax-free bonus for anyone. In the specific case that has led to major works on the Western Isle, it is rumoured that the Euromillion prize in question exceeded two hundred million euro."

"Have you evidence to show that the couple in question ever won a lotto prize? Have you seen champagne being splashed about on the Western Isle?"

"It is generally accepted that is where the money came from. We have even bigger questions to answer if it not come from the lotto. Where else did it come from?"

"As I constantly tell you, Deal in facts, not rumour. Their money could have come from many years toiling in English tunnels or in Middle East high-rise buildings. That is the kind of working which the people in question have been involved in the past."

The Leader of The Opposition appeared to be down but not out in sporting terms. He repeated his question about the lotto, declaring that it was not aimed at those who had or had not won a lotto and were now living on the Western Isle. It could be a good earner for the Revenue. "Will you consider it for the next budget? It could cut the homeless figures in half if there was another jackpot of that magnitude in this country."

"All sensible suggestions will be looked at in pre-budget negotiations," the Taoiseach answered like a man in a hurry to be somewhere else.

Chapter Twenty-Four

Word that Nora, wife of Tadhg Rua and mother of Tsunami Tom had died in the Nursing Home on the mainland came as a shock to her family as well as to the close-knit community on their island. Her grandchildren were at school while Tom and Róisín were dealing with the glazing of the grow-houses which was nearing completion.

It was her husband Tadhg who answered the call from the Nursing Home: "Did you get the priest for her?" was his instinctive reaction. "Nora was a religious woman."

"The priest anointed everyone who would take it from him at the weekend. He can't be here all the time."

"I would not like her to be without the priest. That is the sort of woman she was." Tadhg said.

"The priest will be here after a while." The Matron went on to discuss arrangements, saying that there was no need for a post-mortem as the doctor was well aware of her ailments. "But she will need to be embalmed."

"Go ahead with that and we will get back to you. You know yourself the difficulties involved in island life."

"At least the weather will be good for the crossing."

Tadhg rang his son, Tom on his mobile phone: "She is gone," he said.

"Who is gone? Is it that bloody dog again?"

"It is your mother."

"Did she escape from the Nursing home? I thought the door

was supposed to be always with locked?"

"She passed away this morning."

"You mean she is dead? Not mother?"

"They just rang me now from the Nursing Home. They did not expect it either. It came as a shock. I didn't know what to say either. She was not well, but I didn't think that she would go just like that."

"I had it in my mind to go and see her soon," Tom said, "but I kept putting it on the long finger."

Tadhg did not say anything, knowing that his son was hurting. Tom asked him: "Have you told Róisín?"

"I thought you should do that, and the children too."

"The children" Tom mused absentmindedly, as if wondering how or what to tell them: "Won't that he soon enough after school?"

"Word could be spreading at lunchtime. I think you should pick them up before then."

"You are right," his son said. "They should hear it from us."

"I will leave that to you and Róisín," Tadhg said. "I will make the arrangements for bringing her home on the boat. We will take it from there after that."

Tom seemed awkward and unsure as he said: "I'm sorry for your trouble."

His father sounded like he did not know what to say either: "It is your trouble too. She was your mother."

"I am so ashamed of myself that I did not go to see her in ages. I found it hard to look at her the way she was. So, I blamed not visiting her on being too busy. I am a coward."

"Nobody who knows you would call you a coward," his father said. "None of us were expecting this."

"I will never forgive myself."

"That is not what she would want. She was always proud of you. You were always her pride and joy. Ways will. Nothing will change that."

"Except death," Tom said. "She is gone forever."

"You have your own beliefs about that, they will be thinking their Mamó is in a better place. That will give them some comfort, and are we going to take that from them? Don't upset them with arguments about God. Leave those matters for another day, when they have grown up a bit more."

"But I don't like to tell them lies or fairy tales either," Tom answered.

"Do things in your own way," his father said. "You are a big boy now. Those matters have been argued about for thousands of years and are we going to find answers now while your mother is in her coffin? You will have the rest of your lives to deal with those matters. One day at a time, as they say."

Tears came to Tadhg's eyes when he looked around in his own house. There were pictures of Nora everywhere. It was as if he had avoided looking at them while she was in the Nursing Home. He had known in his heart of hearts that she would not be coming home alive, but at least he could go to visit her on the mainland. Things were different now. The dreaded words: "She is dead," were real now. She would only be coming back for her wake and funeral. Maybe Tom was right, that there was no other life, but his father did not want to accept that. He wanted to see her again, young and beautiful as he had first met her, with age and Alzheimer thrown by the wayside. "She should be shining the way Jesus was at Easter, as he had heard a priest saying once, like a butterfly flitting around from flower to flower."

There were practical things to be done, Tadgh thought, things that would take his mind off the realities of life and death for a while. There were arrangements to be made. He went to the wardrobe in the bedroom to take out his best suit, his only suit, as it happened. He brushed it off and hung it out on the line for a while to freshen it up. That too brought Nora to mind. It was for Tom and

Róisín's wedding that they had bought the suit together about a decade earlier He had never worn it since, nor had he ever a reason to do so. That disease had come on her, and where would he be going dressed up to the nines? It was a tunic that zipped up to the throat that a man needed when travelling by boat.

It was then that the thought struck him: "I will have nobody to talk to anymore. Except the children, of course. Had he a serious conversation with a grownup in recent years?" He would keep the items of news that he had until he visited Nora in the Nursing Home. She might not understand everything, but it gave him something to talk about.

Talking to the children was different, and even though he loved it, the truth was that it was childish. He would exchange pleasantries with Róisín and Tom, but they were busy all the time as you would expect from people of their age. He got a glimpse of himself in the mirror above the fireplace and said: "It is talking to myself I will be from now on."

His son, Tom, rang then to say that Róisín and himself would be happy to have the wake in their house. Tadhg thanked him but said: "I would like her to spend her last night on this earth in her own house."

"Our house is ready for people to walk into," Tom said: "You will have an awful lot of readying to do."

"No doubt some of the neighbours will give me a hand. And all of them will understand that an old man on his own might not have a place that looks like a palace. I know that your house is a lot bigger and cleaner, but this is your mother's home, and it is here I want her to be." He asked Tom then: "Have you spoken to Jacob and Cliona yet?"

"We are going to the school now. We wanted the wake sorted out first."

It did not seem to come as much of a shock to the children that their grandmother had died. "Poor Dadó," Cliona said with a sigh, while Jacob suggested that it would not be long until her husband joined her in heaven.

"Dadó is old, but he is not sick," Clíona said from the backseat of the jeep that she shared with Jacob, with their mother and father in front.

Jacob had his own theory: "Mamó might send for him, or he might want to go and stay with his wife and all the angels and saints."

"I hope that he stays here for another while to look after us," was Cliona's answer.

Jacob leaned forward to ask his parents: "Will Mamó be coming home in one those boxes?"

"They are called coffins," his mother told him.

"We know," Clíona replied. "We often see them on scary films on the TV."

"My friend's granny in Dublin got burnt," Jacob said. "They set fire to the coffin and let it burn until all that was left was dust."

"Dust and ashes," his sister said. "Why is Mamó not going to be burnt?"

"Because we are more civilised," her mother said.

"What is civilised?" was Clíona's next question.

Róisín struggled with her answer: "We know better. We have a bit of class about us."

Tom offered his ideas on the matter: "There is nothing wrong with cremation, or burning a body as you call it. It is done in many places all over the world. But that is not what your Mamó wanted."

Jacob tried to help his father to answer the question: "Mamó wanted to be put down in a hole in the graveyard, so that her bones would be holy. Like the saint she was minding the blessed bone for."

His father decided to let things go: "Something like that,"

he said.

Jacob had another question: "Is there a smell like rashers and sausages when somebody is burning in their coffin?"

Róisín hedged the question: "I don't know, because I was never at a cremation except in India. There was so much incense and other perfumes burning that you could not smell anything else."

Róisín added: "They have a special fire that is very very hot. It happens in a special room, so people outside do not get any smell."

"If we keep telling them soft stories," Tom said to Róisín, "they will never be able to grasp the realities of life."

"Too much realism they get on television and computer games," his wife reminded him, "Did you hear that stuff about scary stories? That stuff is far worse for them than our traditional step by step approach. They will find out the rest for themselves when the time is right."

They stopped the jeep at Tadhg's house and both children and parents went in to sympathise with him. Jacob and Clíona had their own hugs for Topsy as well: "She was your Mamó too," Cliona told the dog. "We will bring you to see her grave when the funeral is over next week."

The priest had come to the island, and he arrived the house to sympathise with Tadhg and his family and to organise arrangements for readings, prayers and other aspects of the funeral Mass. He shook hands with everybody, and Tom took his own opportunity to express his own disappointment in the clergyman: "I hear that you were not there to say the prayers for the dead?"

"A man can't be everywhere, and priests are scarce, especially in island and coastal areas. I anointed her with everyone else in the Nursing Home last week and said the other prayers as soon as I could after she passed away."

Fearing a confrontation, Róisín ushered the children from

the room to the yard outside when she noticed that Tom was getting more angry by the minute.

"Some of you have no problem being in places you are not supposed to be. But can't be found when you are needed."

"What do you mean by that?" the priest asked.

"Read a few of the reports about child abuse, and you will know," Tom said.

The priest tried to be understanding in the circumstance: "It is natural for a person to be angry at a time like this. We all know how much your mother suffered because of the Alzheimer." "You don't understand anything," Tom told him. "If you did you would know that there is no God and no heaven or any of those fairy tales you tell the people to keep them in ignorance. Fuck yourself and your God. You are nothing but a joke."

"I will see you later," the priest said quietly to Tadhg Rua as he ignored Tom's rant and walked slowly out of the house.

Tadhg followed him and tried to apologise. He said his own view was not that of his son: "He was an only child and very close to his Mum. It is not that he saw her as often as I would have liked but she loved him dearly and his heart is broken."

"When did he see her last?" the priest asked bluntly.

"A couple of years ago, maybe, three, six. I don't know. He was busy building the wall at the top of the cliff."

"And he is the one giving out to me because I was not there the minute his mother died?"

Neither of them knew what to say next so nothing was said for a while. It was Tadhg who broke the silence: "Come in and have a cup oof tea. Whatever else, we have a funeral to organise. Anything else can hold."

Tom had left by the other door and had brought Róisín, Jacob and Cliona with him. Tadhg and the priest arranged a time for the funeral mass. The parish council would organise the rest. The priest drank a glass of whiskey and headed for the ferry to be in time for duties awaiting him on the mainland.

"I am not going to say anything," Róisín said to her husband Tom when he attempted to discuss what had happened between him and the priest. "You are so stubborn," she said to him. "You only see one side of any argument. I never felt so ashamed of you. Where are we going to find a priest now for the funeral mass?"

"I thought you said you were not going to say anything," Tom answered. "Isn't that what you said a few minutes ago? I will bury her myself if I have to, priest or no priest."

"What would your mother think about that?"

"My mother is dead," Tom said bluntly.

"I am aware of that," was Róisín's sarcastic answer. "Dead but not buried. She would not want to be buried without a priest. Are you going to carry the coffin on your back?"

Tom was still being awkward: "I can bring the coffin on the forklift from the boat to the cemetery. I have men working for me. They will do what I tell them."

"What about your father, if you have no respect for your mother?" his wife asked him.

"Nobody ever had as much respect for a mother as I had."

"Don't upset everyone so," Róisín said: "Think if Jacob and Cliona. Think of your father. They are heartbroken too. As I have said already, Think of your mother."

"She knows nothing about it. She is lying cold in her coffin."

"That is not how your children see it. They think she has gone to a lovely place full of peace and happiness. Why upset them?"

Tom replied: "It is past time for them to wake up and learn a lesson about the cruelty of life and of death."

Róisín put her arms around him when his voice started to break. He cried uncontrollably for a while, his body shaking with grief: "I let her down," he said. "I let her down so badly."

Róisín hugged him and said: "Nobody was ever as proud of you as she was. Except me, maybe," she added with a smile.

Tom shook his head, and asked: "Why did I not visit her even once in that place?"

"I don't know. You didn't want to see her in the way she was in recent years. There are few things in life as difficult, I'm sure, as someone's mother not recognising them. To tell you the truth," she said, "I thought it was like talking to a ghost when I went in there with the children."

"Were the kids scared?" Tom asked.

"They accepted her as she was. Their Mamó, their grandmother who was not well. I'm sure they thought that none of it was her fault."

"I suppose it is not the priest's fault either that I am in such a mess," Tom said. "He was trying to do his job and I treated him like shit. I suppose I will have to apologise to him, even if I hate what he stands for."

"He is not the worst," Róisín said. "He is big enough and ugly enough to know that it is a broken heart that has a go at him on occasions like this. I heard him talking one time I brought the children to mass. He spoke of a man he knew in another parish. A religious enough man but he used the 'F' word when his father died suddenly."

"'Fuck God,' is what the man said. Needless to say, that brought a groan or two from some of the congregation, but the priest said that was actually a good prayer in the circumstances, a person talking to God straight from the heart."

"If that is the case," Tom said, "I can curse him again," and he did.

"Does a curse work?" Róisín asked, "If as you say you don't believe in what you call that rubbish?"

"Whether you believe in it or not, it gives a man a bit of

satisfaction." After a while he said: "To tell you the truth I don't know if I believe in some of it or not. It does not impinge on my life or work most of the time. Sometimes I long to have the simple faith of the children."

"There is a bit of magic to it at their age."

"A magic that seeps away with the passage of time," Tom said. "Still, I suppose that my mother never lost it. Or my father either, I suppose, but it is hard to know. He is not easy to read."

"He is a man of his time," Róisín said: "He will want everything at the funeral to be done in the traditional way, the way in which it was always done."

As things turned out, the funeral did not proceed in the traditional way. The captain of the ship from Amsterdam that had brought the glass and frames for the grow houses to the island the previous week offered to bring Nora's body from the mainland to the island for her funeral. As the water was not deep enough for the ship to dock at either pier, smaller boats and churches were organised to bring the coffin and passengers ashore. This did not cause any problem to islanders who were used to such arrangements. Island children were delighted to have the opportunity to travel on such a large ship.

"I am sure that Mamó is delighted," Cliona said, "because she was never in a ship as big as this one."

"Maybe she was on the Titanic," Jacob said. "It was much bigger than this."

Clíona corrected him: "If she was on the Titanic, she would be dead already.

"Not everyone that was on the Titanic died," Jacob told her, "Only millions of people. The rest were saved."

"A person can only die once, so Mamó only died yesterday."

Jacob's answer was immediate: "What about Jesus?"

"He was different. He was God."

Jacob mused out loud: "I wonder did Jesus shows his heart to Mamó when she got to heaven?"

"How do you mean?" his sister asked.

"You know that picture in Dadó's house, and Mamó's house too, the picture of Jesus with his heart in his hand?"

"Maybe he had a transplant," Cliona suggested.

Their conversation continued as the ship ploughed through the deep waters, rising and falling a little because of a gentle sea swell. Almost before they knew it they were lying at anchor beside the Western Isle, as their local ferry and smaller boats took the coffin and the people ashore.

"It is a great honour to you," Róisín said to her husband Tom, "that they sailed across to bring Nora home."

"A great honour to my mother," he said, "and a well-deserved one."

Her body was brought home to the house to which she had moved on her wedding day. Neighbours had gathered earlier to scrub and clean the house for her return. Cobwebs had been removed from places in which they had resided peacefully since Nora had gone to the Nursing Home. The fire had been lit, sandwiches prepared, with tea and coffee on standby. There was no alcohol served as there had been a general acceptance in recent times that such beverage caused more trouble than it was worth on occasions like that. Stories were told which led to laughter and jokes, none of which went down well with Cliona.

"Why are people laughing?" she asked her mother, "when poor Mamó is lying dead in her coffin?"

"I am not laughing," Jacob who was standing nearby, said, "And I don't like it either. Poor Mamó."

"They are not laughing about your grandmother," Róisín said. "Just laughing about funny things that she said and did when she was younger and in her health. You were not even born then, so you never really saw her as she was when she was younger. Before she got ill." Their mother went on to explain as well as she could that death was more natural when a person was old and had lived their life. It was nice to remember things that had happened in the past.

"Like when they killed the pig?" Jacob said.

Cliona was quick to correct him: "It was not Mamó that was there that day. It was Maggie."

"Your grandmother liked to have a bit of fun too," Róisín told them.

Cliona asked: "Was she joking when she gave the holy bone to Topsy?"

"Ssssh," her mother said, as if suggesting that they already had enough trouble for that day: "Nobody knows where the bone is at the moment. She must have put it in a safe place, and then she had to go away to live in the Nursing Home."

After all that had been said already, Jacob thought it would be no harm to introduce a bit of fun to the proceedings: "I know where the bone is."

"Where?" his mother asked, and Clíona got excited: "Tell us, tell us."

"In Topsy's tummy," Jacob answered.

"Don't make a joke about that," his mother said.

"Why not? Isn't every else joking and laughing?"

"Some things are jokes, and others are not," his mother tried to explain, but suddenly questions were coming from every side about the bone. Róisín asked her friend Gearóidín who was among those who had cleaned and readied the house had they seen anything in the many shoeboxes that had been under the beds.

"They all looked so old that we took them straight to the bins," she said.

"We will have to go through those bins carefully after the funeral," was Róisín's response.

Jacob and Cliona were carried to the beds they used in their grandfather's house when they could no longer keep their eyes open. Róisín asked Gearóidín how her romance with the big sailor from Liberia, Patrick, was going. "I didn't have time to talk with you for days," she explained, "because all of this came on us so suddenly."

"He is a right little dote."

"Have you done him yet?" she asked in a loud whisper.

"What a question to ask."

"That is not an answer."

"No, so. We have walked out together as they used to say in days gone by. I have never walked the beach from end to end so often."

"So he has not made a move?"

"Not that kind of move anyway."

"Maybe he is gay or bi, or both?"

"Listen to yourself, because everyone else is listening."

"So you are telling me nothing else happened?"

"Nothing. It as if he has too much respect for me. I think he belongs to a culture that is not as liberal or as free as ours has become."

"Where is all this free and easy attitude? Here in the west?" Róisín asked.

"Here as much as anywhere else in the so-called free world. The countries that have rejected religion. There is actually something refreshing about meeting a man who has morals and self-discipline."

"Says she that can't wait to take the pants off him."

"That was all talk," Gearóidín replied as if she was offended.

"I'll bet you were wearing your best knickers, and you ready for action?"

"What makes you think I was wearing one at all?" her friend joked. They were having a laugh about that when they noticed a woman opposite to where they were sitting listening intently to their conversation. She stared at them with what looked like a mixture of shock and hate as she spoke to a younger woman beside her. "I see now how the little girl complained about people laughing at a wake. If the poor woman who is lying in her coffin opposite us could hear those two, she would be turning in her grave."

Gearóidín and Róisín rose from their seats as they found it difficult to contain their laughter. "More tea, Missus?" Gearóidín said as she walked past the other woman, but she did not even wait for an answer.

The other woman was heard to say to her neighbour; "No sooner have some of them gotten rid of a man but they try and install another one. It seems that chasing after one of the black fellows that one is at the moment. Some people have no shame."

"I am not racist," the woman beside her replied, "but a lot of them don't care what colour a man is, black, blue or yellow."

"They don't mind what colour they are so long as they are good in the saddle."

Her neighbour replied: "I never did understand what a saddle has to do with it, and I don't want to know."

Tsunami Tom sat beside his mother's coffin with his head lowered most of the time except when someone came to shake his hand and whisper a few words of consolation. His own workmen were in and out, strong rangy men who had worked in the most difficult of conditions for many years but now seemed awkward in the face of death. Some of the ship's crew attended the wake too and compared it with the way death was dealt with in their own countries. Some said that people in their culture would already be in their graves at this stage because of heat and danger of disease. That was not to say that they would not have a wake with music and song and dance. They too would tell stories about the person who had passed and pray for a safe journey to a better world.

Some of the island people remembered the time that alcohol had played a big part at wakes. Things went too far sometimes. A particular funeral was remembered at which the women had to carry the coffin to the graveyard because not enough men were able to stand up without stumbling. That was the turning point. Alcohol was banned at wakes, but of course people could go to the local public house for a drink if they so desired.

Róisín asked her husband next morning as they got ready to go to the funeral mass: "Are you going to apologise to the priest for the hurtful things you said to him the other day? You said yesterday that you would try to be nicer to him at the funeral?"

"Why should I apologise? Will he apologise to me for the thousands of years of superstition that he and others like him imposed on people? Is he going to apologise for all the children that were abused, or the women who got pregnant that were turned into slaves in the laundries? I will stay out of his way, but he will get no apology from me."

Róisín said: "Whether we like it or not we will have to deal with him or whatever priest that comes in his place. Do you want to keep the children from first holy communion and confirmation? It will upset Cliona and Jacob if you are constantly fighting with the priests."

"What is it they call confirmation in Irish?" Tom asked with a lot of irony: "Going under the hand of the bishop. They named that well alright. We all know where the hands and more than the hands were."

"You can't tar all of them with the same brush."

"You and I can do what we like. We have money literally to burn. There are very few people that we can't buy or sell. We will always be in the driving seat, To hell with the lot of them," Tom said.

"You are beginning to sound like Stalin now."

Her husband was in a wild and almost crazy humour: "That

is the first time you said I was like a stallion."

"You know I am talking about Joseph Stalin, the dictator in Russia or the Soviet Union as it was called at the time. Someone told him that the Pope disagreed with one of his policies." He asked: "How many divisions has the Pope? In other words, how big of an army has he?"

"Too bloody big," Tom answered.

"He does not have an army," Róisín answered, "but he has moral authority."

"Doesn't he have those blokes in pyjamas with funny hatchets guarding the doors? Or have they done away with them?"

Róisín shook her head: "You have an answer to everything but lay off the priest. For the sake of the children People like and respect him and it would not help any of the projects either of us are involved in to turn him against us."

"Don't worry," Tom answered. "I will steer clear. I will not be going under his or any other hand ever again."

"What are we going to say if he asks about that blessed bone your mother used to mind?"

Tom laid on the sarcasm: "Tell him it has been eaten by Saint Topsy."

"I never saw you so giddy," his wife commented. "There will be neither sense nor reason out of you until this funeral is over. I hope you get rid of the nerves by then."

"Nerves?" he said: "What have I to be nervous about?"

"You tell me," Róisín said. "You are like a wound-up jack-in-the-box."

Tom answered bluntly: "My mother is after dying. How do you expect me to be? I only had one mother."

"And you are filled with shame that you did not go to see her before she died. I think that more than anything that is the cause of your nerves."

"Are you turning into a psychologist to a psychiatrist now?"

Tom asked.

"There are things you ned to face up to," Róisín said. "I am the person nearest to you and I know what upsets you most. It is time to let go of hurts and hatreds abouts priests and bishops and Popes that are not really relevant to our lives most of the time. You have to face your own demons."

"So you are calling my mother a demon?"

"Nothing of the kind," Róisín said, "but you ned to ask yourself what stopped you from going to see her in the Nursing Home."

There was silence for a time, Tom sitting, half-dressed on the bed, seemingly deep in thought, or was he just too stubborn to attempt a reply. Róisín sat in front of the mirror as she dealt with her hair and her makeup.

Tom spoke quietly then: "I could just not bear to see my mother like that. She was no longer the mother I knew. The mother that reared me and looked after me until I grew up and left home. She was gone and there was like a ghost in her place. I had worked away for years, England, America, the Middle East, even Australia for a while. When I came back it was as if my mother had been taken away. There were a lot of stories when I was growing up about fairies stealing children and leaving what were called changelings in their place. It was as if my mother was a changeling when I came back. She had been turned into an old fairy who could no longer talk sense. That is how it came across to me."

Róisín sat on the bed and put her arms around him: "I understand how you felt a little better now. We will talk more about it in the next few days, but it is important that we concentrate on the funeral now."

Tom shook his head: "I don't know can I even face it."

"You are not a coward. You never were," his wife told him. He stood up and began to get himself ready.

As normally happens when things have been carefully

organised, the funeral mass and everything to do with it went according to plan. Róisín read from the scriptures. Jacob and Clíona said prayers of the faithful. Their grandfather thanked friends, neighbours and the captain and crew of the ship from Amsterdam for all of their help and support and invited all to the local public house after the funeral.

Nora's body was taken to the cemetery then and laid down beside a grave dug deep in the sand. The expertise of Tom's workers was evident in the way in which the inside of the grave had been shored up with timber to prevent the sides collapsing. The priest read the prayers and threw a shovel of sand on the coffin as he repeated the age-old prayer: "Dust you are and into dust you shall return, but the Lord will raise you up again on the last day."

Jacob and Clíona had carried the little plastic shovels with which they made the sandcastles with them and that led the traditional throwing sand or clay into the grave. The tradition of filling the grave as part of the funeral service had lived on in the Gaeltacht areas, especially in Conamara and on the islands while most other parts of the country covered the grave with false grass and filled the grave later.

Tsunami Tom took a shovel and tackled the pile by the graveside as if the island was in danger running short of sand. His father joined him for a while as did some of his employees, and soon the grave was neatly filled and finished.

Tom went across to the priest when he finished the final prayer and formally shook his hand: "I am sorry I was a bit rough with you the last day, "he said, "but a lot of this stuff doesn't mean much to me."

"It is a free country," the priest said. "I am long enough in this job to know that death is a traumatic time especially for families. I did not know your mother in her heyday, but I am tod that she was a great lady. It is unfortunate that she had to endure what she did in later life. I know all about it. It affected my mother and my sister and my great-grandfather too, I am told. He died in what was called the Mental Hospital in Castlebar. So, it is unlikely I am going to avoid the Alzheimer's myself."

The two men stood in silence for a while, men of very different backgrounds and life experiences with seemingly nothing to say to each other. It was the priest who broke the silence as he grew increasingly uneasy.

"You have got a lot done with the big wall?"

"What do you think of it?" Tom asked.

"I think it is completely stupid," the priest answered bluntly, "but it is a great job of work." Suddenly both of them were laughing.

"At least you are honest," Tom said.

"You think what I do is stupid too," the priest said, "so we can agree to differ."

Chapter Twenty-Five

A particularly severe weather forecast spurred on the wok on the glazed structures on the Western Isle. A big storm was brewing in the Atlantic, the tail-end of a weather system that had originated in the West Indies. It was not so much the damage that might be done on the island itself that worried the islanders, but that the ship that had travelled from Amsterdam would lose its anchorage and be washed on to the rocks. Most of the glass as well as the steel and wooden frames had been floated ashore on pontoons by now, but some had been left on board to prevent them being damaged onshore by people who might be bent on mischief such as had been previously tried on lorries and machinery.

A big effort was underway to bring the rest of the materials ashore so that the ship could sail, if not back to Amsterdam but to shelter in Galway Bay or perhaps the Shannon Estuary. Patrick from Liberia informed his friend Gearóidín by phone that he would be leaving the island within the week.

"I will miss your company," she told him. "I have come to like you an awful lot. I suppose that you will be so busy from now until the time that you leave that I will hardly see you at all."

"Those of us working in the galley or the kitchen have some free time when the main meals are over. When the Sunday lunch is over on board, I will be free until the late evening. Noah is on duty for dinner in the evening."

"It would be nice to walk up to the cliffs and walk along the top of the wall there," Gearóidín suggested. "There are wonderful views from there."

"What if you fall off the wall?" he asked. "Will I have to jump into the sea after you?"

"You have such long arms," she joked, "that all you will have to do is reach down and pull me out of the waves." She went on to explain that there was a waist high safety wall on either side at the top of the wall.

"Just like the great wall of China?" he asked. "Have you been there?"

"No, but I have seen the pictures," Gearóidín said.

"Would you like if I brought a lunch for a picnic?"

"That would be wonderful," she said. "I will bring the wine and the glasses."

The traditional calm before the storm was in evidence when they met on the following Sunday afternoon. It was a beautiful sunny day with blue skies and hardly a hint of wind.

"They must have been just trying to get the big ship sailing away when they announced that storm," Gearóidín said. "I have not seen a better day for a very long time."

"The weather forecast on the ship is the same as the one on the shore," Patrick said. "It is only a matter of time until it reaches us."

"Do storms like that scare you?" Gearóidín asked. "Especially when you are out on the high seas?"

"Scare is probably too strong of a word," Patrick answered. "Any kind of a storm worries a sailor. But we get used to them. We hope to be in shelter for this one."

"Were you ever in danger of drowning?"

"We were off South Africa once," he said. "Rounding the Cape, one of the most dangerous seas in the world, and certainly the worst I have seen or sailed through. The ship sat on a great wave at one stage, high above deep troughs. It could have tipped either way, but it didn't. She slipped back down with the wave, and we were safe," Patrick paused for effect: "Until the next big wave."

"You must have all been scared shitless?" Gearóidín said.

"We were certainly scared foodless, because almost everyone was seasick."

"They say around here that is good for you, that it cleans out the insides?"

"I would not wish that storm on anyone," was Patrick's reply. "My memory of it afterwards is that everyone was weak and barely able to do their work for a few days."

"I'm sure it would not help to be working in the kitchens at a time like that. Was it the worst voyage you ever experienced?" Gearóidín asked.

"I was more scared off the coast of Florida."

"The Bermuda Triangle?"

"I never feel safe on that side of the Atlantic, especially in hurricane season. They can be horrendous."

"I love the Gaelic wors for it –spéirling. It seems to sum up those whirlwinds you see going around and around on television. It is a word that sounds magic to me."

Patrick shook his head: "I don't like magic of that kind. It is too much like black magic. You don't know what is going to happen next."

"Do you pray at times like that?"

"It reminds me of Jesus in the boat during a storm. I ask for help."

"You have a strong faith?"

"A strong fear of storm and high seas more than anything. I will step into the island chapel tomorrow to pray against the storm they promise."

"You can do it now if you wish. I am in no hurry."

Patrick laughed as they turned their steps towards the chapel: "It was the Irish nun that brought me to believe. There was only one of them left in the parish when I was growing up, but she was a strong woman. Kind too but strong of heart. Strong in her faith."

"Maybe she scared you more than the hurricanes did?"

"I still remember her as a kind of, how do you say, Your mother's mother?"

"Your granny," Gearóidín answered: "Mamó they call it here."

"A lovely word, Mamó,"

They had reached the little island church. The way in which Patrick spread his arms in prayer and held them like that for a long time amazed Gearóidín who felt a sense of shame that she had nothing to say to God, if he or she had a presence there. A story came to her mind of an island man who had gone to pray inside the same backdoor some years earlier. Thinking there was nobody around but himself and God, he shouted out: "Do you know who I am?" The priest happened to be in the sacristy, and he often spoke on subsequent years of what he used to call: "the best example of prayer I have ever heard."

Feeling no spiritual connection whatever, Gearóidín slipped out of the church, lit a cigarette and waited for Patrick to come out of what seemed like a trance. When he emerged with a smile on his face, he said that, living on ships most of the time, he missed attending Sunday mass.

"They only have it here once a month," Gearóidín told him, because priests are scarce.

"It is like that too in my country. It always was."

"We will never get to the cliffs at this rate," his companion said.

Patrick picked up his picnic bag and said: "Let's go. Soon his long strides were making it difficult for Gearóidín to keep up with him and he slowed down to her pace."

"Did you manage to put a hex on the hurricane with your prayers?" Gearóidín asked.

227

"I cannot stop it. It is part of life, part of nature. All I can do is to make sure that it does not catch me unawares out on the high seas."

The sheer size of the wall across the island clifftop surprised both of them. It had not seemed as impressive at a distance. Looking upwards from the island lowlands it tended to blend in with the grey limestone rock on which it was built. Seeing that it was more than four times Patrick's size and topped by a three-foot safety wall on both sides, it seemed to tower above the cliffs. "This will be a wonderful attraction for tourists," Gearóidín said in amazement.

They stood for a while to take in the beauty and majesty of their surroundings as seagulls of many species circled about their heads. Gearóidín dodged her head now and again as she sensed that some of the birds were coming too close: "I hate those bloody terns," she said. "They would take the eyes out of your head."

"You do have lovely eyes," Patrick said. "If we feed the birds," he added, "they might go away."

"It is more likely that all of their friends and relations will come to join them," was Gearóidín's verdict.

"They seem to be easing off a little now," he said after a while. "Perhaps they were just excited at seeing us."

"I don't think exciting is either of our middle names."

"Who cares? The day is lovely. The sea is like a mirror. There is not a cloud in the sky. Who would believe that there is a storm coming to threaten us?"

"You are right," Gearóidín said. "We should enjoy it while we can. She was wondering what to make of this tall handsome man who seemed to have so little interest in her as a woman. 'He must see me like a sister,' she said to herself, but that thought was drowned in a mental picture them making love here high above the cliffs, sheltered and hidden by the safety wall, black and white, bodies hugging and kissing, and making love with a pure passion,

passion being all that was pure about it."

"I just need to make it happen," she said to herself.

"Are you ready for the picnic now?" His words broke into her daydream.

"I am ready for anything," she heard herself say. "I mean that I am hungry enough to eat a horse."

"I forgot to bring the horse," Patrick joked as he opened the picnic box: "There are sandwiches. There is salad, and of course there is the wine that you brought." He explained that he was not a drinker, but he would join her in a glass of wine.

"I would not have bothered with wine at all," Gearóidín told him, "If I knew that you are not a drinker."

"Alcohol is a dangerous companion on a ship. I have known too many men who allowed it to wreck their lives."

"You are certainly a man of many surprises."

"In what way?"

"No bad habits. You are the cleanest living man I have ever met."

"Wait until you see me after glass of wine," Patrick joked.

"Wait until you see me after the rest of the bottle. I intend to launch it out to sea when it is empty. One empty bottle is hardly going to pollute the atmosphere."

"It could be allowed," he said, "if the bottle carried a message."

"Hold on to the cork so, or it will fill up with water and sink to the bottom."

"Think of what you want to say," Patrick said, "and we will write our messages after the picnic."

"I have neither pen nor paper," Gearóidín said.

He tapped his breast pocket: "I have some here."

"Do you write poetry or something?"

"I wish. Just notes to remind me of this or that." He thought for a while: "We should not read each other's notes. The ones in the bottle, I mean."

"I have nothing to hide," Gearódin said.

"Nor I either, but it will be more romantic like that."

"I like romantic," she said. "The chance that anyone will ever see or read what we write? A chance in a million? Or a billion? This week's storm could take the bottle to the other side of the world."

Patrick answered: "What we write is not for anyone else. Just for us."

"What good is that if we do not get to read it?"

"It is magic. It is different. It is romantic."

"I think I will just smash the bottle," Gearóidín said. "Like someone launching a ship. But not until I drink what is inside it."

"I thought you were on the side of the environmentalists." Patrick said, "against the polluters, in favour of slowing down climate change? Is that not what you and your friend Róisín are not trying to achieve. Throwing bottles off the cliff and smashing them into the tide is hardly going to be good for the green agenda."

"It was you that came up with the idea of the message in the bottle."

"That is different. That is romantic."

"The only romance I am interested in at this moment." Gearóidín said "is romance with a sandwich and anything else in that box. I am starving."

"The angels are back," Patrick said, as seagulls gathered above them as they ate the sandwiches and an African salad.

"They are more like white devils," was Gearóidín's answer.

"They will probably fly away again as soon as we finish," Patrick said hopefully. He refused a second glass of wine, as Gearóidín poured herself another. She looked at the bottle: "You are right about not breaking it," she said. "Somewhere, sometime the broken glass could wash up on a beach." She told of how she had cut her foot on such a piece of broken glass when she was a child. "I will show you the scar later when I take off my shoes as we walk back across the beach."

"I will be really looking forward to that, he joked."

"You are a right tease," she said.

"Tell me when you are ready to write the note to put in the bottle."

"Give me time to think about it. I will do it when the wine is gone, and the bottle is empty."

Patrick took a small notebook with a pencil in its spine from his pocket: "Now what am I going to write?"

"Something nice and romantic, I hope."

"We are not Romeo and Juliet."

"Just as well, maybe. Things did not work out too well for them, if I remember correctly."

"Nobody would remember now if they lived happily ever after." Patrick commented. "Just as nobody will remember today's sunshine during the coming storm."

"We should make the best of it while we can." Gearóidín leaned over to try and give Patrick a kiss. Because of his long neck and the way he leaned backwards, she did not succeed. They did hold hands as they walked along after taking a little while to write their notes before putting them in the bottle. Patrick had fired it out over the ocean. They listened to hear if it had smashed on the rocks or landed in the water, but they heard nothing.

"It is too far down to hear anything," Patrick said.

"I am surprised that you did not let me read what you wrote," Gearóidín mentioned as they walked along.

"I did not read yours either."

"You had the choice, I didn't."

"It is not a big deal. They will seem twice as romantic when they come ashore somewhere."

"It is very unlikely that either of us will get to read them," Gearóidín answered.

"It is not the end of the world."

"It is probably the end of our world. You and me." she said.

They walked along, their difference in height even more obvious since she had taken off her shoes and carried them in her hand. Neither spoke for a while, each thinking the other was annoyed with them. Gearóidín suddenly asked:

"Would you like to have a walk on the beach?"

"Why not?" As soon as they got close to the water Gearóidín started to strip off all of her clothes: "Come on," she said. "There is nobody around." She swam powerfully for a few minutes, careful not to get out of her depth. Then she stood up and shouted to Patrick: "Come on in. The water is lovely."

To her amazement Gearóidín found that Patrick hag dozed off by the time she finished her swim. She lay beside him to allow the sun to dry her off. "This is the life." she said to herself and soon she had nodded off too.

Both of them awoke around the same time. The sun had clouded over, and they felt cold: "Put your arms around me." Gearóidín said. "I am shivering with the cold. Soon they were kissing, Patrick's long tongue reaching far into her mouth. Soon he was kissing her cheeks, her forehead, her shoulders and her breasts."

"Come back to the house," she said: "Quick." She wondered why she was whispering, but she sensed that someone, or more than one person watched in the background. Gearóidín began to dress and said: "I can't wait to make love to you."

"I'm sorry." Patrick said, as he leaped into a standing position and started to run, towards the pier, to take the rubber dingy out towards the big ship in the bay.

"What have I done wrong now?" Gearóidín asked herself: "Is he married? Is he gay? Has he been hogtied by religion?" She knew that she would never know.

Gearóidín was coming to terms with the events of the day to

some extent when she checked her social media account later in the night: One word stood out even when it was spelt in three different ways: "Hoor, hure and whore."

"I am out of here," she said to herself. "I have enough of this lousy place." She thought of a man whose advances she had spurned again and again because he was married. She texted him to say that she had a problem for which he had the remedy. She would have all night session, she promised herself, even if it was not with Patrick.

Chapter Twenty-Six

The person who named the forecast hurricane "Storm Fanny" had much to answer for in terms of bawdiness and toilet humour, not just in the Western Isle, but throughout much of the western world. Comments were made, such as: "They will probably call the next storm, 'Storm Bollix' or 'Storm Asshole.'" That kind of dark humour was seen by many as a "whistling past the cemetery" exercise, as people tried to avoid the enormity of the potential damage such a hurricane could cause by having a laugh about it.

One forecast worse than the last emanated from various television and radio stations. The effects of global warming and the lack of care for the environment were highlighted, even though the naysayers too were quoted by some who just wanted to sit back and let nature take its course. Still, it was hard to ignore the wildfires particularly in Australia and California, floods in Madagascar and the southern States of the US.

Those who dismissed such evidence harked back to the ice-age which was not that long ago in age of the world terms. There were no cars or lorries on the roads then, or no roads for that matter. There was talk of the "Night of The Big Wind" in 1839, of the blizzard of 1947, the big snows of 1962 and '63 which could hardly have been blamed on The Beatles who were upsetting a few apple carts at the time.

People on the Western Isle realised that the new glazed grow houses were about to get their first real test in the oncoming storm. Róisín and Tom were in constant touch with their insurance providers to ensure that all angles were covered, even though Tom complaints that: "The insurance will cost nearly as much as the glass." There was relief on the island that the big ship from Amsterdam was safely anchored in Galway Bay.

Róisín and Tom found it difficult to sleep during the storm. It was not that their house was not well built or that windows or tiles rattled. It was just basic worry for themselves and their family and the people of the island generally. They had seen enough examples from the United States down through the years of towns and cities being razed to the ground but tornadoes and hurricanes. They had seen the devastation in Haiti and other places. There was always the fear that forecasters would get things wrong, that the worst ever storm would ensue and that would be the end of life as they had known it.

"Ignore it," Tom said to Róisín, who was nervous as the storm broke. "It will be over when we wake up."

"We should have stayed on the couch in the sitting room. At least there would be another floor between us and the storm."

"Don't worry about the roof," he said: "It was me that put it there."

"But if it goes during the night, you could have the whole world looking in on top of us."

"I don't know what you have in mind." but I am too tired for anything."

"You have such a dirty mind." she said.

"Tell that to Storm Fanny."

As it happened this time, the forecasters had overestimated rather than underestimated the storm. Not a pane of glass was shattered, although some slates and sheets of galvanize were blown off houses and barns. "I knew that it would be all over when we woke up." Tom said in the morning.

"You didn't wake up, because you didn't sleep." Róisín said. "I lay awake listening to you tossing and turning all night. Was there something bothering you?"

"Only the storm," he answered. "What else could there be?"

"You had black rings under your eyes before you went to bed at all. You stayed out too long the night before trying to make everything safe before the storm."

"It is always hard to judge how bad it is going to be."

Róisín remarked: "It is amazing how relaxed you have become since your mother passed away," Róisín said.

"What makes you say that?"

"Nothing happens unknown to me. I hadn't realised that it hurt you so much that she had to put up with that disease."

"I should have gone to see her more often."

"Don't beat yourself up about it. You knew she would not be getting better. I can understand what you would not want to see her the way she was."

"If there is a better place, as you say, I hope that she is there." Tom said.

"I suppose it relaxes you too to know that the two big jobs are nearly done. The wall and the grow houses. And the storm is over now as well."

"We don't know what damage it has done yet."

"At least there is still a roof over our heads." They lay back and dozed for a while. Then Tom sat up suddenly in the bed.

"What is it?" Róisín asked.

Tom could not admit that he had been dreaming about Gearóidín; "My mother," he said. "I saw her in the dream."

"What was she like?"

"Like she always was."

"Did she say anything?"

"No, but a brilliant idea came from nowhere. She must be in that place. The better place you are always talking to the children about."

"What makes you think that?"

"Windmills. Windmills on the wall. Not big high ones like you would see on the hills and in the bogs. Short stumpy ones the storms would not bend over. How come I never thought of that?"

"It is what they call an epiphany." Róisín said.

Tom laughed. "First we have storm Fanny and now we have epiphany."

"Don't joke about sacred stuff," his wife told him.

Tom was talking out loud to himself at the same time: "Little windmills a hundred metres apart. It will keep the island in electricity, and we may be able to sell some to the mainland. A brilliant idea, even if it is not my own. Thanks Mom."

"Do you know what you should do now?" Róisín asked before answering her own question. "See to it that the blessed bone is found. For your mother's sake."

"I'm on to it." Tom said excitedly. "Money no object. If we can't find the old one, we will invent a new one."

"That completely defeats the purpose. How can you recreate a bone that is more than a thousand years old?"

"Nobody needs to know the difference."

"We can deal with all of that again," his wife said. "We need to check on Jacob and Clíona first."

The children were still asleep, so they left them where they were. The school was closed because of the bad forecast. It only took a glance out the window to sea that there were huge waves breaking along the shoreline. From that distance it was impossible to see if any of the houses had been damaged. Tom used his binoculars to scan the distant wall on the top of the cliff Surf was rising in the air above but the waves themselves did not seem to reach that height. There was a constant thump of wave against cliff to be heard, but that was common in stormy weather. He looked too at the roofs of the houses and the glass on the grow houses.

There was no major damage to be seen.

"It is a long time since we had a such laidback breakfast," Róisín said, "without one or other of us being busy or the children under our feet. I am looking forward to the time it will be like this every day."

"When will that be?" Tom joked: "When the next hurricane comes? When the next storm Fanny comes our way?"

"I hope that you will not be using gross language like that in front of the children."

"I am not completely stupid," Tom answered. "They are asleep just now."

"I would prefer them not to be wakened up by that kind of talk."

"They could hear worse."

"Not from me, they won't."

"Next thing you will have me putting curse money in the jar." Róisín wondered aloud after a while what should they do for an official opening and launching her environmental project.

"Is there any need for it?" Tom asked.

"It would be a way of thanking all of those who helped out along the way."

"Local people will just look at it as if we are getting above our station. Again."

"Gearóidín and myself were talking about inviting Greta Thumberg. It would cut the politicians out of the equation."

"You mentioned her a while ago, but will she not be yesterday's news in a few months' time. Young people could do anything. Swing from condemning global warming to welcoming it because 'it makes the garden grow.' At least the politicians are stuck in their ways for the most part. They are unlikely to swerve off the beaten track. And we may need them for planning permissions."

"I thought you were alright for that for the moment." Róisín said.

"That is before I got the idea for the windmills. Fair play to my mother."

"Amen," was Róisín's answer to that.

Her husband set the record straight: "I was not saying a prayer. I don't do prayers. I am a rogue. Isn't that how the Dublin papers describe me, 'the rogue builder?'"

"And don't you love the publicity?"

"We don't have to decide all that stuff today," Tom said. "It is enough for one day to get past the storm, with ourselves and the children safe."

"What about the children?" Cliona's sleepy voice asked. She had slipped into the kitchen without a sound. "Is the roof still on the house?"

"As far as we know nothing stirred in the breeze," his mother answered. "The wind was a bit noisy, but it seems that Jacob and yourself slept through it all."

"Did it knock the school?" was Cliona's next question. "I was praying that the school would fall down when I heard that there was going to be a very big storm."

"It would have been on the radio if it had been knocked," her mother told her. "But you have no school today anyway because of the bad weather."

"Will Jacob and myself be going to Dadó's house to see himself and Topsy I hope that they were not blown away either?" Jacob arrived in from his bed just then, rubbing sleep from his eyes with the knuckles of his hands: "is the storm finished?" he asked.

"It is," Cliona answered disappointedly, "but the school was not knocked. Maybe God did not answer our prayers because Mamó lost the holy bone."

"Is God as silly as that?" his father asked.

"I am not sure," Jacob said, "but it seems that he has his

own way of doing things. Maybe he did not bother to knock the school this time, but he would let us have something else instead. He might let us get our bone back."

"He will give back the bone for sure," Clíona said. "Mamó is in heaven now and she will make him give it back."

"Maybe he doesn't know where it is anymore than herself." her father commented.

Clíona had no doubt: "God knows everything. I hope that he gives Mamó back her memory."

"I think he did," her father said. "I was dreaming about her, and I thought of a wonderful idea."

"Was it an idea about the whole family going on holiday together to Lanzarote?"

"It was something closer to home. It was about putting windmills along the wall on top of the cliff in order to generate electricity."

Jacob interrupted: "Will there be big white sails on them like the ones you would see in films?"

"Don't be daft," Clíona said. "The big storms would just blow away the sails."

Their father sidestepped their argument: "They will be like the ones you would see around the country, with a small propeller on top like you would see on an aeroplane."

Clíona joked: "If they are like parts of an aeroplane the whole island might take off and fly to someplace else."

Her brother added: "This island might fly off to Lanzarote, and you would get your wish to go to your favourite place."

"Mamó will probably make our wishes come true." Clíona added.

Sometime later Jacob had a question for his father: "Is electricity that comes from a windmill different than what comes from something else, like that big water place on the Shannon that was on television?"

"Different in what way?" Tom asked.

"Is it going round and round inside the wire?"

"I doubt it. I don't think the wires from the Shannon have water inside them either. But it is a good question. Keep asking questions. That is the best way of all to learn."

"I have a question too," Clíona said. "When are we going to Lanzarote again?"

"Who knows? When the wall is finished and the fruit is growing under the glass, maybe."

The children high-fived and cheered. Jacob raised his hand as if he was at school: "Can I ask another question, Dad?"

"You don't need permission to ask a question," his father said. "Ask away."

"I heard you saying that clean electricity would come from the windmills. Is some electricity dirty?"

"It does not dirty the kettle when we plug it in to boil, or the clothes when we plug in the iron. But if it is generated from coal or oil or turf or the burning of rubbish, you could say that it is dirty because of the fossil fuels used to generate it. On the other hand, seawater is clean as is the wind that turns the windmills."

"So, Storm Fanny does not make it dirty?" his son asked.

Róisín interrupted: "What kind of dirty talk is that, Jacob? Don't ever let me hear you say those words again."

Her son was perplexed: "But that is what they called it on the radio? Storm Fanny. I heard the woman on the weather forecast saying it. Why did she say it on the radio if it is a bad word?"

"It is a word that I don't want to hear again." his mother insisted.

"You are as bad as the bloody church now." Tom told her. "Making a sin out of something completely harmless."

"What do you know about the church?" Róisín asked angrily. "A man who never crosses the threshold of such a place."

Tom decided that it was prudent to avoid a row. He asked

the children: "Let's go to see if your Dadó is alright after the storm."

"And Topsy as well?" Clíona said.

"We will be a while," Tom said to Róisín: "I will take them to visit the grave as well. Put on your coats," he told the children: "It will be cold after the storm."

When the children were on their way out to the jeep, Tom went over and gave Róisín a kiss: "You can't win every battle," he said.

"Get out of here," she said in mock anger: "Yourself and your fanny."

Jacob and Clíona gad their little plastic shovels in the jeep since the day of the funeral. They carried them with them as they went into their grandfather's house, to give him a hug and ask him was everything alright after the storm. Topsy jumped up on them excitedly and followed them out to the sandpit. After many days away from the sand, they dug in enthusiastically as they started to fill their buckets and build their sandcastles.

Jacob was struck by an idea he had not thought of previously: "I wonder could the blessed bone be under the sand?"

"Who is going to throw a bone on the ground and spill a lorryload of sand on top of it?" Clíona asked.

"Doesn't Topsy often hide a bone after our dinner? Maybe he hid the saint's bone in the sand?"

"But where?" his sister asked. "There is the full of a lorry of sand here. It would take us a year to go through it all with those little shovels."

"Why don't we ask Dad and Dadó to help us?" Jacob asked. "They would like to find it too for Mamó's sake. And she might help from where she is looking down from heaven."

The children were excited as they ran into their grandfather's house to announce: "We know where the bone is." Jacob said and before the words were fully out of his mouth, Clíona added: "Topsy hid it under the sand."

"What makes you think that?" their father asked. "Where did Topsy find it?"

Jacob had his own logic: "In the place where Mamó hid it. Come on out and help us. Your shovels are bigger than ours. We need your help to find it."

Tadhg Rua looked at his son, Tom before he asked the children the question: "What kind of help are you talking about?"

Clíona tried to demonstrate with her hands: "Just move each shovel of sand from here to there."

"That is a big job," her grandfather said. "There are tons of sand out there."

Tom winked at his father: "I will do it with the shovel on the small tractor. It won't take long."

The children were not satisfied. "You will have to do it with shovels because the bone would get lost in the shovel on the tractor. It would pick up too much sand at one time."

Clíona added: "And it might smash the holy bone. Mamó would not like that."

The grown-ups looked at each other: "Are you busy today?" Tadhg asked his father.

"Are you up to working a shovel yourself? After the week you had?"

"All we need to do is turn it over, shovel after shovel. Like we used to prepare a mix in the old days. There is no need to tackle it like madmen. Like you did in the cemetery the last day."

"I needed to be doing something."

Tadhg looked at the sand when they came out to the yard: "I don't think the bone is under there," he said to Tom. "It was missing for a long time before you delivered the sand. But it will satisfy these two if we go through it."

"It will probably disappoint them as well," Tom said.

"At least they will know that we looked."

Tadhg Rua and Tom approached their task in an easy-going but effective way. They just moved each shovelful a foot or two aside, emptied it in a way that they and the children knew that it did not contain a bone. They repeated the same task again and again, with the children watching with anticipation at first which gradually turned to boredom.

Their interest was ignited every time that Topsy wandered in through the sand: "He knows very well where the bone is," Clíona said, "He is just playing a game."

"He is just teasing us," Jacob added.

"Topsy's game is certainly making us sweat," Tom said, as he peeled off his jumper. "Do you need a break?" he asked his father.

Their grandfather winked at the children: "An old-timer can outdo a youngster any day of the week," he said. "It is all in the technique. When you have it, you don't lose it."

"Machines were invented," Tom said, "so that people don't have to work like slaves anymore."

"Can we help?" Cliona waved her little shovel.

"Say a prayer," her father said.

Tadhg Rus leaned on his shovel to draw breath: "Alleluia," he said. "My son has found God."

"The children tell me that they work sometimes and do not at other times. And I am pretty sure that this is one of those times." He tore into what was left of the sand as his father continued in his own methodical way. The heap of sand looked refreshed, but there was no sign of any sacred bone.

Tom threw his shovel on top of the pile of sand: "A waste of time," he said. "Where is your God now?"

His father was of a different viewpoint: "Was there any serious damage done by last night's storm?"

His son Tom answered sarcastically: "We are back to the old story again. God does not shut one door without opening another." He called to Jacob and Clíona: "Say thanks to your Dadó for searching through the sand." He said to his father: "I promised to take them to the cemetery to visit the grave. Do you want to come with us?"

"I'm ok," he said. "I was there first thing this morning."

The children were disappointed that they had to leave: "But we didn't have Dadó's pizza yet?" Clíona said.

"We will have pizza at home later. You got up late and had a late breakfast. You couldn't be hungry again."

"I don't like pepperoni in my pizza," Jacob said. "Dadó never has that in his pizza." He gave a spit of disapproval: "I hate it."

"What kind of childish pets am I rearing at all?" Tom asked in frustration.

His father asked: "Why don't we all go to the cemetery together? We can have the pizzas then when you are really hungry."

"But you were there already? Tom said.

"What else have I to do?" His son realised how much his father needed the company, but he was still impatient: "Your Mom will be expecting you home," he told the children.

"Give her a ring," Clíona said. "She won't mind. But don't tell her about the pizzas until we have them eaten."

Her father gave her a little hug: "I think that the youngest must be the boss in every house."

Tom drove the jeep to the big wall at the top of the cliffs first to check for any possible cracks in the wall after the first real battering it had got from high seas. There did not seem to be a crack anywhere.

"It is probably the first of many storms that it will have to survive," his father said. "Imagine that your wall could stand there for a million years or more?"

"I would be happy with a thousand," Tom joked.

"It is not impossible. Some of the old Dún castles on the other islands must be there for three thousand years, and there is not a trace of cement or steel in any of them."

"It is hard to know with Dún Aenghus in Inis Mór for instance. Was it built in the way that it is now, with the cliff as protection on one side? Or was it an oval shape like Dún Chonchúir in Inis Meáin but half of it collapsed with the cliffs into the sea?"

"Questions we will probably have an answer to," his son said.

Their archaeological and philosophical musings were interrupted by an enquiry from the back seat of the jeep: "When are we going to have the pizza?"

"As soon as we visit your Mamó's grave," her father answered as he got the jeep into gear: "I just needed to check that the wall had not been damaged by the storm."

"Storm Fanny," Jacob whispered to Clíona.

"I'll tell Mom. She said never to say that word again."

"I will give you half my pizza if you don't tell."

"I will think about it." Clíona answered.

When they reached the cemetery, all four of them stood side by side in silence beside Nora's grave, deep in their own thoughts. Jacob broke away from the group when he say Topsy enter the small ruined chapel.

"Leave him alone," his father said. "Say your prayers or whatever you are supposed to do."

"I think that Topsy might have found the blessed bone." Jacob said in a low voice so as not to disturb anyone's thoughts by the graveside.

"We already had one wild goose chase today," his father answered. Jacob suddenly started to run towards the little chapel, at the door of which Topsy stood, wagging his tail, a bone in his mouth. Jacob grabbed the bone and started to shout: "Cliona, Dad, Dadó. Topsy has found the holy bone."

The others hurried towards him: "Could it possibly be it." Tadhg Rua asked as he examined it carefully. "I suppose those marks are from Topsy's teeth," he said as he handed it to his son, Tom: "Do you think it could be the right bone?"

"It will do," Tom said. "It is a bone, and it looks old."

"A DNA test would tell us its age," his father said. "But would the locals be happy to give it that kind of a test?" he asked himself more than anyone else.

"Would the priest have any idea?" Tom asked.

His father's answer surprised him: "I wouldn't be bothering the priest with questions like that."

"You mean he might know if it is genuine or not?"

"I will put it like this," his father said. "There is the priest's religion and there is the people's religion. They are the same a lot of the time, but there are times that they are not."

His answer intrigued his son, Tom: "In what way?" he asked.

"People never had priests in places like this for hundreds of years. Maybe they were scarce. Maybe they saw islands like this were too isolated. There were exceptions of course, like MacDara who had his own island off the coast at Carna. But the bishops and those in authority did not approve people like that, and they tried to close down the pilgrimage in his honour. One bishop even had a cross belonging to him buried on the island. It is probably still there someplace."

"That could be a job for a metal detector," Tom said.

"As far as I know it was a wooden cross. Anyway what I am trying to say is that people out on the fringes kept their own faith in their own way, with holy wells and saint Bridget's crosses and relics like the bone of saint Gregory. That is why it was passed down through the people and not the priests."

Tom asked: "Are you telling me that the priests had no say in the sacred bone or whatever you call it?"

"In fairness to them they left things like that up to the people. They left it to sit on the altar on the saint's day but that was it. You could say they were not for it or against it. They tolerated it and left it like that."

"All that is certainly new to me," Tom said.

"As far as I know it is much the same as that in so far as some of the great shrines of the world are concerned," his father commented: "People are free to believe in them or not. No big deal."

"So how come my mother got to have the bone?" Tom asked. "Was there some kind of an election?"

"She came home one day with the bone in a plastic bag, and she said it was given to her to look after for the rest of her life."

"But who gave it to her?" Tom asked with some impatience.

"Whoever was in charge, I suppose. It was none of my business If she was happy, I was happy. I suppose it was an honour to her in a way."

"So, you had no choice in what your wife was asked to do?"

"They didn't ask us to have separate beds or anything?"

"Could they do that?"

"Religious people are a funny lot. Look at the way they don't allow priests to get married."

"Are you telling me that is why I am an only child?"

"I am telling you that we were lucky to have you. You were half-way into the world when something went wrong. Your mother was bleeding, and the weather was too bad for even the Aran lifeboat to come. The first helicopter to ever land on this island was the one that brought the doctor to save your life."

"Are you listening to that, Jacob and Clíona?"

"Listening to what, Dad?"

"Listening to what a special person I am?" He told them what his father had told him.

"You always lived close to the wind," his father, Tadhg Rua said.

"So, Mom was not able to have any more children?"

"She was lucky to be alive. Lucky to have you. I think that might be why they gave her the sacred bone to mind."

"Because she was lucky?"

Tadhg Rua shrugged: "Because she had a miracle baby."

"More of the same old poppycock," his son remarked.

"All I know is that she was grateful to God to have you," Tadhg said.

Clíona and Jacob danced around holding hands as in 'ring-aring-rosy' singing: "Dad is Americal. Dad is Americal." Cliona asked: "Will you bring us to Disneyland in America when the wall is finished?"

Tom corrected the children's version of the story: "We are not talking about America. But about a miracle."

"We know," Jacob answered. "It just sounded like the same thing, so we made up our own rhyme."

Tom shook his head ruefully as he said to his father: "I never know with those two. One minute they are crying about their grandmother. The next they are making up nursery rhymes about the illness that was nearly the cause of their father's death before he was even born."

His father's dry humour came to the surface: "We were never able to get the silver spoon out of your mouth."

"It looks like it was not a silver spoon that I was born with," he said, "but with a big dirty old bone sticking out of my mouth."

"A hard chew for a hard chaw."

"You are outdoing yourself with the smart remarks today." Tom shook his head: "It is hard for me to say it or believe it, but it looks as if mother's death is bringing the two of us closer together."

"We were never apart," was his father's seemingly thruway

remark.

By now the children and their dog, Topsy were chasing each other around between the headstones of the graveyard. Clíona and Jacob were playing hide and seek, with Topsy sniffing out the hiding place as soon as one of them thought they were out of sight. "Is there any sound in the world nicer?" Tadhg Rua asked, "as the sound of children playing. "Even if it is in the field of the dead."

Just then Jacob and Cliona came back to where their father and grandfather stood talking: "Is it time for pizza yet?" Clíona asked.

"I am dying with the hunger," Jacob announced, bending over to add to the exaggeration.

Tom answered: "Sit into the jeep and we will go to your Dadó's house."

"Did you tell Mom that we will be late getting home?" Jacob asked.

"I did. She is calling over to Gearóidín's house to have a cup of coffee."

When they reached Tadhg's house, he switched on the TV for the children and continued the chat he had with his son in the cemetery. He felt that it was the longest one to one talk they had together for years. He had a question for Tom: "On the way back from the top of the cliff earlier I was wondering would it be a nice thing to have special little box built into the big wall to hold the sacred bone?"

"You mean a kind of a little shrine?"

"You could call it that. I was thinking of a kind of a box with a strong glass at the front of it that would keep out the bad weather, or for that anyone that would be minded to throw a stone at it."

"It would not be difficult to get a bit of bullet-proof glass," Tom said.

"I doubt if anyone would start shooting at it."

"I might have had a pot-shot if it was there in my younger days."

His father could not resist the temptation: "That was a long time ago."

"But still not as far back as your younger days. Are you talking about something like a tabernacle in a church?"

"You have got it in one. That kind of a box, with a window through which the bone could be seen by the public. That would even draw a few tourists. They love chopped off heads and things like the head of Saint Oliver Plunkett in Drogheda. Your mother and I went to see it once."

"And I thought that it was to Benidorm you brought her," Tom joked.

"That would be more like your kind of a shrine." Tadhg was thinking out loud: "There would need to be a key for it. It would need to be taken out on the pattern day, or if there was someone seriously ill."

"There is nothing like the rub of the relic."

Tadhg ignored what he considered his son's crass comment: "I suppose we would need to get permission from someone."

"Do you mean the priest?" Tom asked.

"I know you don't like him..."

Tom interrupted him in mid-sentence: "It's not that. I would have no problem in asking him to bless the little box. But there are some questions that it is better not to ask a priest, because you are putting him on the spot."

His father was confused: "What spot?"

"Giving him a decision to make that should not be his decision. If he says no, which will probably be his first instinct, you are at full-stop. If the bone or the relic or whatever you want to call it belongs to the people, leave it to the people to decide. Priests come and go but there will be people here as long as the Western Isle is inhabited."

Tadhg seemed to be between two minds: "People always had respect for the priest on this island."

"There are not many of them left," Tom said. "Anywhere. But you will always have the old wells and shrines and relics."

"Religion without a priest," his father said, "It is hard to imagine it."

Tom was already onto his next train of thought: "Róisín was only talking this morning about having a big day for the opening of the glasshouses and the finishing of the wall. I thought there was no need for any of that, but I think now that it might not be a bad plan at all. We could get the priest of Rome to bless the installations, for want of a better word, and we could leave the holy relic in the hands of the people."

Chapter Twenty-Seven

Róisín had not heard anything from Gearóidín since the day of the funeral. She was aware that her friend had a date with Patrick from the Amsterdam ship before the boat sailed and the storm was due. She would have loved to have had an account of how the date had gone, but felt it was a sign of sensitivity that the last thing her best friend wanted to do was to, as she said to herself "rub my nose in it when the family and I were in mourning for Nora."

Róisín checked her friend's social media platform but there were no entries since the "This could be the day," anticipatory one on the day that Patrick and herself were due to meet.

"Has she taken off with him?" she asked herself, followed by every kind of wonder and emotion from: "Did he stay and the two of them have been flaking away ever since?" to "Have they fallen off the cliff and drowned unknown to everyone?" The even darker thought that Gearóidín had drank herself to death or even taken an overdose because she felt abandoned surfaced too, but even as she shrugged it away, she had fears for her friend's welfare: "We have never gone this long without talking," Róisín reminded herself: "Something must be wrong. Maybe she has the hump with me for some reason?" she told herself. "The best thing to do is to ring up and ask her is everything alright after the storm. The phone had rung out so often that it came as a surprise that it was answered this time."

"I thought that you had gone away with the fairies," Róisín

said.

"I was not in a position to deal with anything," her friend answered. "There are lots of messages, but I have not opened any of them yet. I needed a break."

"We all battened down the hatches for the storm," Róisín said.

"Was there a storm? I was three or maybe four sheets to the wind and didn't notice anything. I brought a couple of bottles to bed with me. There were lots of dreams. Lots of nightmares. I managed to get to the en-suite a couple of times to throw up or the other one. I just needed to get away from it all."

"Do you feel better now?" Róisín asked.

"I don't feel anything at all. It is the best feeling in the world. This must be how it feels to be dead." She paused: "Sorry, I will rephrase that. I know that you are all sad at this time."

"Is it because of Patrick that you are feeling like that?"

"Patrick was no more than a figment of the imagination. To put it mildly, he did not, or could not perform. I did meet someone who did, and what a performance. It was lovely while it lasted, but when the bubble burst, he was gone. So, I just drank myself into oblivion. What else does a girl need when her heart is broken?"

"A friend to talk to," Róisín said quietly.

"You had enough on your mind, so my best friend was the bottle. With another bottle of vodka to follow. Is that what they call a threesome?"

"A dangerous thing to do," Róisín said, "but I hope it is over now."

"You hardly think I was going to do with myself because of a man?"

"Accidents can happen."

"So, Patrick did not cut the mustard?"

"You have a nice way of putting it. But I am not faulting him. I have no one to blame but myself. I just wanted to give him the time of his life before he sailed away. For my own sake, of course. There is an old saying about offering it to someone on a plate. Well, I was that plate, but there he was. Running away from me as fast as he could. You would think I had a disease, and I suppose that I had: The horny disease."

"The bloody idiot. He does not know what he missed."

"But someone else does. Someone that was in the right place at the right time to catch the apple falling from the tree. But someone who does not want to know me now."

"There I was," Róisín said, "thinking that everything had worked out hunky dory and that yourself and Patrick were all loved up for the weekend. When I heard nothing from you, I even wondered had you sailed away with him?"

"Things were bad enough, until the dirty comments started on social media. I was called every kind of name. They were sexist and racist because I was seen out with a coloured man. To make it worse someone saw me running naked into the sea for a swim. I am surprised that you had not heard about it."

"Even the gossips zip the lip when they meet someone that is in mourning. I did look at your own platform, but nothing had been posted except a few excited words the day you were going to meet Patrick."

"I think some of the other stuff seems to have been taken down. Someone probably threatened them with a lawsuit. Or bribed them."

"Was it locals that wrote the hateful stuff?"

"Who else? I am now officially the whore of Babylon, even though they were not able to spell it correctly. 'Hoor' will probably be in next year's Oxford Dictionary. I will never be able to go out in public again."

"Sue them," Róisín said. "Bring them up before the courts."

"Bring who? This is like trying to deal with ghosts."

"I would prefer to go and hide my head," was Gearóidín's

reply.

"There will be no head hidden while I am around here," Róisín said. "Right now, you are going to take a shower and put on your face and come out with me for a cup of coffee. If anyone even looks sideways at you, I will sue the hole off them."

Chapter Twenty-Eight

Tsunami Tom found a Danish company which would be able to install the small windmills he wanted close to the clifftop on the Western Isle in a matter of months. Connections to the electricity supply and the national grid would take a while longer, he was told, but he knew from experience that once a job was started it tended to take on a life of its own. He had his own ways of hurrying things up, not least of which was bullying those involved in the process to get on with the job at top speed. Some employers considered that kind of bullying a handicap. Not Tom, but then he had the capacity to splash the cash in ways to which it was difficult to say no.

"You are not telling me that you are going to jump the gun with regard to planning permission again," his wife Róisín said to him. "You will get us all into trouble if you keep this up."

"It is just one more time," Tom answered. "We are close to the finishing line. Your grow house is built, and the planting seems to be going well. Planting has been at issue with your project, and I am just trying to improve mine in a way that will be completely pleasing to the environmentalists."

"Be careful how much of the mental you put into that word," she laughed, "or you really will drive them all mental."

"As they say I think that ship has sailed. Everybody knows that they are mental already."

"Don't bother saying that at the official opening."

"I think the best way of hurrying up permission for the

windmills is to ask the Taoiseach to cut the tape. OK, that little girl Goretti..."

"Greta," his wife corrected him, "Greta Thumberg."

"I know," Tom said, "Goretti." Róisín saw no point in correcting him again, now that the young woman was unlikely to be at the official opening.

Tom continued: "There is a big difference between the Prime Minister of a country and a radical young firebrand. Inviting her could even jeopardize our chances of planning permission. The word radical does not sit well with Government ministers and officials."

"This matter has never been discussed properly" Róisín reminded him.

"Well, I know what I want."

"You want to boss everyone. That is what you want. Gearóidín and I thought Greta would be the best and first choice for our project, the grow houses."

"Things have changed now," Tom said, "in the light of that new flu that has been forecast. We have a very small window of opportunity to get things organised properly. We have to fix days and speakers. Now or never."

"Gearóidín will not be satisfied," Róisín said, "and like it or not, she is my righthand woman."

"Fuck Gearóidín," Tom said bluntly. "These are decisions we need to make ourselves. We don't know where she will be this week or the next."

"That is a strange thing to say about my best friend," Róisín said.

Tom shrugged his shoulders: "Did she tell you she was running naked on the beach and into the sea the last day?"

"She did actually, and that is her own business. It is a free country. She has suffered enough on account of it."

"What did she say? Suffered in what way?"

"She has been ridiculed and insulted on social media. I didn't want to tell you about it because I knew that it would anger you. She was called a bitch and a whore and every worse name under the sun."

"I think that she should stay in out of the sun."

"It wasn't just sunburn she was made to suffer. She is lucky not to have been burnt at the stake as a witch."

"It would make a good takeaway," Tom said: "Steak and chips and a witch or is it a bitch?"

"That is not a joke," his wife said, "and if it is, it is one in very bad taste. Your mother would be ashamed of you."

"Leave my mother out of this. She was a decent respectable woman."

"A woman you didn't have time to visit for months in the Nursing Home. If you needed to cry, that was the time to cry. When she was alive. Not when she is dead. You don't believe in life after death anyhow."

"What has got into you all of a sudden? Were you drinking?"

"Do you know what is wrong with you?" Róisín said: "You have no respect for man or woman. All you respect is money. Your ill-gotten money that you didn't pay tax on. Just like you didn't seek planning permission until the matter was raised in the Dáil and you had to?"

This led to a stony silence for a while. Róisín remembered then that Tom was grieving and that this was the wrong time to say some of the things that she was saying. She went over to him and held out her hand: "I am sorry. Sorry for dragging your mother's memory into all of this. What Gearóidín told me hurt me an awful lot. Some men are pigs, and I don't mean you." A little smile escaped her lips: "Most of the time anyway."

"I am sorry too," Tom said, and there was another long silence.

It was he who put a question that had intrigued him for some time, given his own frustrations with planning laws: "How have you managed to get permission so easily for the grow houses?"

Róisín pulled up her long skirts and whirled around: "A woman has her wiles," she answered, "but don't ask me what a wile is."

"I can see exactly what it is."

"A woman has power and influence a man does not have," she said, teasing him with another twirl.

"I thought it was a woman that is in charge of that office?"

"Where have you been for the last twenty years? A woman can be as attractive to one of her own as any man."

"Don't say that in public, or you will have all the 'isms' after you, the feminists and the homophobes and I don't know how many others."

"Seriously," Róisín answered. We got the permission primarily because ours is an environmental project. Rising seas and planet warming are the biggest issues of our time. I assume that is why my application was successful so soon."

"So, you didn't slip the planning officer a million or anything?" Tom joked.

"You would be a lot quicker to slip someone something than I am."

Tom asked: "Is my project not as important in its own way as yours? There is obviously favouritism in some quarter."

"I doubt it. It doesn't help to be so bolshie so much of the time, but I presume you will have no problem with the windmills. That is a genuine environmental project," Róisín said.

"Is a safety wall to prevent or break up a tsunami not just as important or even more so than growing a few avocadoes and tomatoes?"

"Many would see it as a vanity project. A man with money

flexing his muscles and doing his own thing which may or may not ever be needed. Many would see it as a waste of time and money. It will take a big wave to prove them wrong and I don't know how you are going to organise that."

"Vanity project my arse," Tom answered angrily. "Someday the people saved by that wall will be very grateful to me."

"I hope that they are, but that may be in a thousand years' time."

"Now you are telling me all this?" Tom said.

"We had these arguments before we even started. That is why we decided to divide the money, for you to do your thing, and for me to do mine. Anyway, I am not complaining or finding fault. I am trying to see into the minds of people in the planning office or the newspapers. It was one of those that used the words 'vanity project' first."

Tom sighed: "So you are saying that all of my effort is a waste of time?"

"I am not saying that, and neither of us really cares about what is written in the newspapers or said on radio or television."

"Are we not? You certainly remembered the vanity project?"

"That was because it was said to hurt you," Róisín said: "This is the way I look at it. You did your thing with your share of the money, and I did mine. That is what we had arranged: Who is to say that you will not save more people with the passage of time than my project will feed? This is not a competition. Neither of us will be in line for a prize at the end of it all. All I hope is that we will have done some good particularly for this island and its people."

"You should be in Dáil Éireann," her husband said. "They love that old plámás up there. Waste of time, waste of money. That is all I am hearing. It would make a man jump off the cliff."

"Don't say stuff like that. Even in jest. You never know when the children might be listening. Look at the bright side: We have provided lots of work. We have two lovely children. We have prospects of a good long life stretching out in front of us. We still have plenty of money. We will never be hungry, I hope. We have not run out of plans yet."

"Only planning permission," Tom said wryly.

"That will come in time. Who is going to knock what you have built? They might let you sweat for a while, but they know that they need us. They need our money to top up what they have in their own coffers. And anyway, you are still a young man. You have most of your life in front of you."

"Was it the great Alexander that said at the age of twenty-five: 'No more worlds to conquer'."

"There are plenty of worlds out there waiting for you to conquer," Róisín said: "You have already mentioned the Pacific Island that will soon be swamped by the sea. They need walls like the one you have built. What about all the houses that are needed for the homeless? That is a project for you."

"All of those choices mean going away. Leaving here." Tom said.

"You don't have to be hands-on all of the time. You could fly out somewhere and set up a project. Call over every now and then to oversee the work, and then come back home here."

"Anything is possible," I suppose.

"Do you think I would complain about spending a year in the Seychelles when the kids are a bit older? I would never need fake tan again after that."

Tom laughed: "I suppose not, because all of your skin would have been burnt off, I suppose there is work to be done here on the island too. When the big ship from Amsterdam was here, it showed up how much we need a tidal pier. We need a proper pier on this island."

"And an airstrip like they have on the three Aran Islands," Róisín added. "I better not think of anything else in case I have to cancel my year in the Seychelles. That is more than enough to be getting on with for the moment."

Tom asked casually: "Have you heard anything from Gearóidín recently?"

"She is traumatised, just hanging in there. There were some awful things written about her on social media."

"That is the world we live in, I suppose."

"I know that you don't like her," Róisín said. "It is not very civil the way you tend to walk out of a room when she comes in."

"I never said that I disliked her, but put it like this, I can do without her."

"She is my friend, like her or not," was his wife's next comment.

"That does not mean that I need to be on top of her all of the time."

"I don't want you on top of her either, just to be nice."

"I will try. It is just that she makes me nervous or something. I can't put my finger on it, so I keep my distance."

"Don't tell this to a soul," Róisín said, "but she told me that she spent all night riding a fine hunk of a man."

"You mean the sailor, Patrick?"

"No. That fell through. I think she was with a married man" Róisín said. She gave a nervous laugh: "The lucky bitch."

"You seem jealous?"

"Of course, I am not. Haven't I got you?"

"That should be enough for you or any woman," Tom said with an exaggerated swagger.

"It didn't do her much good. I have never seen her as down in the dumps as she was the following day."

"You pay for your pleasure," Tom said in a throwaway manner: "How did you manage to keep that bit of hot gossip to yourself until now. You are usually bursting to tell me something like that as soon as you hear it."

"I didn't think that it was any of your business."

"If it was not my business then, why is it now? I have no interest in any kind of rumour or bitching or backbiting. I never had and I never will. It is very seldom that there is any kind of substance in stuff like that. In the meantime, somebody has been hung out to dry. All the denials in the world do no good. It is back to the 'no smoke without fire' syndrome."

Róisín deliberately mixed up a Shakespearean comment: "Methinks he doth protest too much and for a man who doth not give a damn, he doth overthink a very simple answer."

"Impressive, but just try and say what you want to say."

"Gearóidín will be working with me soon, and we will be doing a lot of secretarial and other work from the house. It will take the pressure of minding the children off your father's shoulders. I would like if you were pleasant and civil with her and not walk out the door every time she comes in."

"I will learn a speech every morning in order to have my 'ps' and 'qs' right and not to say anything that offends feminine or feminist sensibilities."

"Just act normal and leave the social media out of it."

Tom gave a mock salute and answered: "Aye, aye" captain."

Chapter Twenty-Nine

The day the Taoiseach came for the official opening of Róisín and Tom's projects was the biggest day ever in living memory on the island. The windmills had been installed and planning permission received for the wind energy project, with conditional permission for the wall as soon as certain minor adjustments had been put into place. Tom felt that was shorthand for saying: "We can't just let you tell us what to do, but we are not asking to have the wall removed. It could stop a mythical tsunami sometime, so let us just get on with more important stuff."

When the journalist Annette Nic Airt almost literally pinned him to the wall and asked to see a copy of the planning permission for the windmills first. She read and seemingly dismissed that before asking for the real planning permission. Tom produced but kept his thumb over the date the permission was granted.

Annette tried to snatch the document from his hand, and it tore into two pieces.

"Now look what you have done?" he said.

"You did not need to hold it so tightly."

"That is what we do out here on a windy day."

"Show me the date," she said angrily.

"What date?" he asked with mock sincerity.

"The date of the bloody planning permission. I have reason to believe that you have actually not obtained it."

"I will announce the date during my speech," he said, when I am thanking the Taoiseach for all his help and support, given the rabid opposition of certain newspapers, which of course I will not name, out of courtesy to yourself.

In his speech Tom thanked the Taoiseach and other politicians who had made the journey for the official opening. He emphasised job creation and care for the planet as the two most important aspects of their work. He welcomed the local community, the journalists as well as islanders, young and old from Tory Island to Cape Clear. Their ongoing commitment to and fights for the rights of their communities have been an inspiration. He even praised an Aran Island priest who had telegraphed the British Government one hundred and fifty years earlier with the immortal words: "Send us boats or send us coffins."

Tom continued with his prepared speech without any mention of planning permission until Annette got tired waiting. She crossed over to the great white tent erected for the occasion, with the hope of questioning the Taoiseach.

Seeing her coming, Gearóidín said to Róisín: "The bitch is back. I would love to push that one off the top of the cliff."

"Manners and smiles are the order of the day," Róisín replied through gritted teeth, "until we milk every bit of good publicity that we can from the occasion." She shook hands with Annette as if she was her very best friend.: "You are very welcome. I hope you were not seasick this time and that you had something to eat in the reception area."

"My breakfast stayed down, and the brunch was very tasty."

"A bit of seasickness is the best detoxicant of all," Gearóidín said. "You might get to clear out your stomach on the way home."

"I was trying to get an answer from your husband about planning permission," Annette said to Róisín, "but he was much too busy with his speech and everything."

Róisín laughed: "The only answer I ever got out of him was when he said 'I do' in the chapel on the day that we got married."

"Very droll indeed," Annette said, as she zoomed in on the permission question again: "Has he obtained it or has he not?"

"Would the Taoiseach be here if he had not?"

"That is a question for the Taoiseach," Annette said. "Is it an island trait, or what? Why can nobody give me a straight answer?"

"I was dealing with the glazing of the grow houses myself," was Róisín's answer, "and I have to say that the planning office officials were extremely professional. The application only took a couple of months. It was a different story for the wall that Tom built. All aspects of the case had to be thoroughly examined and that took longer."

"A straight answer to a straight question," Annette demanded: "Has planning permission been granted or not?"

Róisín answered by telling the story of a man who had applied for a grant for the house in which he and his mother lived. The old woman died before the grant arrived so he was afraid that he would lose it. When the official put it to him: "Is your mother still alive?" his answer was: "Not at the moment."

"Funny," Annette said impatiently, "but what has that to do with anything?"

"It is a way of saying that there are different ways of answering a question."

"It is a way of saying: 'Fuck off,'" was Annette's angry reply.

"We will excuse the outburst," Róisín said: "You probably have not heard that Tom's mother passed away recently. He was her only child, and he is devastated."

For once Annette seemed short of words: "I'm sorry," she stuttered.

"How were you to know, Annette? Safe home now and enjoy your evening in the ferry."

Gearóidín said with admiration: "You have learned the

game well, since we first started out. It is no harm to put that one in her box."

"Don't worry. She will take revenge in print."

"You could teach a lesson to the Taoiseach on bow to waffle and avoid a question. He will be looking for you to stand for the Dáil next."

"They need to be played at their own games," was Róisín's reply.

"There was fun, laughter and music to be heard in every direction." Clíona was given the honour of presenting a bouquet of flowers to the Taoiseach. Jacob was given the task of showing the sacred bone to him and explaining its significance as best he could to the Prime Minister of the State. "My grandmother took care of it until she died, or else Topsy would have eaten it."

"And who is this Topsy?" the Taoiseach asked.

"Our dog, but he can't be here today,"

"Why not?"

"He would make his wee wee on the leg of your trousers.

"The Taoiseach laughed heartily and asked: "Did Topsy ever eat a full saint?"

"I don't know. I think they stopped making saints and heroes a long time ago."

The Taoiseach used that answer in his speech to emphasise that there were still lots of heroes to be found all over the country. "They do not have swords and shields," he said, "but they have intelligence, computers, and machinery..." He went on to praise Róisín and Tom for the good use they have made of the money they won in the lottery.

Both of them hung their heads to let that wave wash over them as the leader of the State went on to criticise the political opposition for their plan to tax lottery winnings: "If that had happened here there would be no grow houses, no windmills, no wall to break tsunamis," He raised his glass: "To Róisín and Tom, and their family."

When the subsequent round of applause died down, to avoid being questioned by Annette or any other journalist about their supposed lotto win. Gearóidín caught up with Tom on his way: "Those tweets you sent me were terrible," she said.

"What tweets?"

"You know as well as I do. I came when you called. I did what you wanted."

"You took advantage. My heart was broken, my hopes shattered."

"You still managed to put in some performance."

"Look in your Bank account. I have made you a millionaire. That is your pay-off. Get off the island as quick as you can."

"I am not going anywhere. I have a job here and now I have a man."

"What man?"

"You, of course. Not all the time but whenever I want. I will call and you will come, if you want to hold on to your marriage. A bit like Topsy really. Maybe I should think of getting you a lead."

www.ingramcontent.com/pod-product-compliance
Lightning Source LLC
LaVergne TN
LVHW010156070526
838199LV00062B/4389